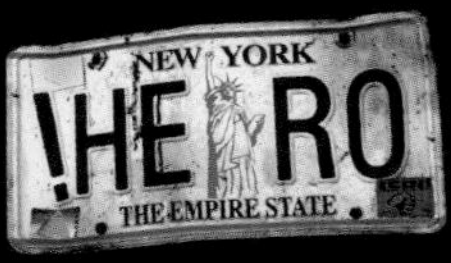
NEW YORK
!HE RO
THE EMPIRE STATE

ONE

Stephen R. Lawhead & Ross Lawhead, Writers • Ross Lawhead, Penciller • Jeff Anderson, Inker • Jonathan Koelsch, Colorist • Jonathan Koelsch, Letter and Graphic Design, with special thanks to Steve Harrison • Jonathan Koelsch, Cover Design and Illustration • Sarah Medina, Editor and Project Manager • Brad Ford, Creative Director • !Hero created by Eddie DeGarmo & Bob Farrell • Published by NavPress

!Hero, Graphic Novel, ISBN 1-57683-500-6
Published by TH1NK books, a division of NavPress, P.O. Box 35001
Colorado Springs, CO 80935. www.th1nkbooks.com

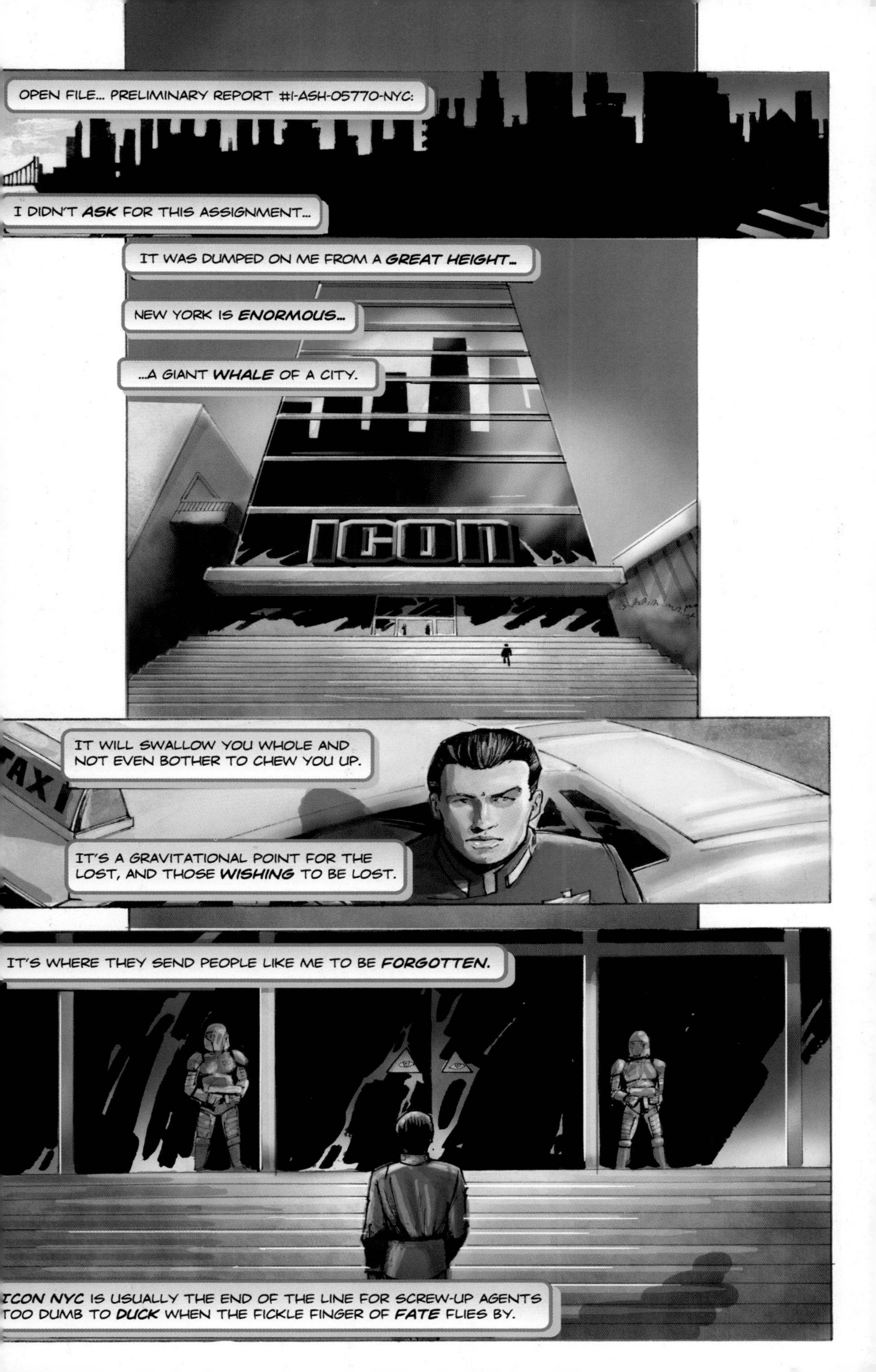
OPEN FILE... PRELIMINARY REPORT #1-ASH-05770-NYC:
I DIDN'T ASK FOR THIS ASSIGNMENT...
IT WAS DUMPED ON ME FROM A GREAT HEIGHT...
NEW YORK IS ENORMOUS...
...A GIANT WHALE OF A CITY.
ICON
TAXI
IT WILL SWALLOW YOU WHOLE AND NOT EVEN BOTHER TO CHEW YOU UP.
IT'S A GRAVITATIONAL POINT FOR THE LOST, AND THOSE WISHING TO BE LOST.
IT'S WHERE THEY SEND PEOPLE LIKE ME TO BE FORGOTTEN.
ICON NYC IS USUALLY THE END OF THE LINE FOR SCREW-UP AGENTS TOO DUMB TO DUCK WHEN THE FICKLE FINGER OF FATE FLIES BY.

NYC COULD BE THE END OF THE LINE FOR *ME*, TOO...

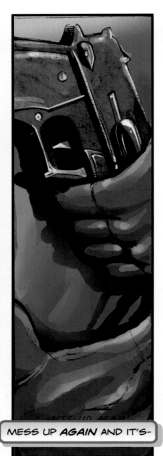

MESS UP *AGAIN* AND IT'S—

PLEASE INSERT YOUR *IDENTITY CARD* INTO THE SLOT.

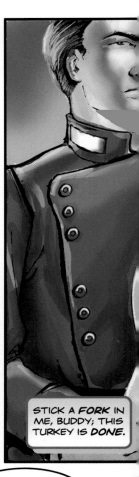

STICK A *FORK* IN ME, BUDDY; THIS TURKEY IS *DONE*.

Hunter, Alexander S.

•05/04/1966•

PIC: TZY-022-567-8040-NO

ICON RNK: •COMMANDER, FREE AGENT, FIRST•

ICON CLSFCN: •AUDITOR•

ICON SVC-RD: •10 YRS•

AWARDS: 5

▶ CITATIONS: 1

WELCOME TO *ICON-NYC*, AGENT HUNTER.

PROCEED TO THE GOVERNOR'S SUITE ON THE 31ST FLOOR.

I'LL HAVE TO WATCH MY *BACK*. EVERY BENT OFFICIAL IS LOOKING FOR A WAY *OUT* OF HERE, AND THEY'LL USE *ME* TO *GET* IT.

DELETE FROM TOP...OPEN NEW DOCUMENT...

WELCOME, AGENT HUNTER, THE GOVERNOR IS EXPECTING YOU. PLEASE, GO RIGHT IN.

ARRIVAL IN NEW YORK: UNEVENTFUL. PROCEEDING DIRECTLY TO MEETING WITH GOVERNOR...

SO! HERE YOU ARE—

ARRIVED AT *LAST.* I EXPECTED YOU *YESTERDAY.*

SORRY. PLEASE EXCUSE ME, SIR. MY FLIGHT WAS DELAYED. I HOPE YOU WEREN'T *INCONVENIENCED.*

THINK *NOTHING* OF IT. I'D HOPED TO SHOW YOU AROUND THE CITY, THAT'S ALL.

THANKS, BUT IT ISN'T NECESSARY. I MUCH PREFER MAKING MY *OWN* WAY AROUND.

OF COURSE. NEW YORK IS A *ROUGH DIAMOND,* TO BE SURE, BUT THERE'S NOTHING HERE FOR THE HIGH COMMAND TO BE *CONCERNED* ABOUT. YOU'LL SEE.

I'M SURE YOU'RE RIGHT. JUST THE SAME, I'LL TAKE A COUPLE DAYS TO LOOK AROUND AND GET TO KNOW THE PLACE.

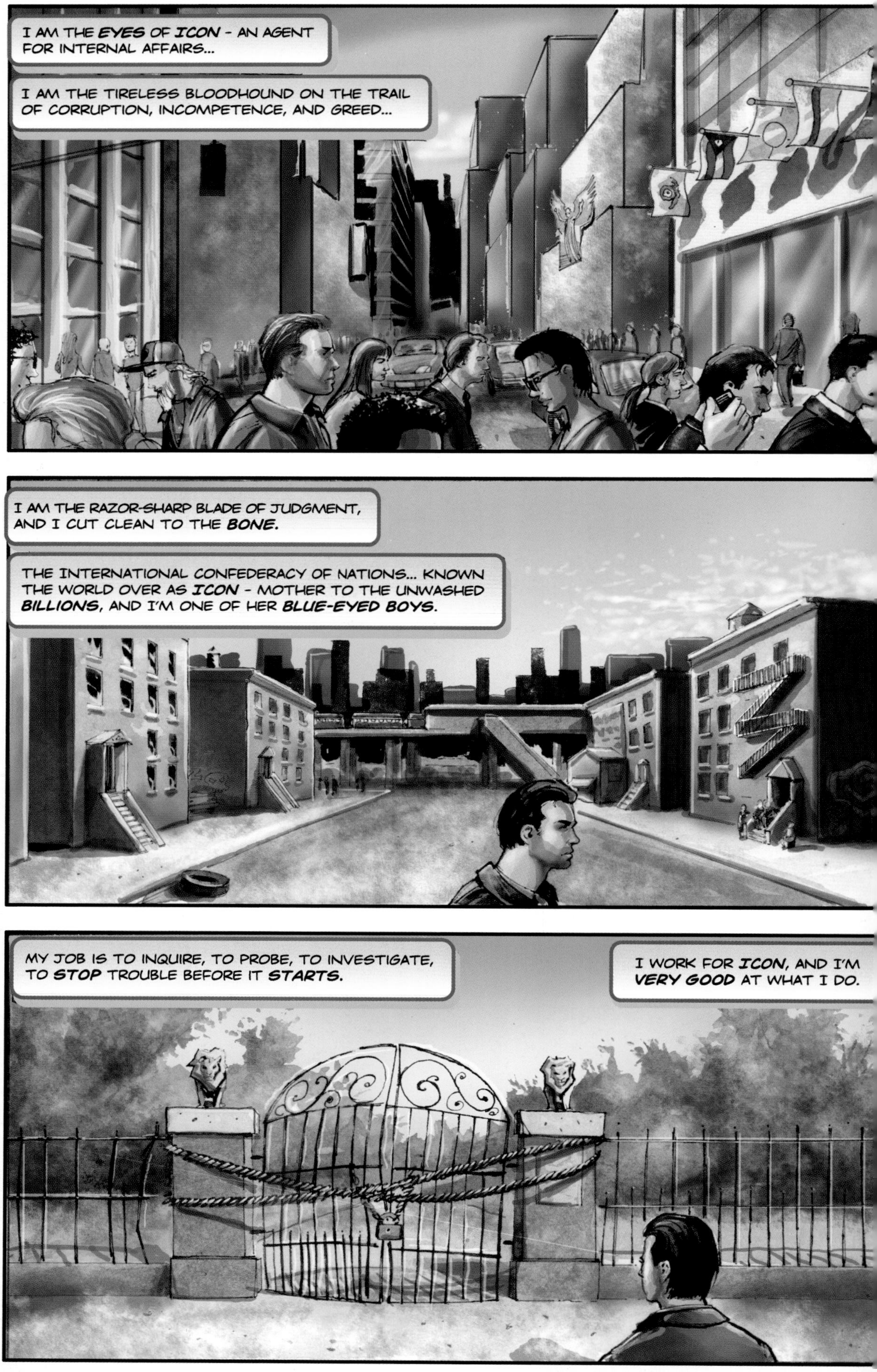
I AM THE EYES OF ICON - AN AGENT FOR INTERNAL AFFAIRS...
I AM THE TIRELESS BLOODHOUND ON THE TRAIL OF CORRUPTION, INCOMPETENCE, AND GREED...
I AM THE RAZOR-SHARP BLADE OF JUDGMENT, AND I CUT CLEAN TO THE BONE.
THE INTERNATIONAL CONFEDERACY OF NATIONS... KNOWN THE WORLD OVER AS ICON - MOTHER TO THE UNWASHED BILLIONS, AND I'M ONE OF HER BLUE-EYED BOYS.
MY JOB IS TO INQUIRE, TO PROBE, TO INVESTIGATE, TO STOP TROUBLE BEFORE IT STARTS.
I WORK FOR ICON, AND I'M VERY GOOD AT WHAT I DO.

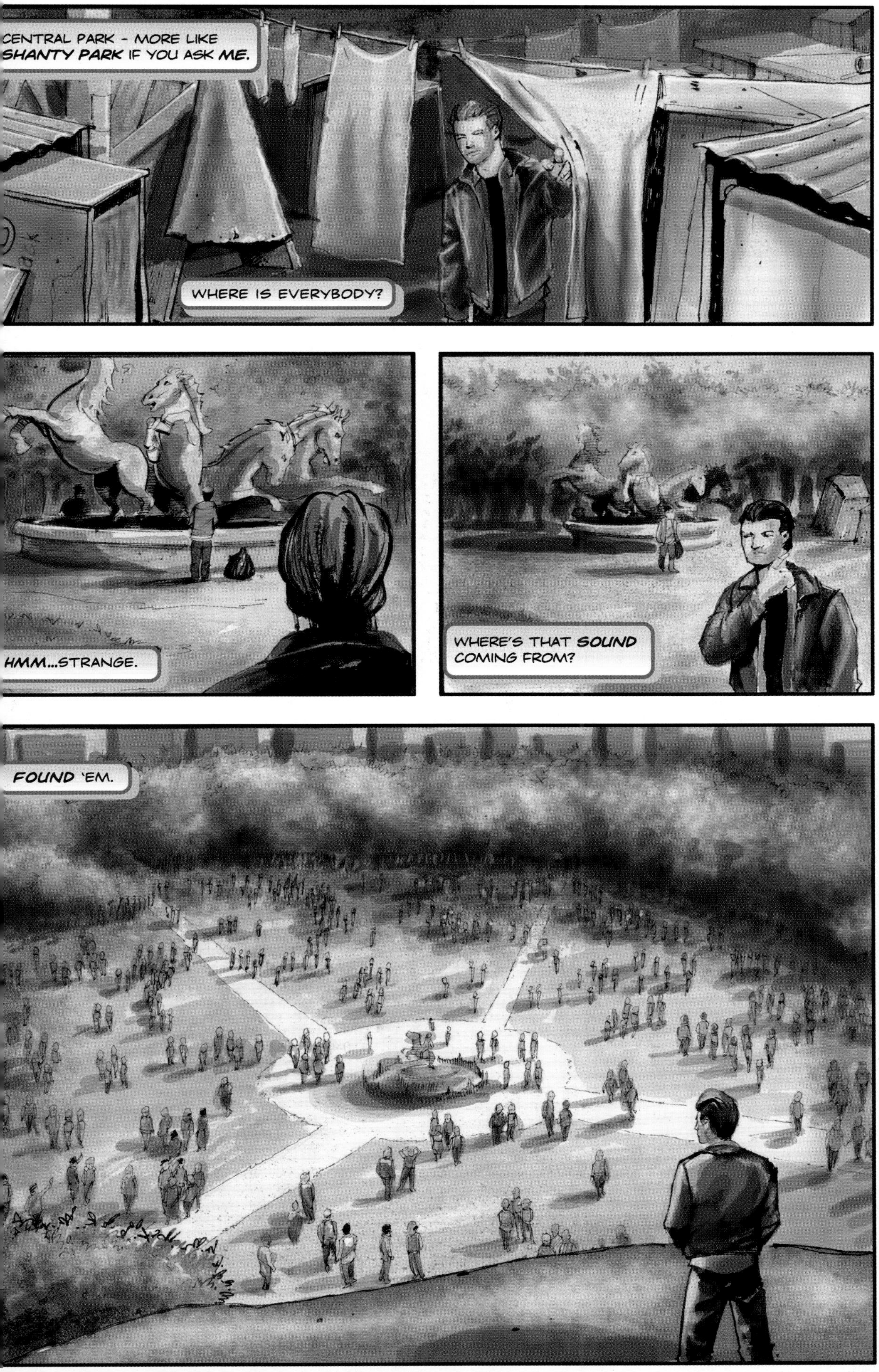
CENTRAL PARK - MORE LIKE SHANTY PARK IF YOU ASK ME.
WHERE IS EVERYBODY?
HMM...STRANGE.
WHERE'S THAT SOUND COMING FROM?
FOUND 'EM.

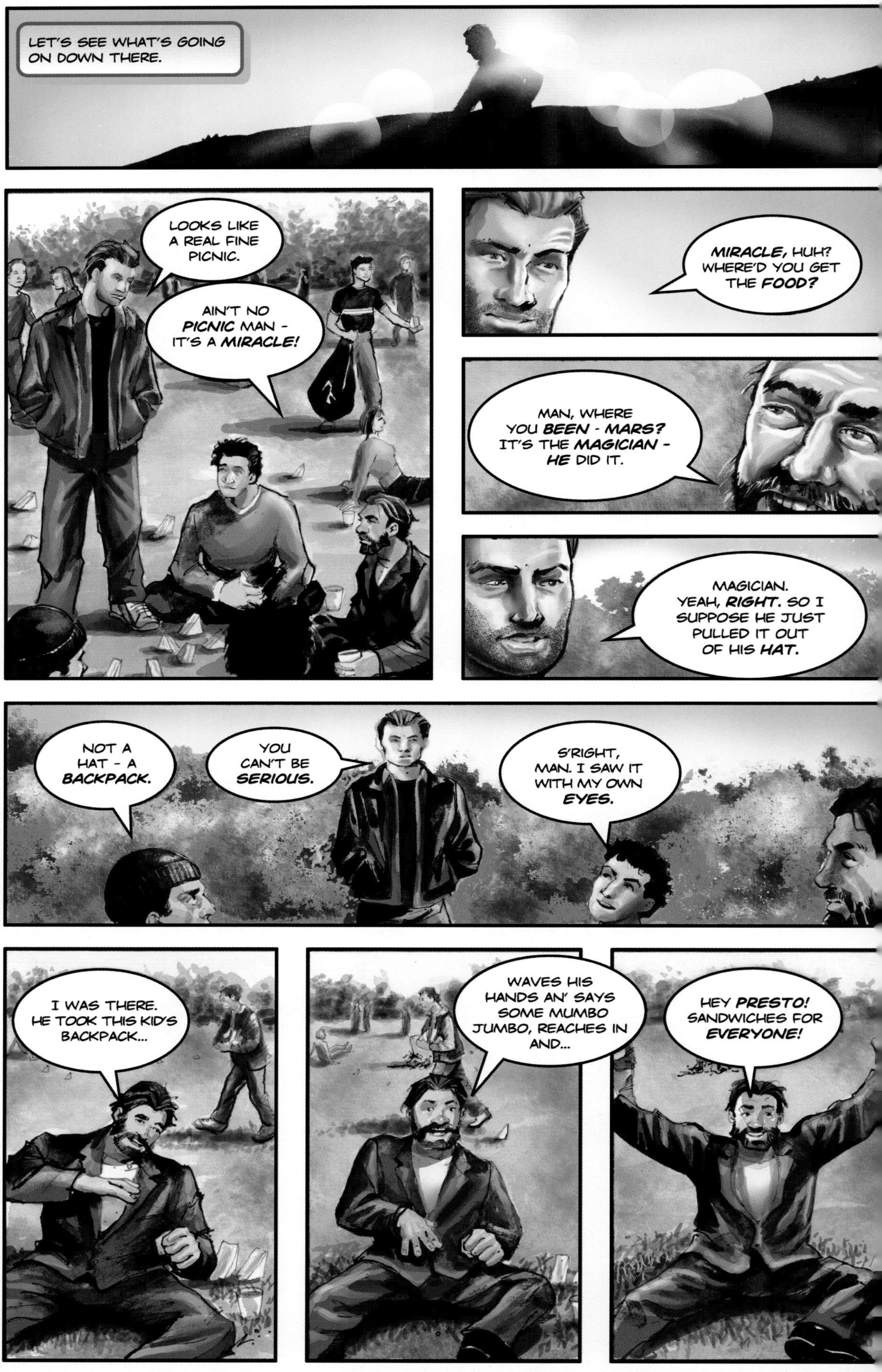
LET'S SEE WHAT'S GOING ON DOWN THERE.
LOOKS LIKE A REAL FINE PICNIC.
AIN'T NO *PICNIC* MAN - IT'S A *MIRACLE!*
MIRACLE, HUH? WHERE'D YOU GET THE *FOOD?*
MAN, WHERE YOU *BEEN - MARS?* IT'S THE *MAGICIAN - HE* DID IT.
MAGICIAN. YEAH, *RIGHT.* SO I SUPPOSE HE JUST PULLED IT OUT OF HIS *HAT.*
NOT A HAT - A *BACKPACK.*
YOU CAN'T BE *SERIOUS.*
S'RIGHT, MAN. I SAW IT WITH MY OWN *EYES.*
I WAS THERE. HE TOOK THIS KID'S BACKPACK...
WAVES HIS HANDS AN' SAYS SOME MUMBO JUMBO, REACHES IN AND...
HEY *PRESTO!* SANDWICHES FOR *EVERYONE!*

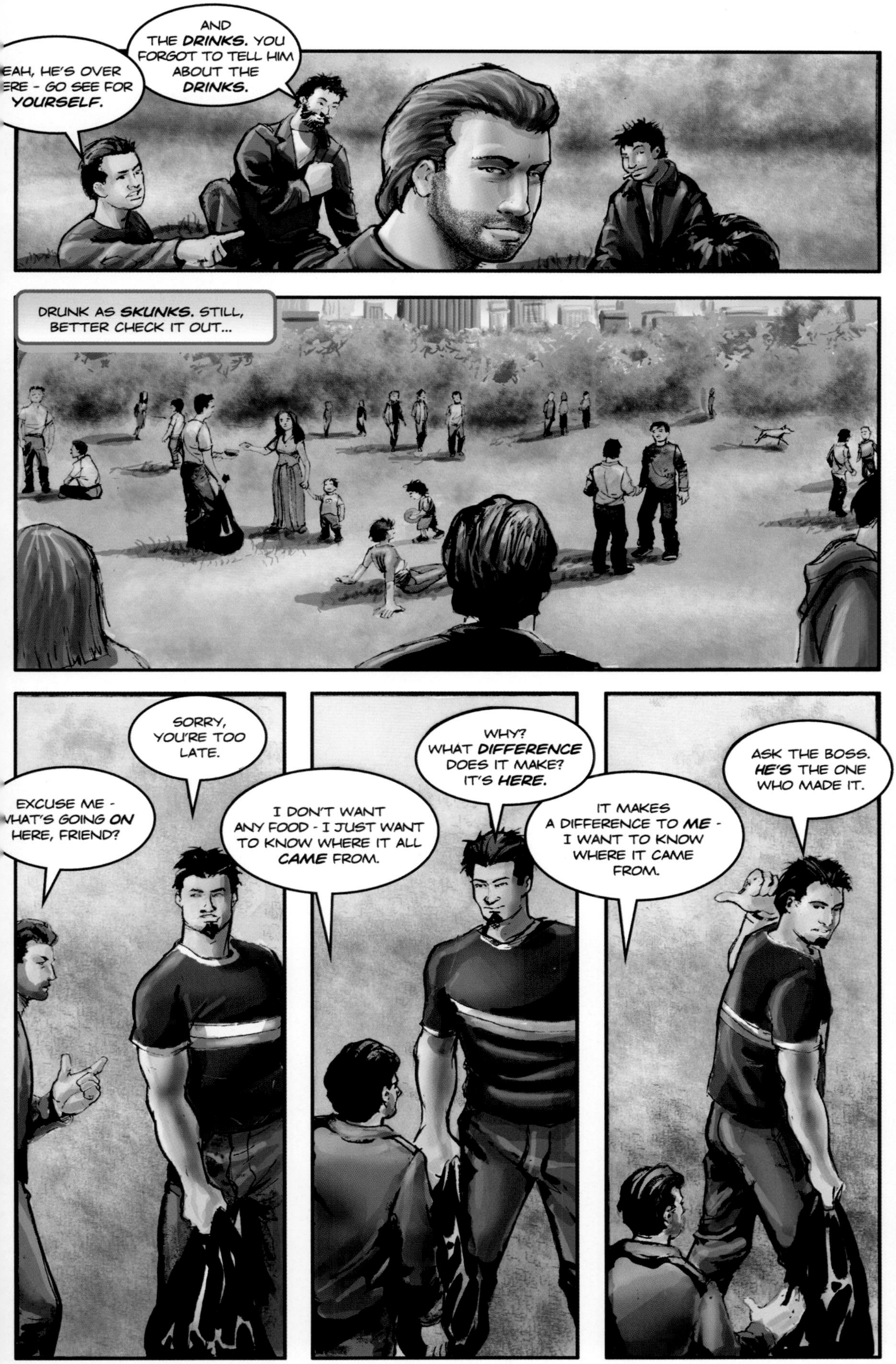
EAH, HE'S OVER ERE - GO SEE FOR YOURSELF.
AND THE DRINKS. YOU FORGOT TO TELL HIM ABOUT THE DRINKS.
DRUNK AS SKUNKS. STILL, BETTER CHECK IT OUT...
EXCUSE ME - HAT'S GOING ON HERE, FRIEND?
SORRY, YOU'RE TOO LATE.
I DON'T WANT ANY FOOD - I JUST WANT TO KNOW WHERE IT ALL CAME FROM.
WHY? WHAT DIFFERENCE DOES IT MAKE? IT'S HERE.
IT MAKES A DIFFERENCE TO ME - I WANT TO KNOW WHERE IT CAME FROM.
ASK THE BOSS. HE'S THE ONE WHO MADE IT.

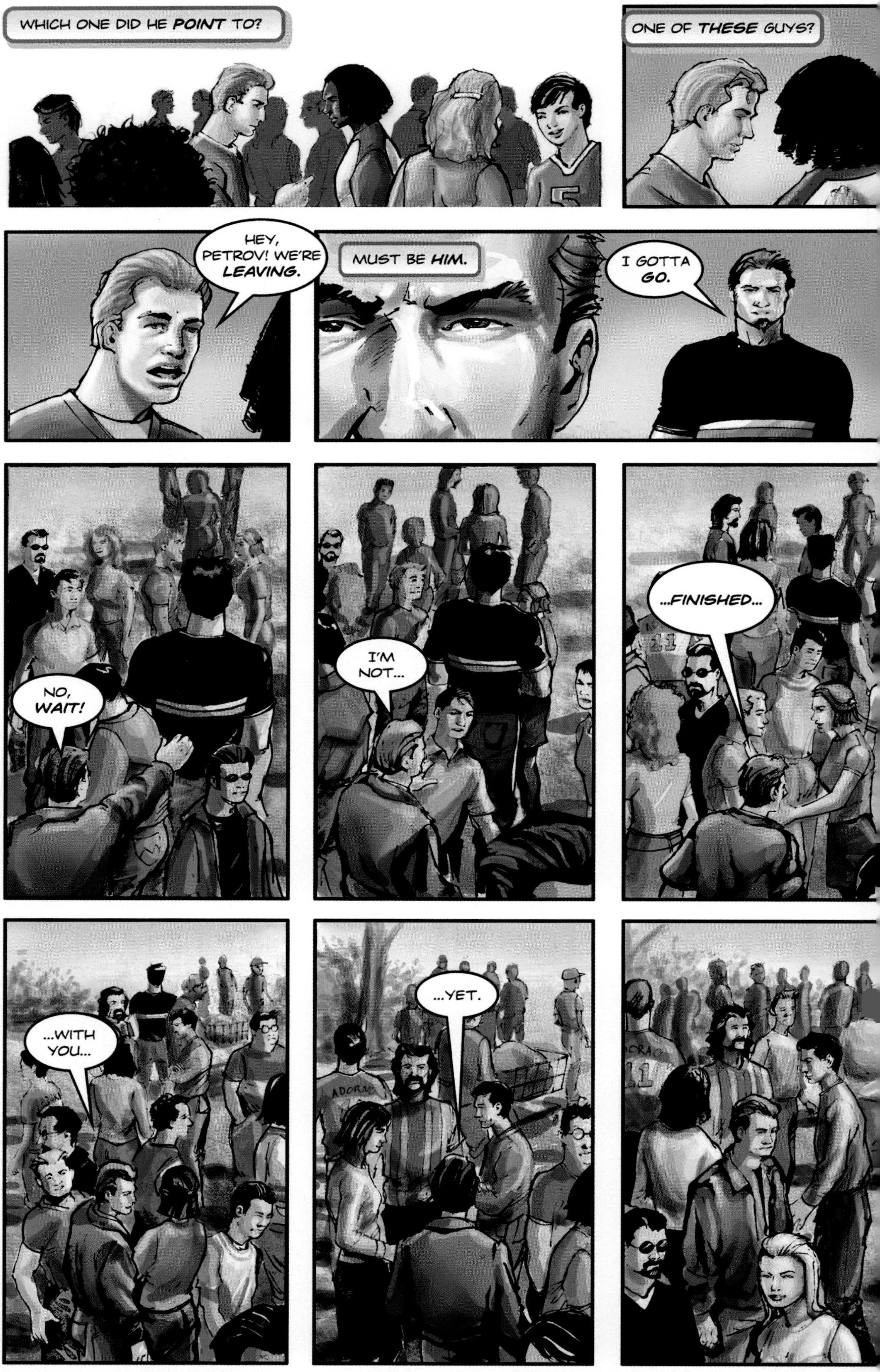
WHICH ONE DID HE POINT TO?
ONE OF THESE GUYS?
HEY, PETROV! WE'RE LEAVING.
MUST BE HIM.
I GOTTA GO.
NO, WAIT!
I'M NOT...
...FINISHED...
...WITH YOU...
...YET.

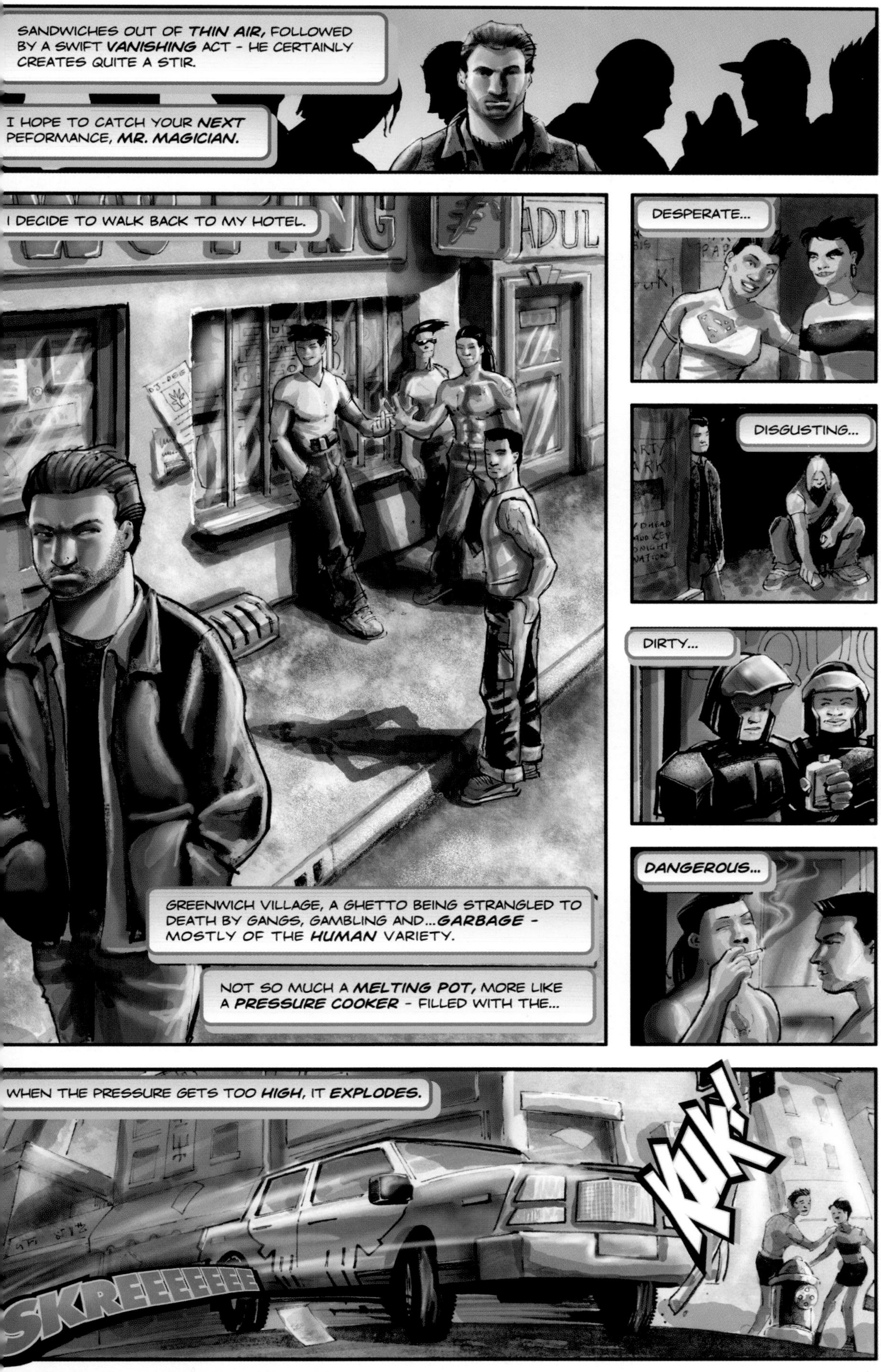
SANDWICHES OUT OF *THIN AIR,* FOLLOWED BY A SWIFT *VANISHING* ACT - HE CERTAINLY CREATES QUITE A STIR.
I HOPE TO CATCH YOUR *NEXT* PEFORMANCE, *MR. MAGICIAN.*
I DECIDE TO WALK BACK TO MY HOTEL.
GREENWICH VILLAGE, A GHETTO BEING STRANGLED TO DEATH BY GANGS, GAMBLING AND...*GARBAGE* - MOSTLY OF THE *HUMAN* VARIETY.
NOT SO MUCH A *MELTING POT,* MORE LIKE A *PRESSURE COOKER* - FILLED WITH THE...
DESPERATE...
DISGUSTING...
DIRTY...
DANGEROUS...
WHEN THE PRESSURE GETS TOO *HIGH,* IT *EXPLODES.*
KUK!
SKREEEEEEE

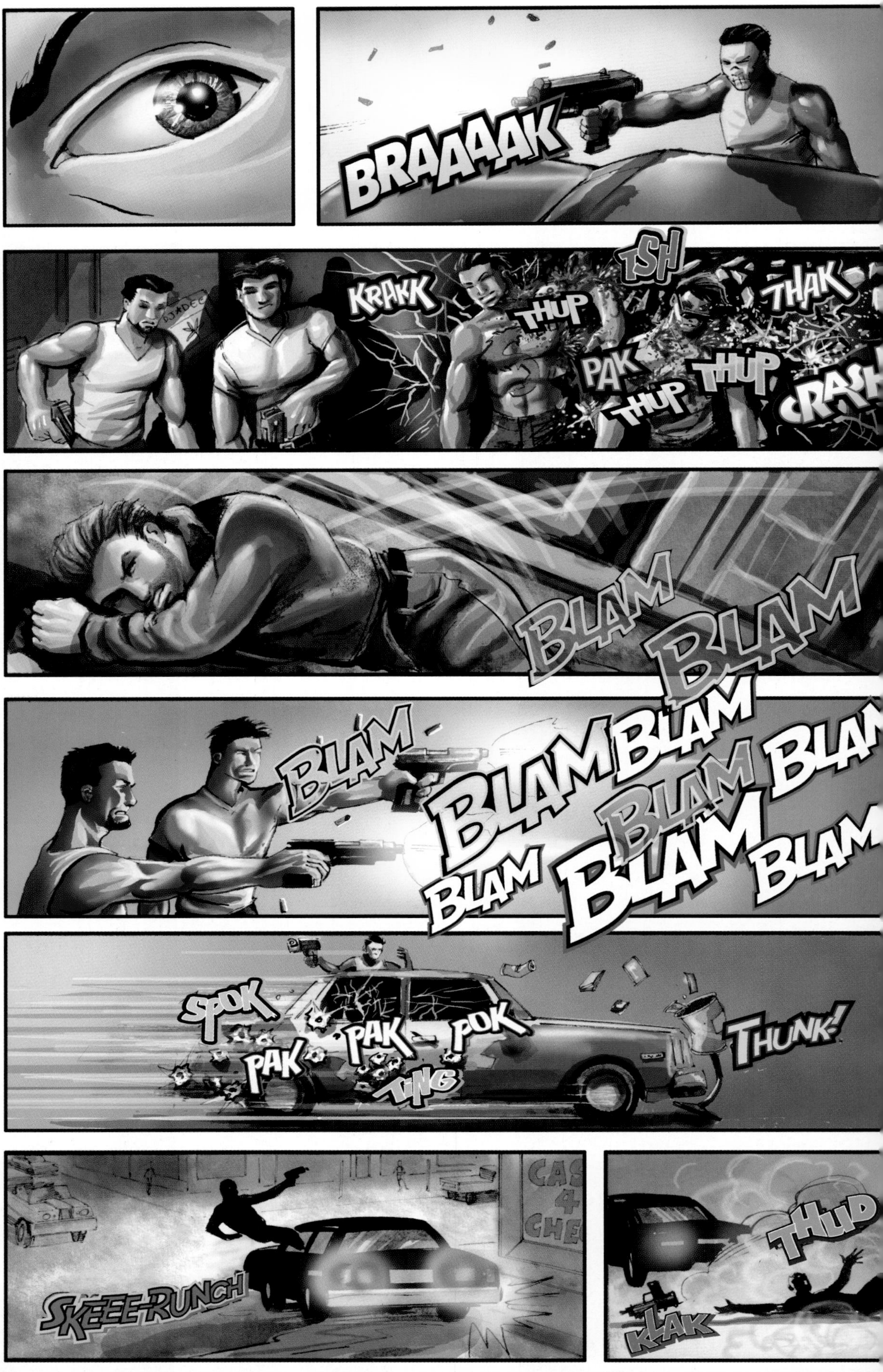
BRAAAAK
KRAKK
TSH
THUP
THAK
PAK
THUP
THUP
CRASH
BLAM
BLAM
BLAM
BLAM
BLAM
BLAM
BLAM
BLAM
BLAM
BLAM
SPOK
PAK
PAK
POK
TING
THUNK!
CASH 4 CHE
SKEEE-RUNCH
THUD
KLAK

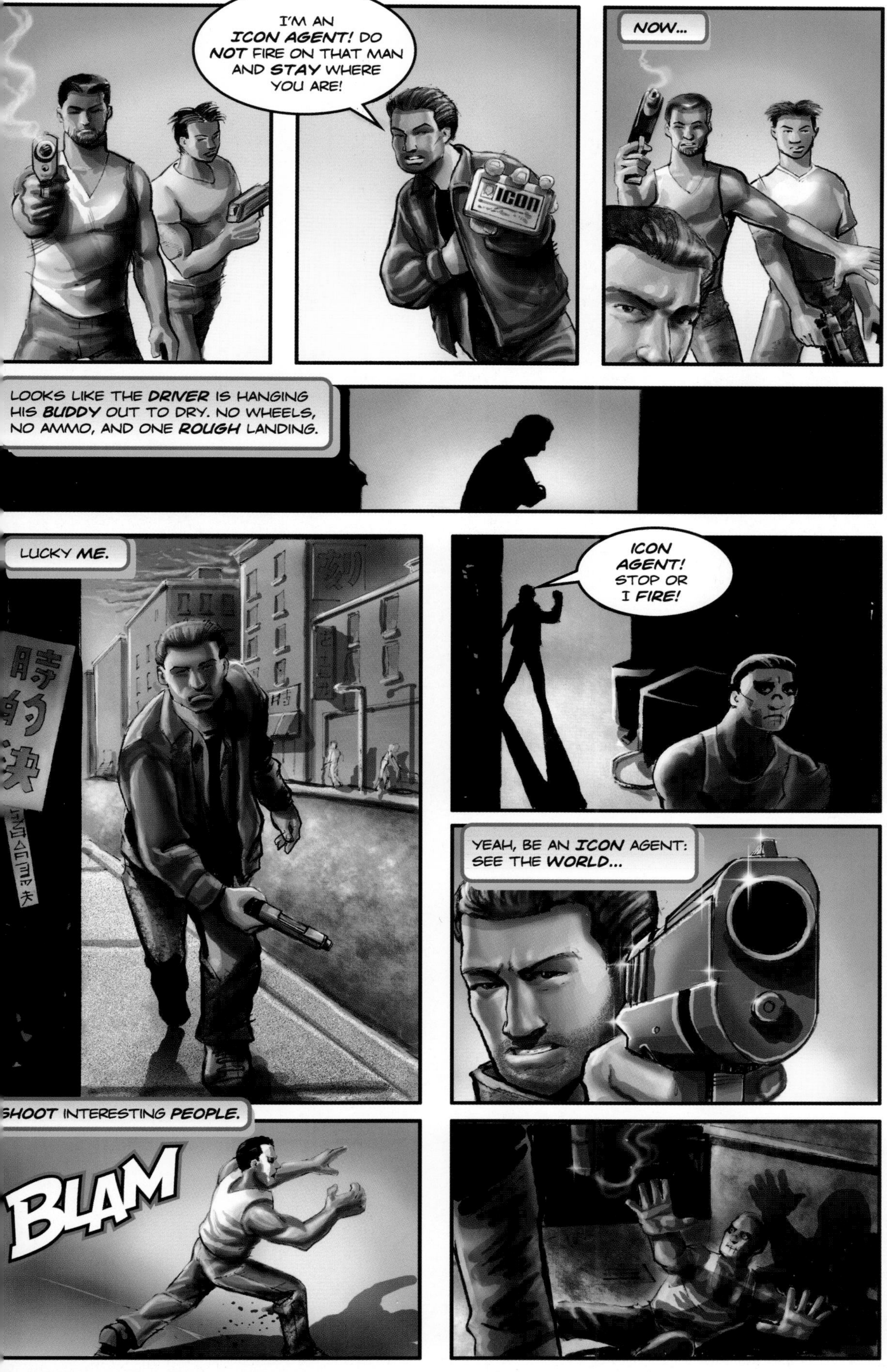
I'M AN ICON AGENT! DO NOT FIRE ON THAT MAN AND STAY WHERE YOU ARE!
NOW...
LOOKS LIKE THE DRIVER IS HANGING HIS BUDDY OUT TO DRY. NO WHEELS, NO AMMO, AND ONE ROUGH LANDING.
LUCKY ME.
ICON AGENT! STOP OR I FIRE!
YEAH, BE AN ICON AGENT: SEE THE WORLD...
SHOOT INTERESTING PEOPLE.
BLAM

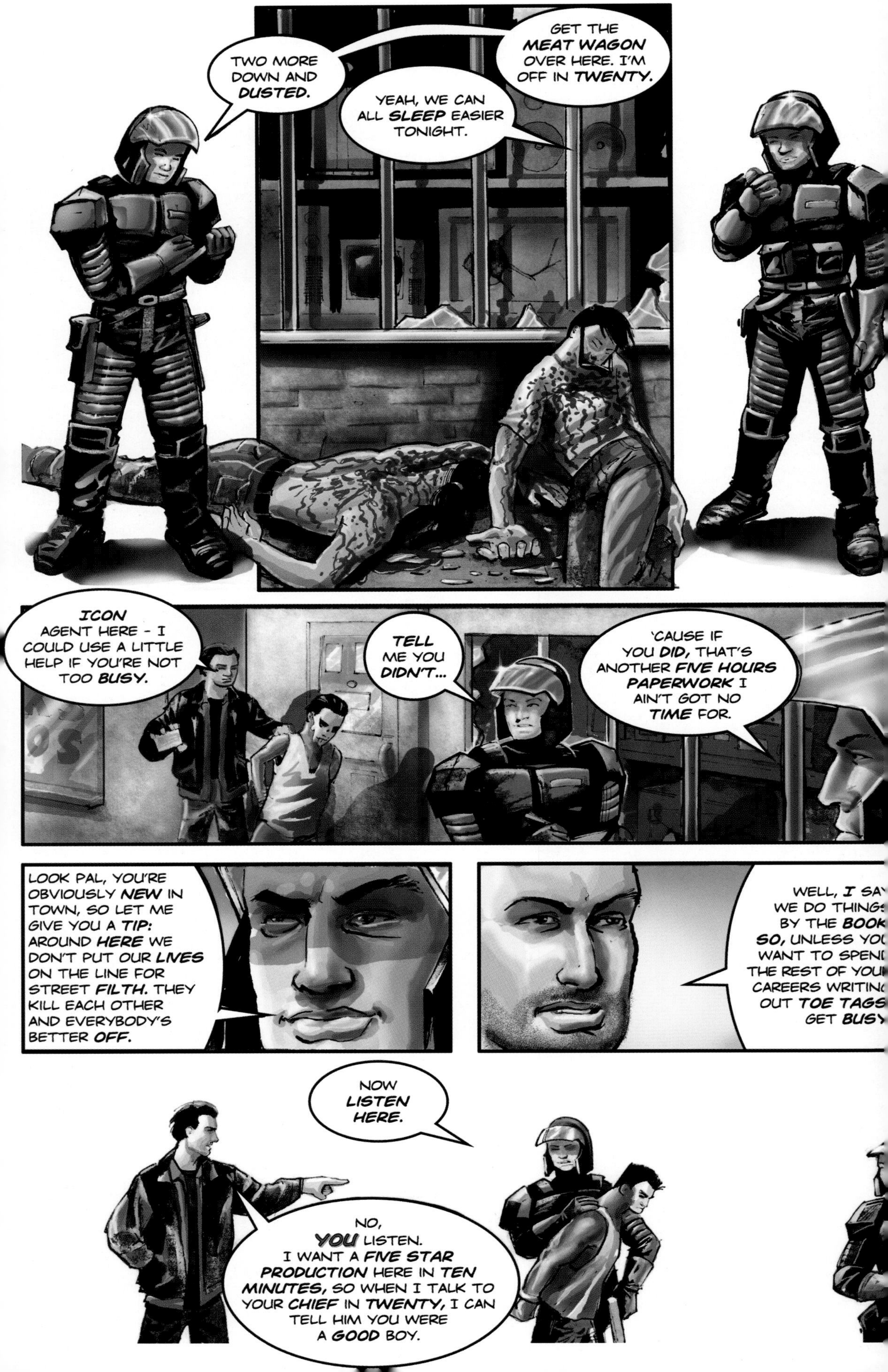
TWO MORE DOWN AND DUSTED.
GET THE MEAT WAGON OVER HERE. I'M OFF IN TWENTY.
YEAH, WE CAN ALL SLEEP EASIER TONIGHT.
ICON AGENT HERE - I COULD USE A LITTLE HELP IF YOU'RE NOT TOO BUSY.
TELL ME YOU DIDN'T...
'CAUSE IF YOU DID, THAT'S ANOTHER FIVE HOURS PAPERWORK I AIN'T GOT NO TIME FOR.
LOOK PAL, YOU'RE OBVIOUSLY NEW IN TOWN, SO LET ME GIVE YOU A TIP: AROUND HERE WE DON'T PUT OUR LIVES ON THE LINE FOR STREET FILTH. THEY KILL EACH OTHER AND EVERYBODY'S BETTER OFF.
WELL, I SA WE DO THING BY THE BOOK SO, UNLESS YO WANT TO SPEN THE REST OF YOU CAREERS WRITIN OUT TOE TAGS GET BUS
NOW LISTEN HERE.
NO, YOU LISTEN. I WANT A FIVE STAR PRODUCTION HERE IN TEN MINUTES, SO WHEN I TALK TO YOUR CHIEF IN TWENTY, I CAN TELL HIM YOU WERE A GOOD BOY.

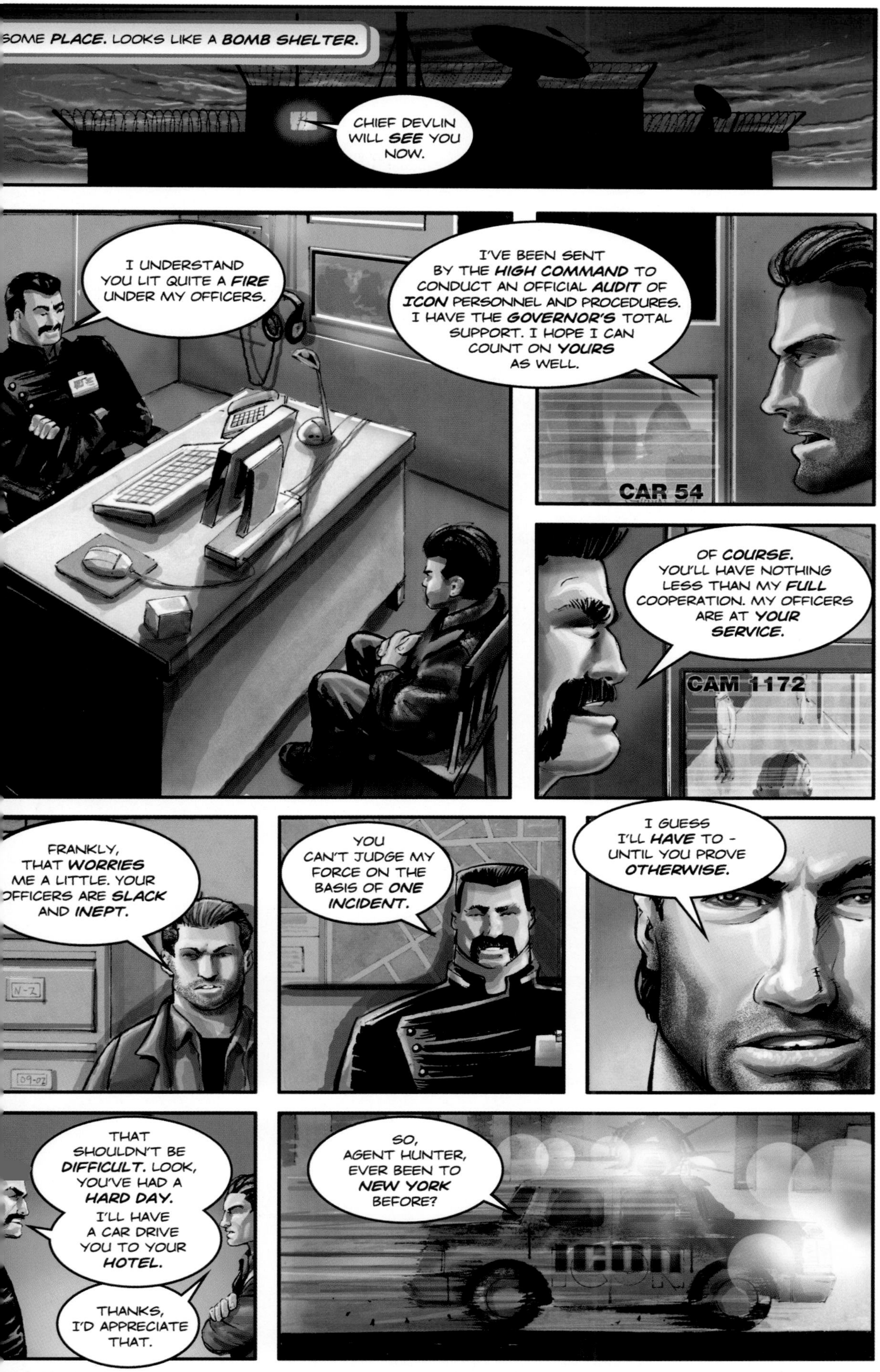
SOME PLACE. LOOKS LIKE A BOMB SHELTER.
CHIEF DEVLIN WILL SEE YOU NOW.
I UNDERSTAND YOU LIT QUITE A FIRE UNDER MY OFFICERS.
I'VE BEEN SENT BY THE HIGH COMMAND TO CONDUCT AN OFFICIAL AUDIT OF ICON PERSONNEL AND PROCEDURES. I HAVE THE GOVERNOR'S TOTAL SUPPORT. I HOPE I CAN COUNT ON YOURS AS WELL.
CAR 54
OF COURSE. YOU'LL HAVE NOTHING LESS THAN MY FULL COOPERATION. MY OFFICERS ARE AT YOUR SERVICE.
CAM 1172
FRANKLY, THAT WORRIES ME A LITTLE. YOUR OFFICERS ARE SLACK AND INEPT.
N-Z
09-02
YOU CAN'T JUDGE MY FORCE ON THE BASIS OF ONE INCIDENT.
I GUESS I'LL HAVE TO - UNTIL YOU PROVE OTHERWISE.
THAT SHOULDN'T BE DIFFICULT. LOOK, YOU'VE HAD A HARD DAY. I'LL HAVE A CAR DRIVE YOU TO YOUR HOTEL.
THANKS, I'D APPRECIATE THAT.
SO, AGENT HUNTER, EVER BEEN TO NEW YORK BEFORE?
ICON

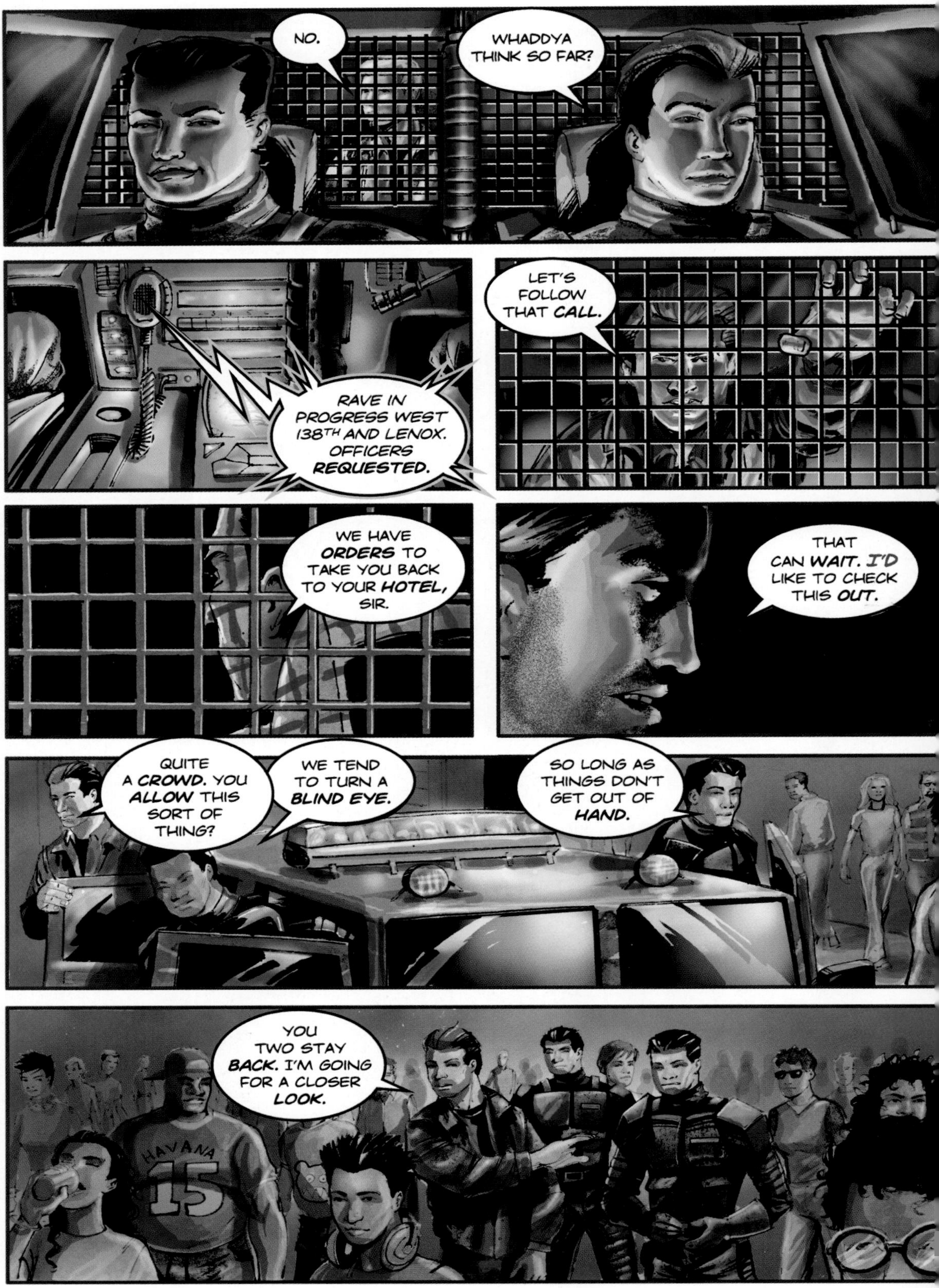
NO.
WHADDYA THINK SO FAR?
RAVE IN PROGRESS WEST 138TH AND LENOX. OFFICERS REQUESTED.
LET'S FOLLOW THAT CALL.
WE HAVE ORDERS TO TAKE YOU BACK TO YOUR HOTEL, SIR.
THAT CAN WAIT. I'D LIKE TO CHECK THIS OUT.
QUITE A CROWD. YOU ALLOW THIS SORT OF THING?
WE TEND TO TURN A BLIND EYE.
SO LONG AS THINGS DON'T GET OUT OF HAND.
YOU TWO STAY BACK. I'M GOING FOR A CLOSER LOOK.
HAVANA 15

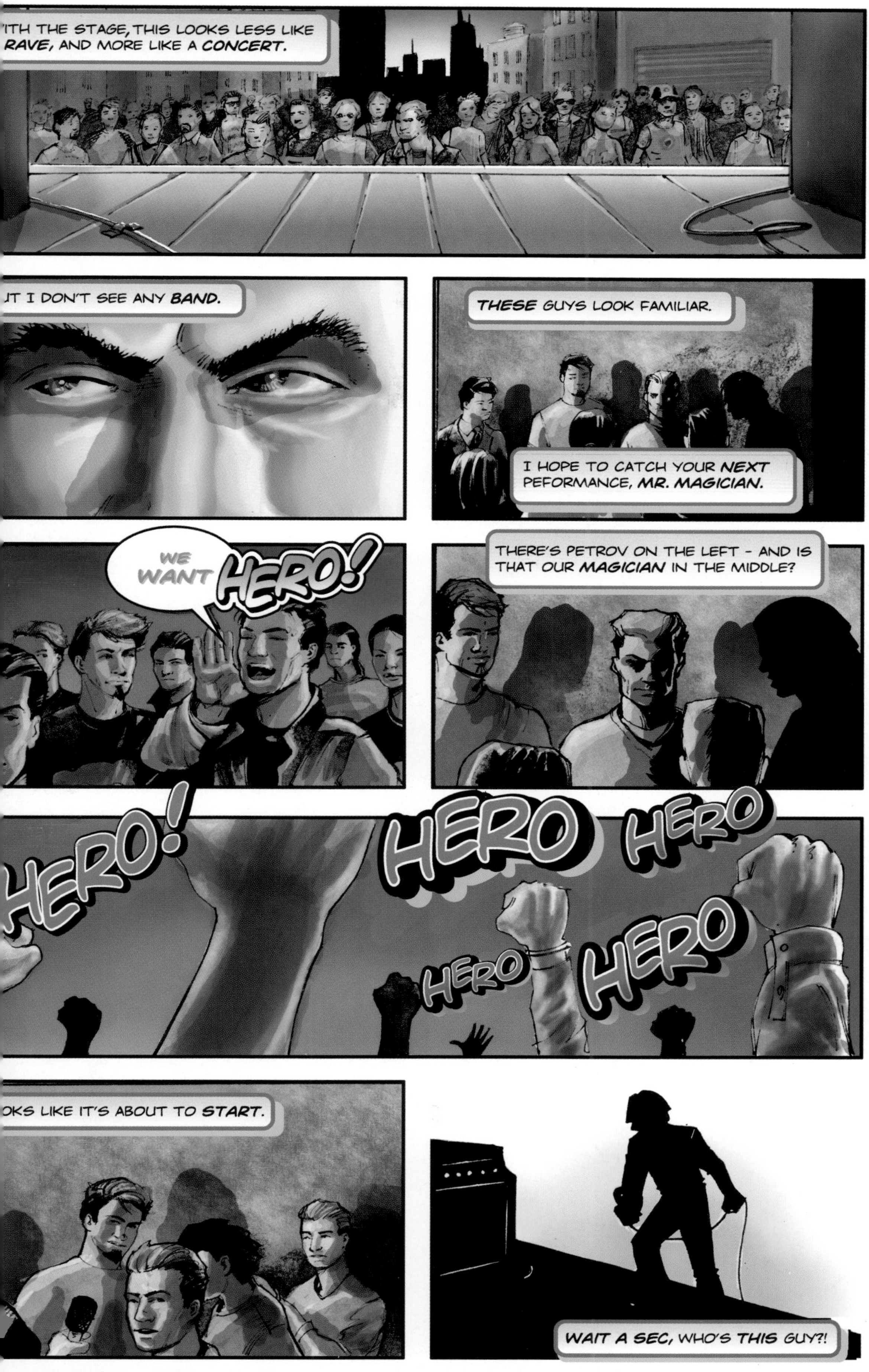

ITH THE STAGE, THIS LOOKS LESS LIKE RAVE, AND MORE LIKE A CONCERT.
UT I DON'T SEE ANY BAND.
THESE GUYS LOOK FAMILIAR.
I HOPE TO CATCH YOUR NEXT PEFORMANCE, MR. MAGICIAN.
WE WANT HERO!
THERE'S PETROV ON THE LEFT - AND IS THAT OUR MAGICIAN IN THE MIDDLE?
HERO!
HERO HERO
HERO HERO
OKS LIKE IT'S ABOUT TO START.
WAIT A SEC, WHO'S THIS GUY?!

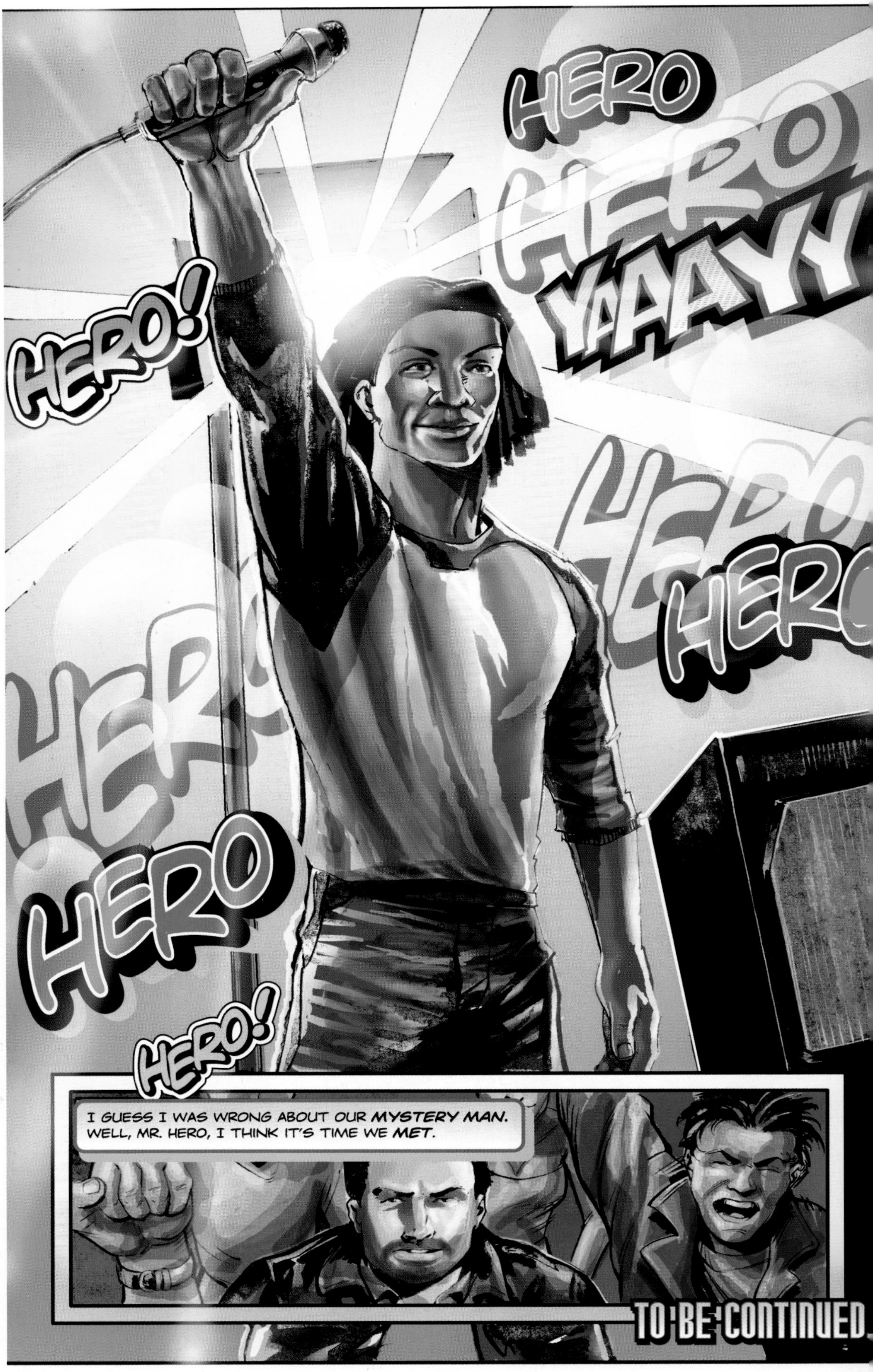
HERO
HERO
YAAAYY
HERO!
HERO
HERO
HERO
HERO
HERO!
I GUESS I WAS WRONG ABOUT OUR *MYSTERY MAN*.
WELL, MR. HERO, I THINK IT'S TIME WE *MET*.
TO BE CONTINUED.

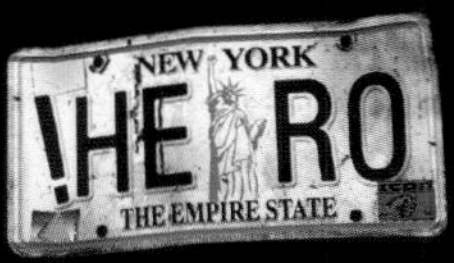
NEW YORK
!HE RO
THE EMPIRE STATE

TWO

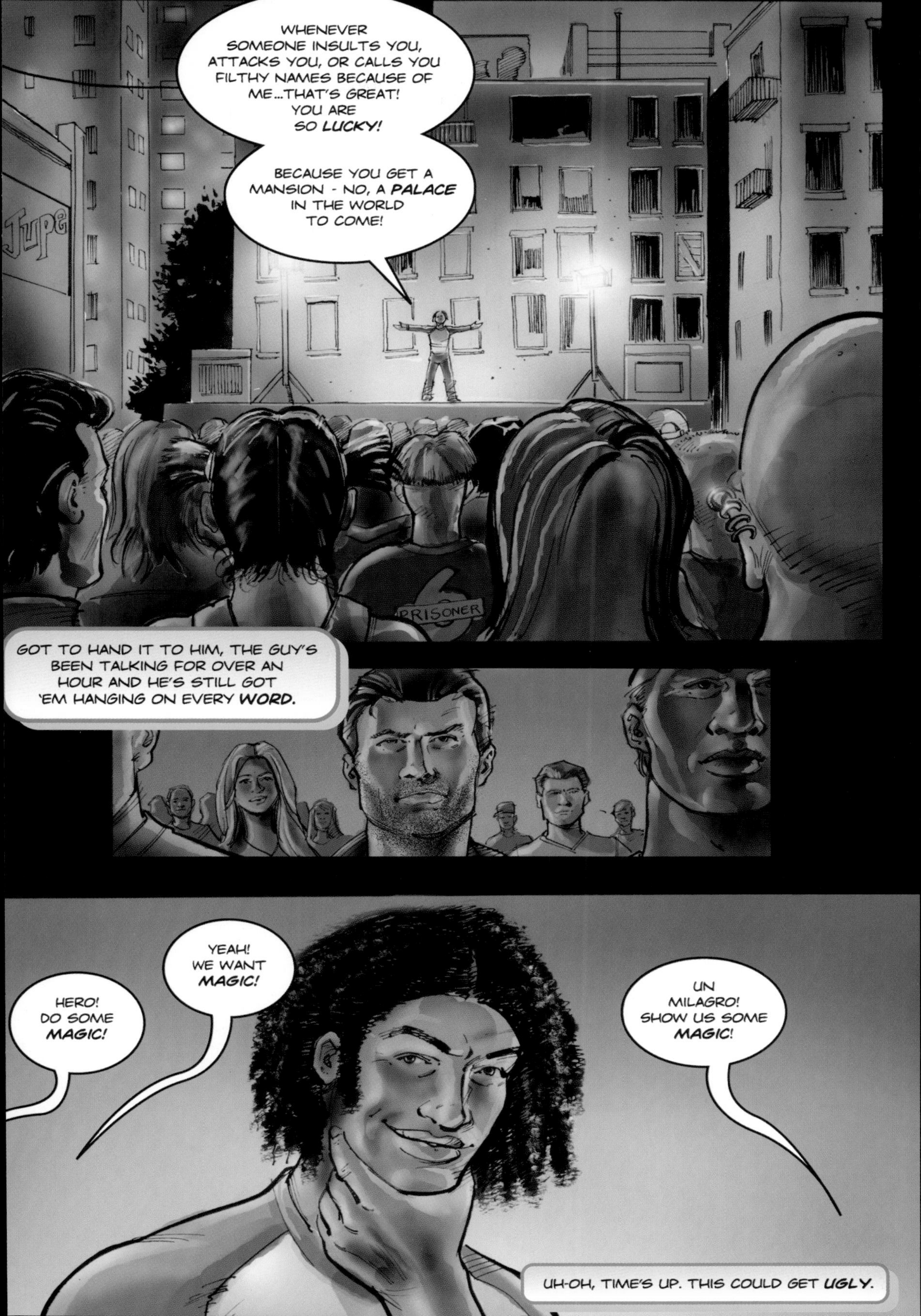
WHENEVER SOMEONE INSULTS YOU, ATTACKS YOU, OR CALLS YOU FILTHY NAMES BECAUSE OF ME...THAT'S GREAT! YOU ARE SO LUCKY!
BECAUSE YOU GET A MANSION - NO, A PALACE IN THE WORLD TO COME!
Jupe
GOT TO HAND IT TO HIM, THE GUY'S BEEN TALKING FOR OVER AN HOUR AND HE'S STILL GOT 'EM HANGING ON EVERY WORD.
HERO! DO SOME MAGIC!
YEAH! WE WANT MAGIC!
UN MILAGRO! SHOW US SOME MAGIC!
UH-OH, TIME'S UP. THIS COULD GET UGLY.

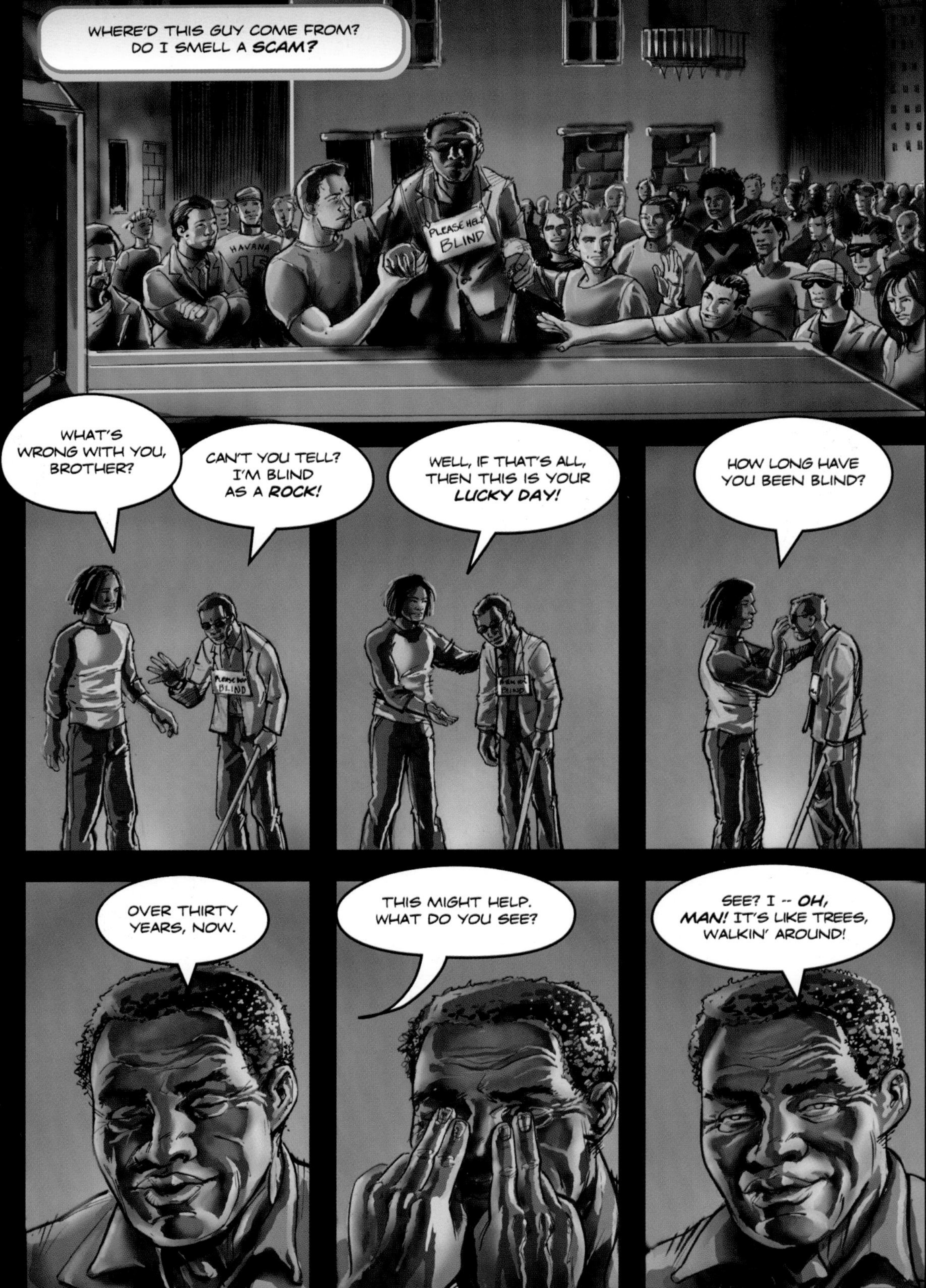
WHERE'D THIS GUY COME FROM? DO I SMELL A SCAM?
PLEASE HELP BLIND
HAVANA
WHAT'S WRONG WITH YOU, BROTHER?
CAN'T YOU TELL? I'M BLIND AS A ROCK!
WELL, IF THAT'S ALL, THEN THIS IS YOUR LUCKY DAY!
HOW LONG HAVE YOU BEEN BLIND?
OVER THIRTY YEARS, NOW.
THIS MIGHT HELP. WHAT DO YOU SEE?
SEE? I -- OH, MAN! IT'S LIKE TREES, WALKIN' AROUND!

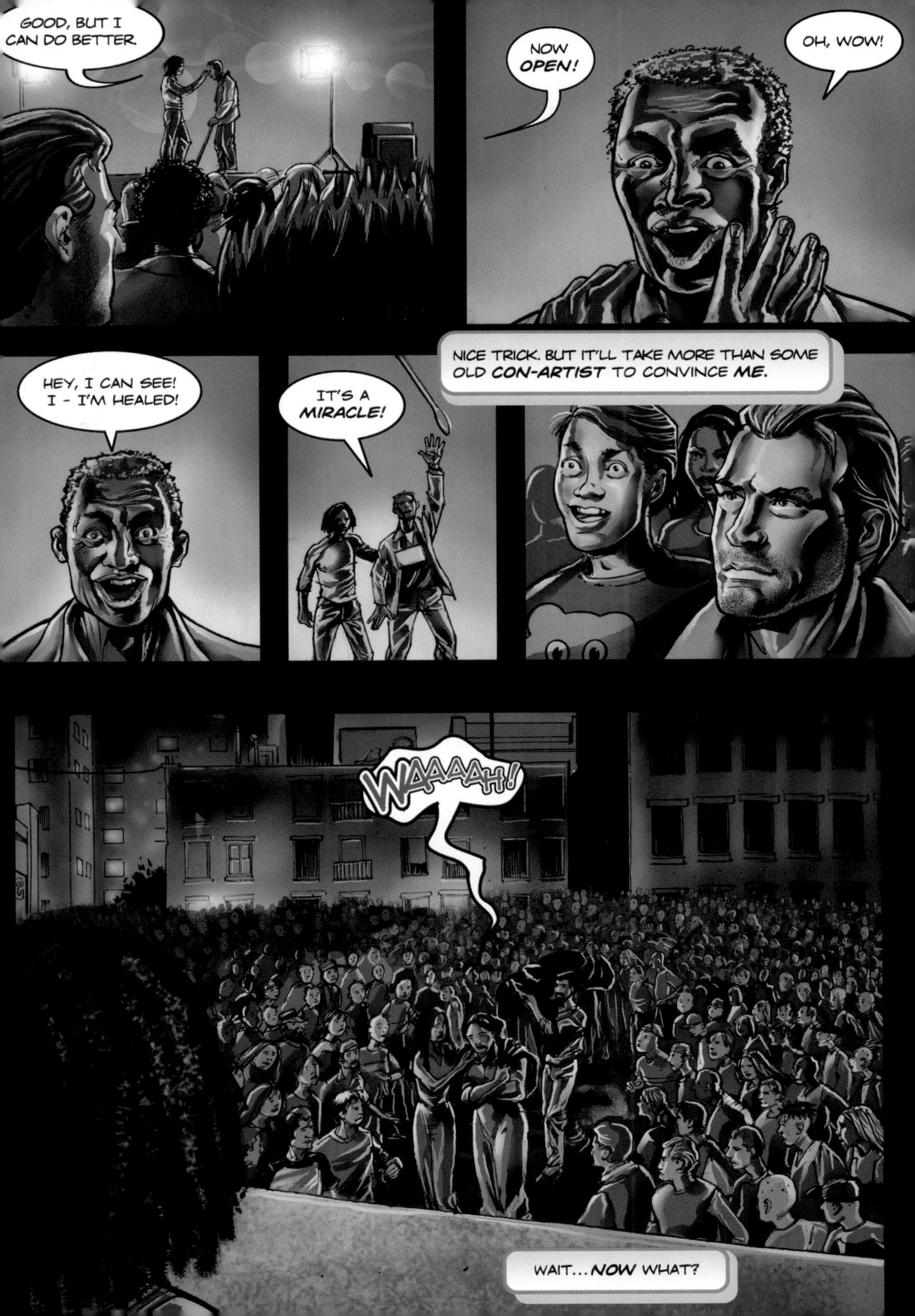
GOOD, BUT I CAN DO BETTER.
NOW OPEN!
OH, WOW!
HEY, I CAN SEE! I - I'M HEALED!
IT'S A MIRACLE!
NICE TRICK. BUT IT'LL TAKE MORE THAN SOME OLD CON-ARTIST TO CONVINCE ME.
WAAAAH!
WAIT... NOW WHAT?

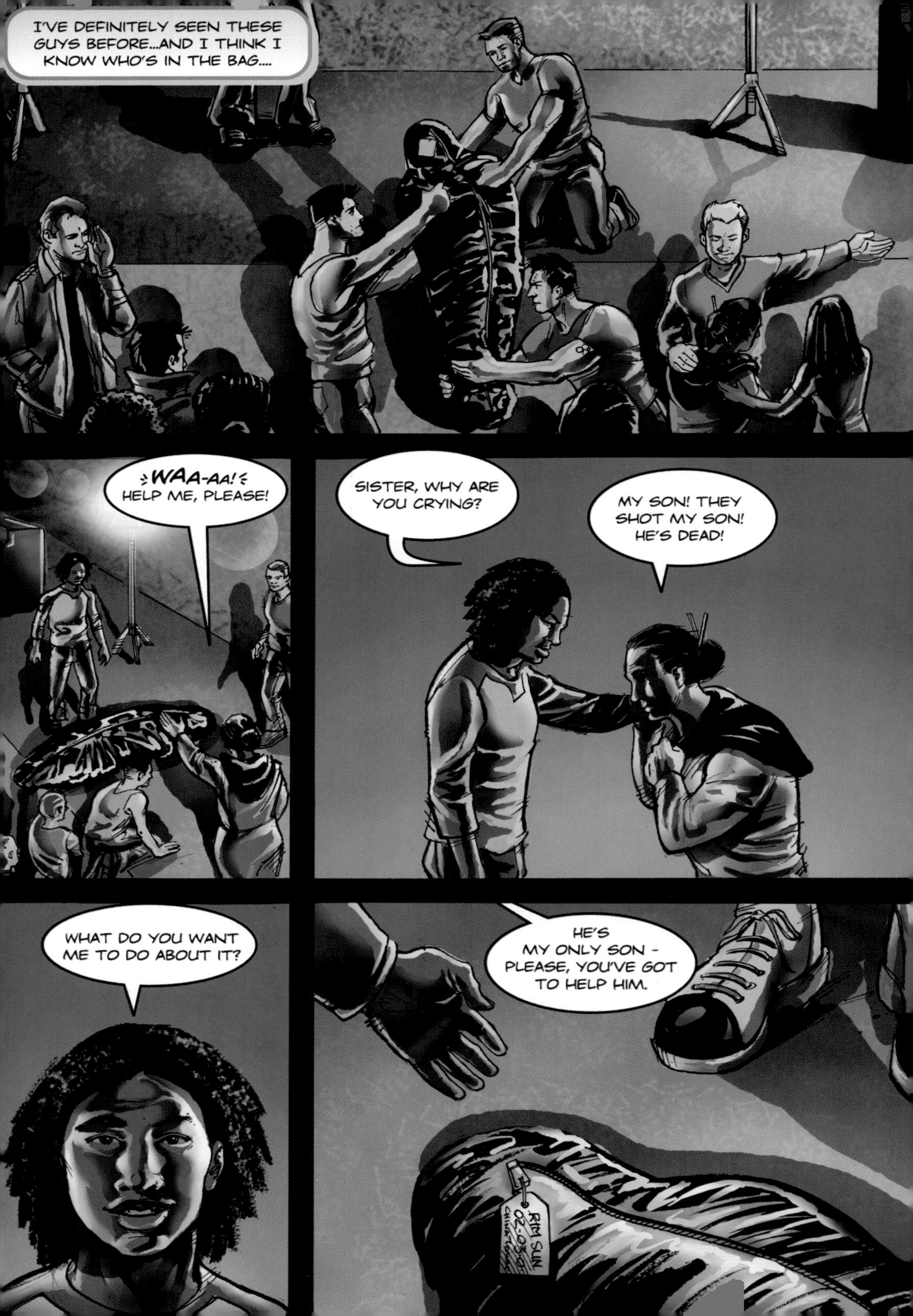
I'VE DEFINITELY SEEN THESE GUYS BEFORE...AND I THINK I KNOW WHO'S IN THE BAG....
WAA-AA! HELP ME, PLEASE!
SISTER, WHY ARE YOU CRYING?
MY SON! THEY SHOT MY SON! HE'S DEAD!
WHAT DO YOU WANT ME TO DO ABOUT IT?
HE'S MY ONLY SON - PLEASE, YOU'VE GOT TO HELP HIM.
RIM SUN

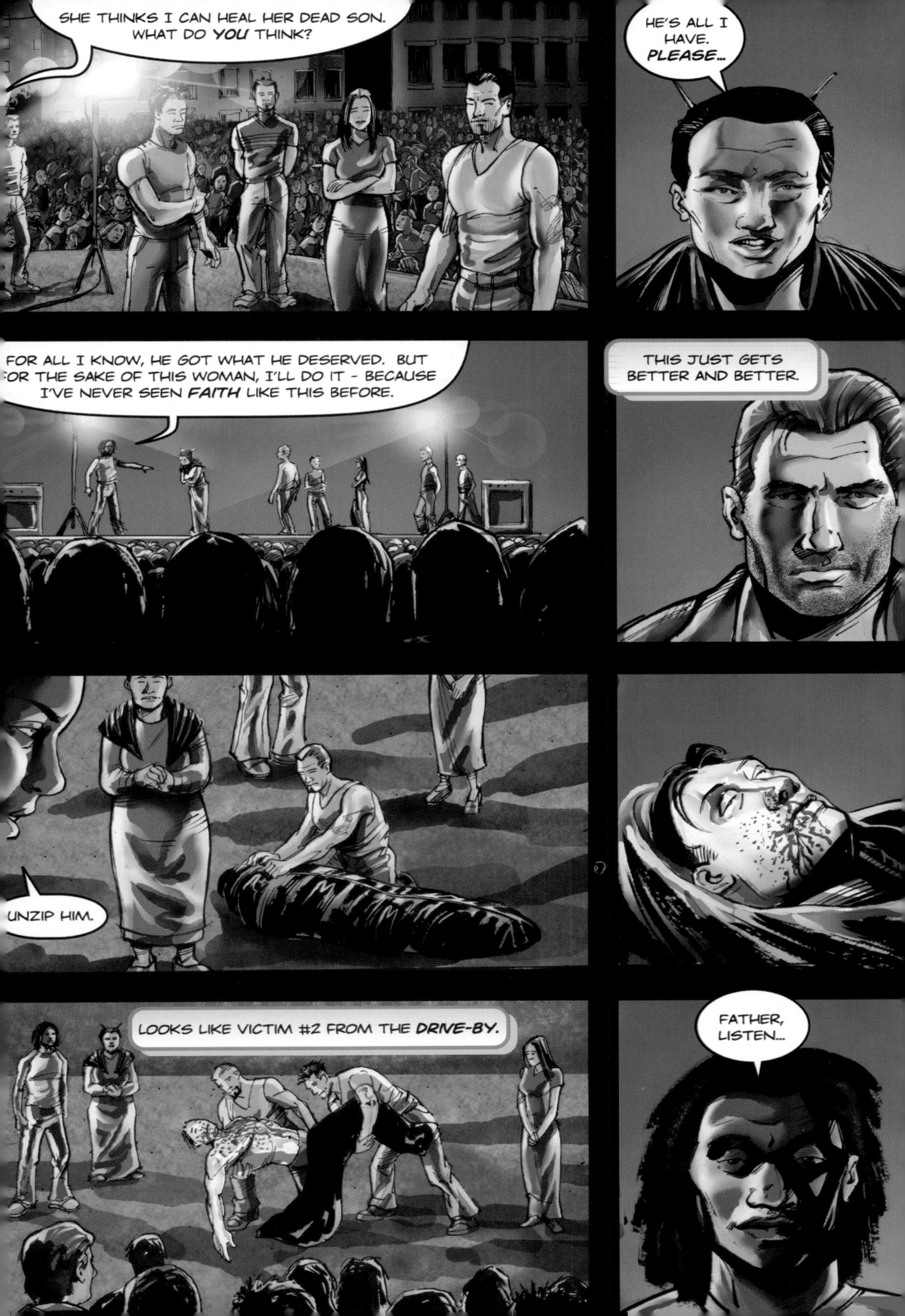
SHE THINKS I CAN HEAL HER DEAD SON. WHAT DO YOU THINK?
HE'S ALL I HAVE. PLEASE...
FOR ALL I KNOW, HE GOT WHAT HE DESERVED. BUT FOR THE SAKE OF THIS WOMAN, I'LL DO IT - BECAUSE I'VE NEVER SEEN FAITH LIKE THIS BEFORE.
THIS JUST GETS BETTER AND BETTER.
UNZIP HIM.
LOOKS LIKE VICTIM #2 FROM THE DRIVE-BY.
FATHER, LISTEN...

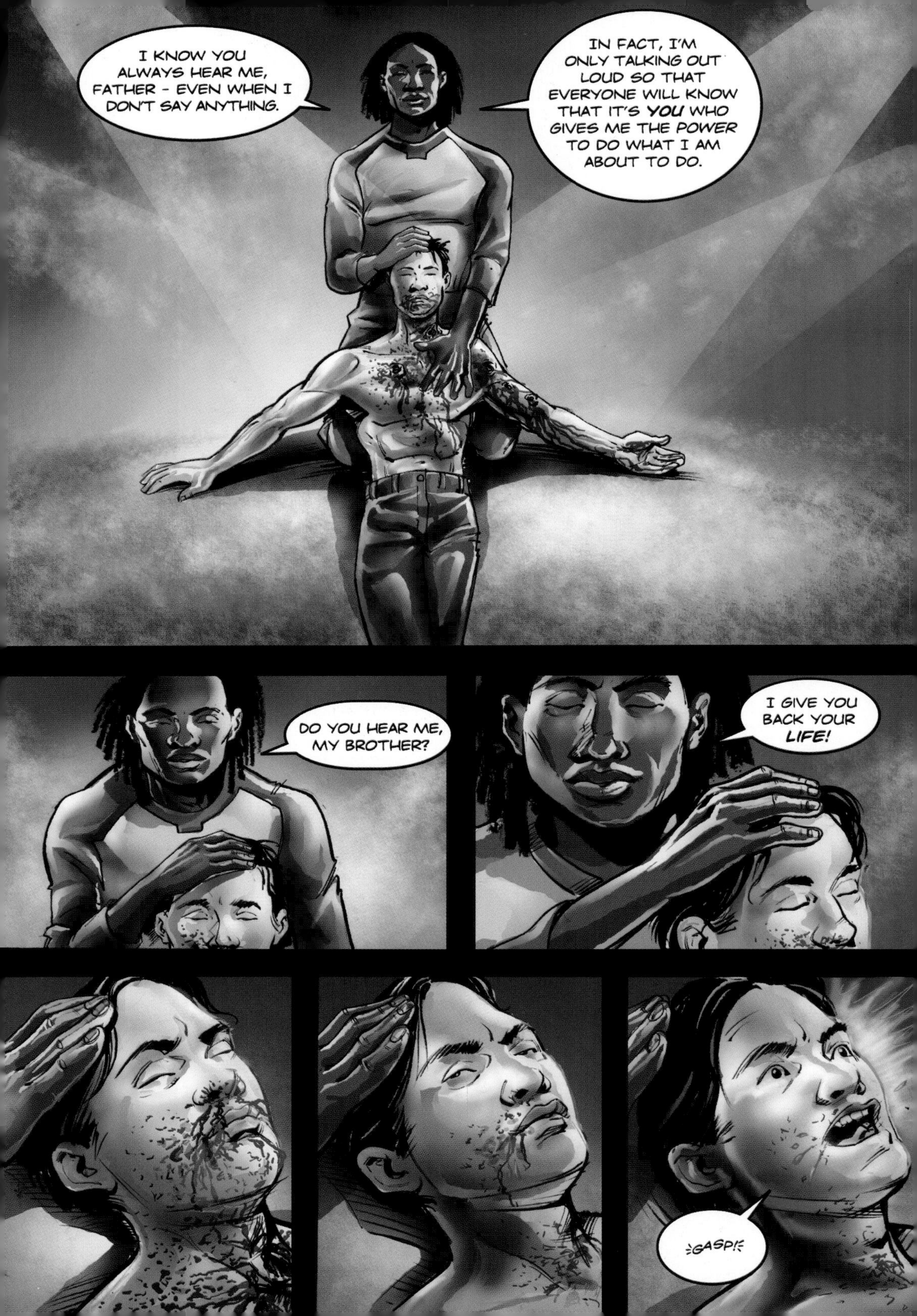
I KNOW YOU ALWAYS HEAR ME, FATHER - EVEN WHEN I DON'T SAY ANYTHING.
IN FACT, I'M ONLY TALKING OUT LOUD SO THAT EVERYONE WILL KNOW THAT IT'S YOU WHO GIVES ME THE POWER TO DO WHAT I AM ABOUT TO DO.
DO YOU HEAR ME, MY BROTHER?
I GIVE YOU BACK YOUR LIFE!
GASP!

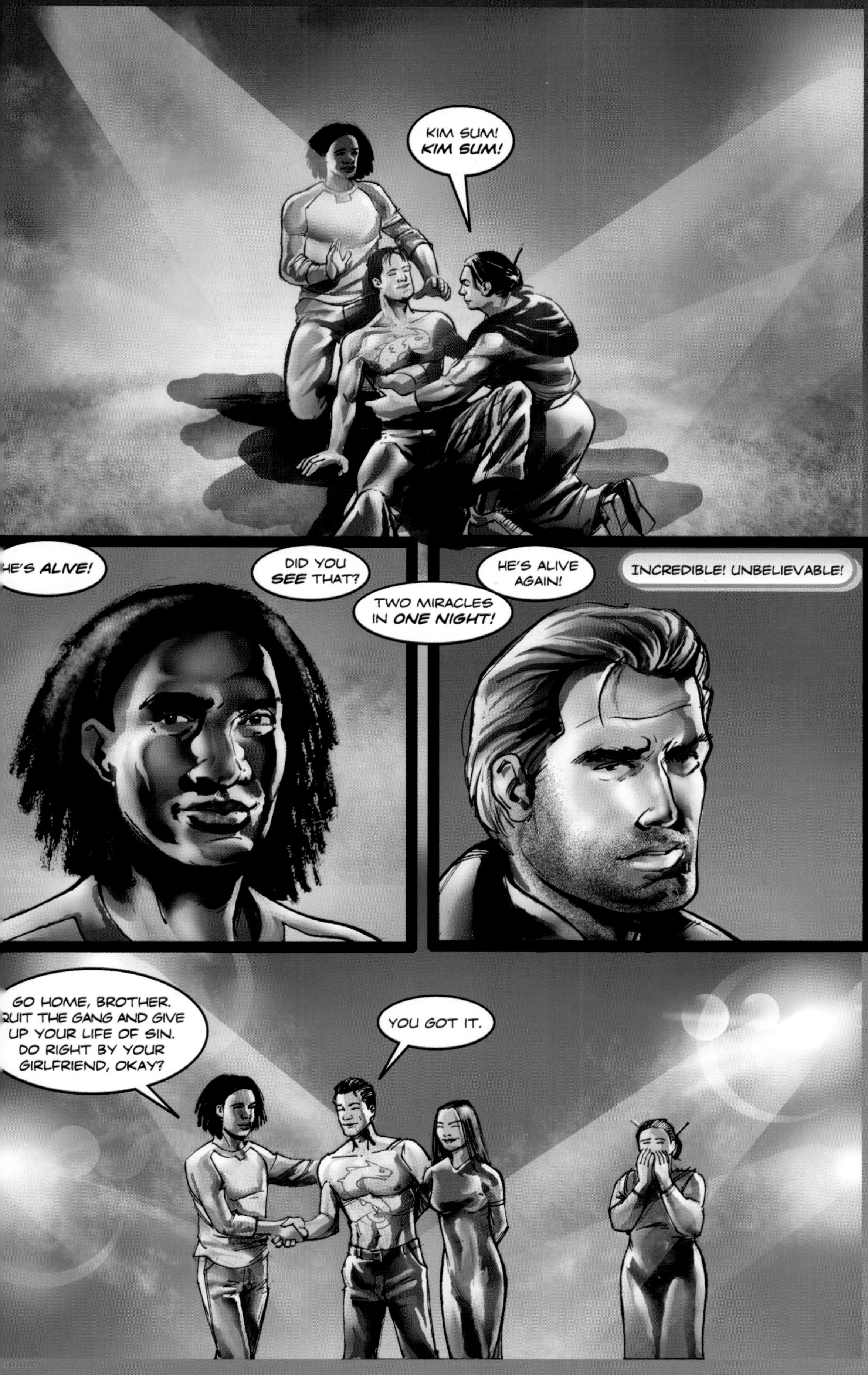
KIM SUM! KIM SUM!
HE'S ALIVE!
DID YOU SEE THAT?
TWO MIRACLES IN ONE NIGHT!
HE'S ALIVE AGAIN!
INCREDIBLE! UNBELIEVABLE!
GO HOME, BROTHER. QUIT THE GANG AND GIVE UP YOUR LIFE OF SIN. DO RIGHT BY YOUR GIRLFRIEND, OKAY?
YOU GOT IT.

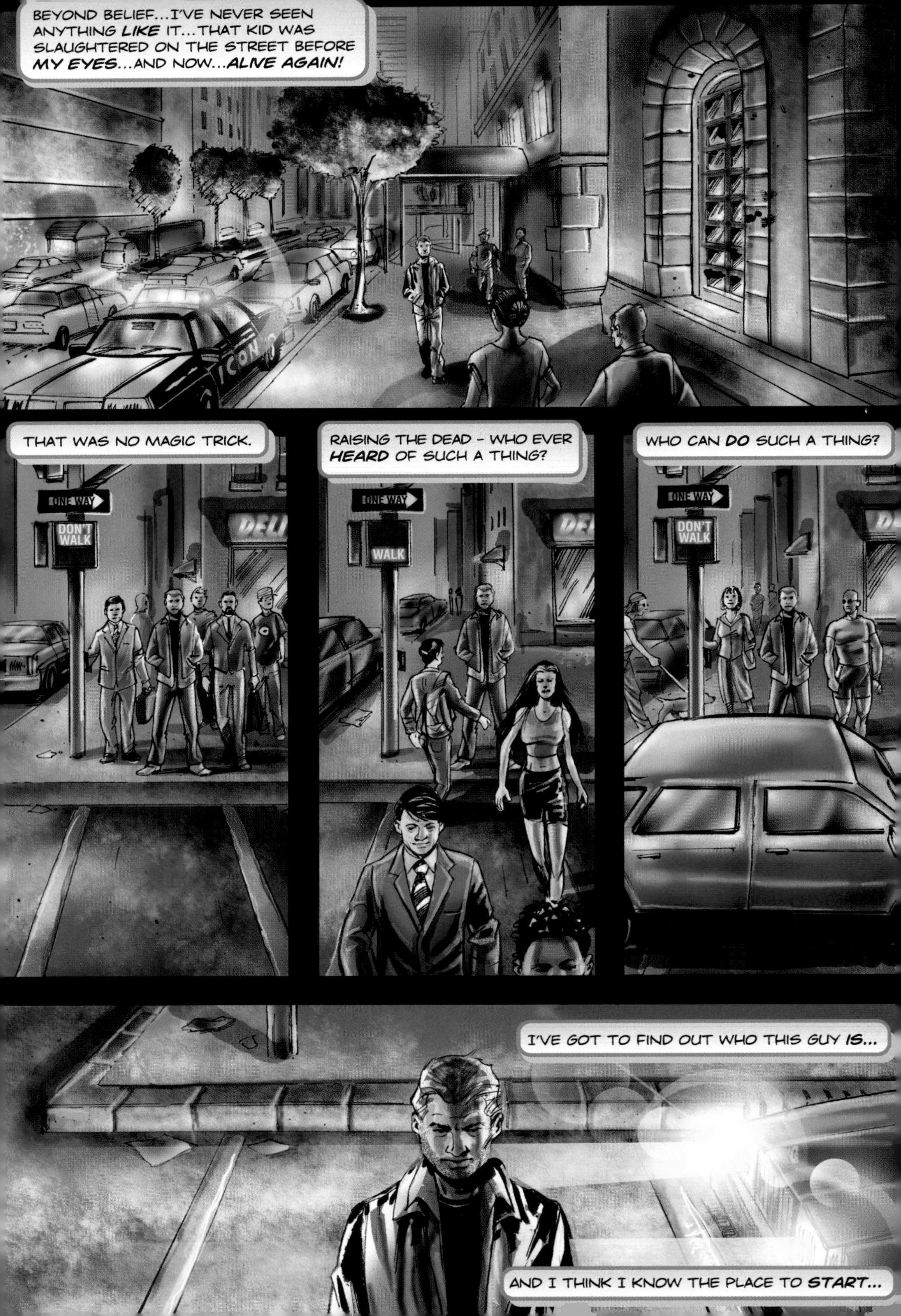
BEYOND BELIEF...I'VE NEVER SEEN ANYTHING LIKE IT...THAT KID WAS SLAUGHTERED ON THE STREET BEFORE MY EYES...AND NOW...ALIVE AGAIN!
THAT WAS NO MAGIC TRICK.
ONE WAY
DON'T WALK
DELI
RAISING THE DEAD - WHO EVER HEARD OF SUCH A THING?
ONE WAY
WALK
WHO CAN DO SUCH A THING?
ONE WAY
DON'T WALK
I'VE GOT TO FIND OUT WHO THIS GUY IS...
AND I THINK I KNOW THE PLACE TO START...

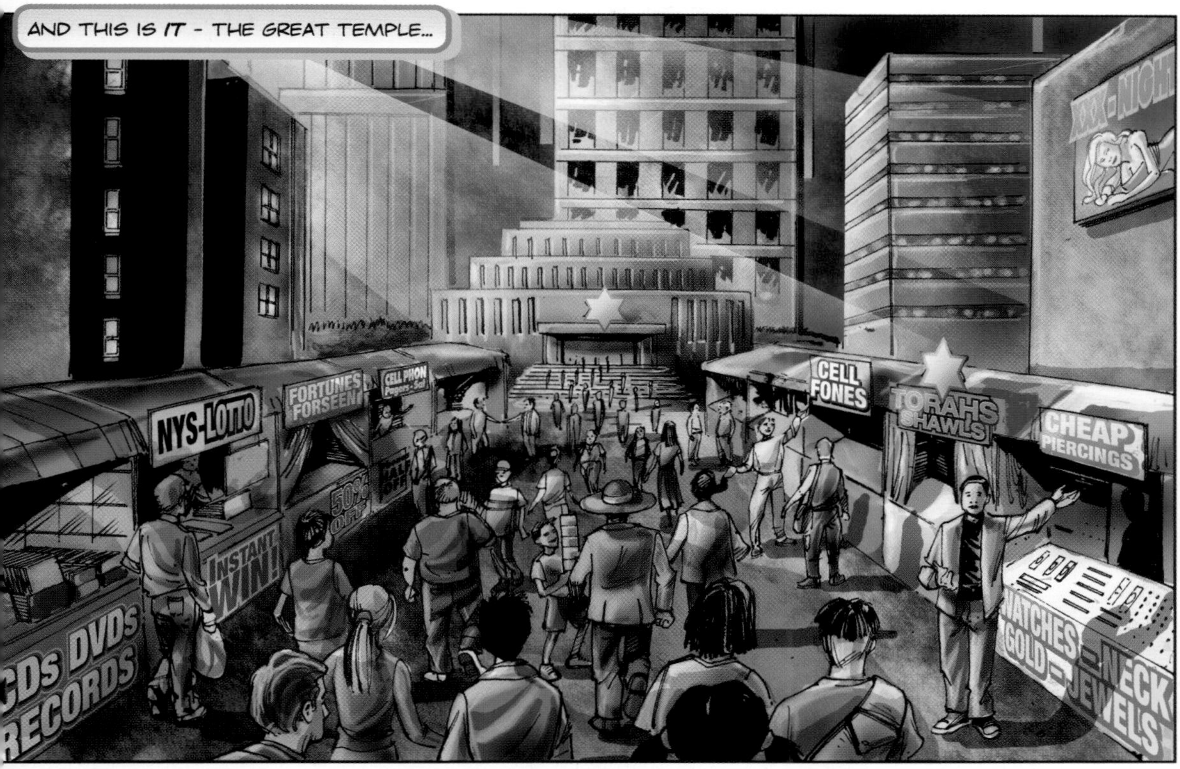
AND THIS IS *IT* - THE GREAT TEMPLE...
NYS-LOTTO
FORTUNES FORSEEN
50% OFF
INSTANT WIN!
CDs DVDs RECORDS
CELL FONES
TORAHS SHAWLS
CHEAP PIERCINGS

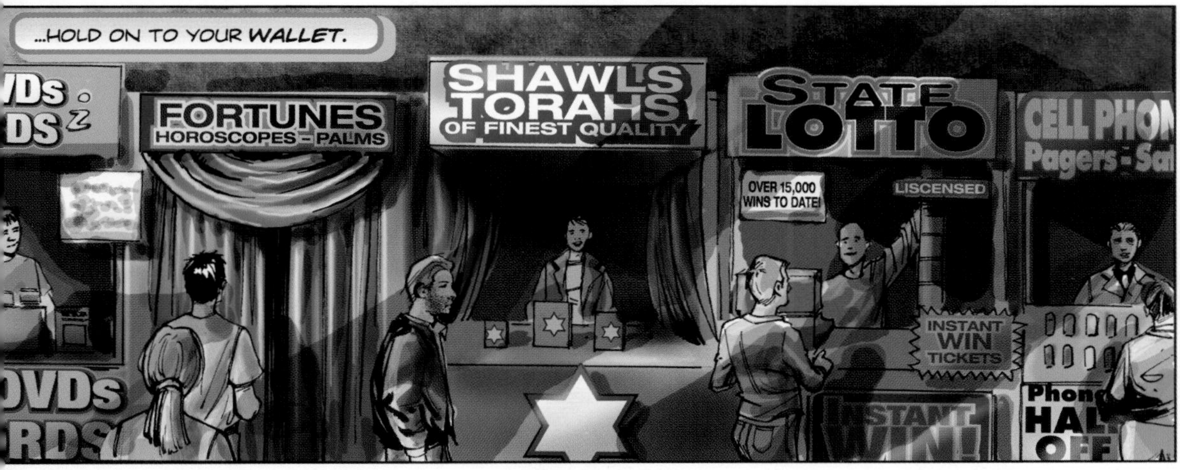
...HOLD ON TO YOUR *WALLET*.
FORTUNES HOROSCOPES - PALMS
SHAWLS TORAHS OF FINEST QUALITY
STATE LOTTO
OVER 15,000 WINS TO DATE!
LISCENSED
INSTANT WIN TICKETS
INSTANT WIN!

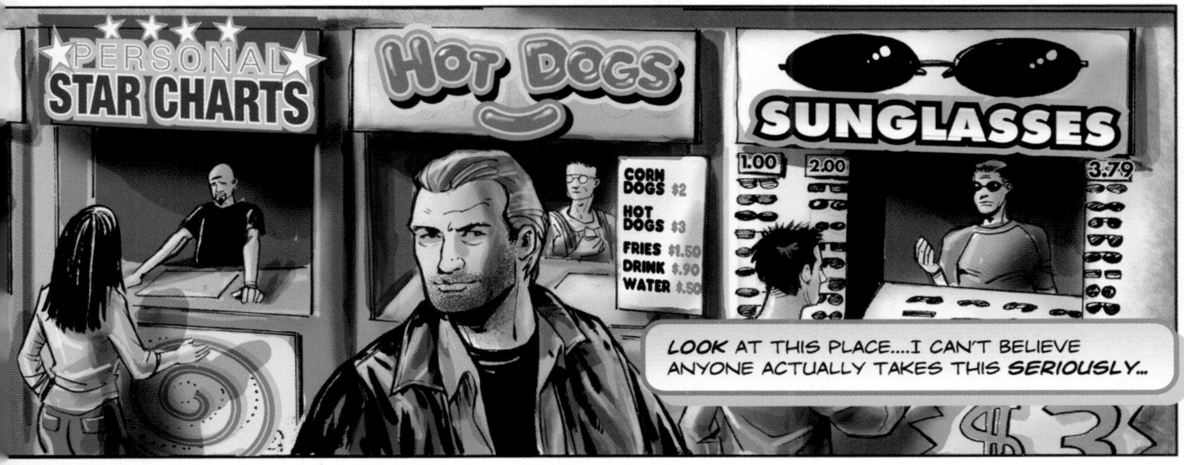
PERSONAL STAR CHARTS
HOT DOGS
SUNGLASSES
1.00
2.00
3.79
CORN DOGS $2
HOT DOGS $3
FRIES $1.50
DRINK $.90
WATER $.50
LOOK AT THIS PLACE....I CAN'T BELIEVE ANYONE ACTUALLY TAKES THIS *SERIOUSLY*...

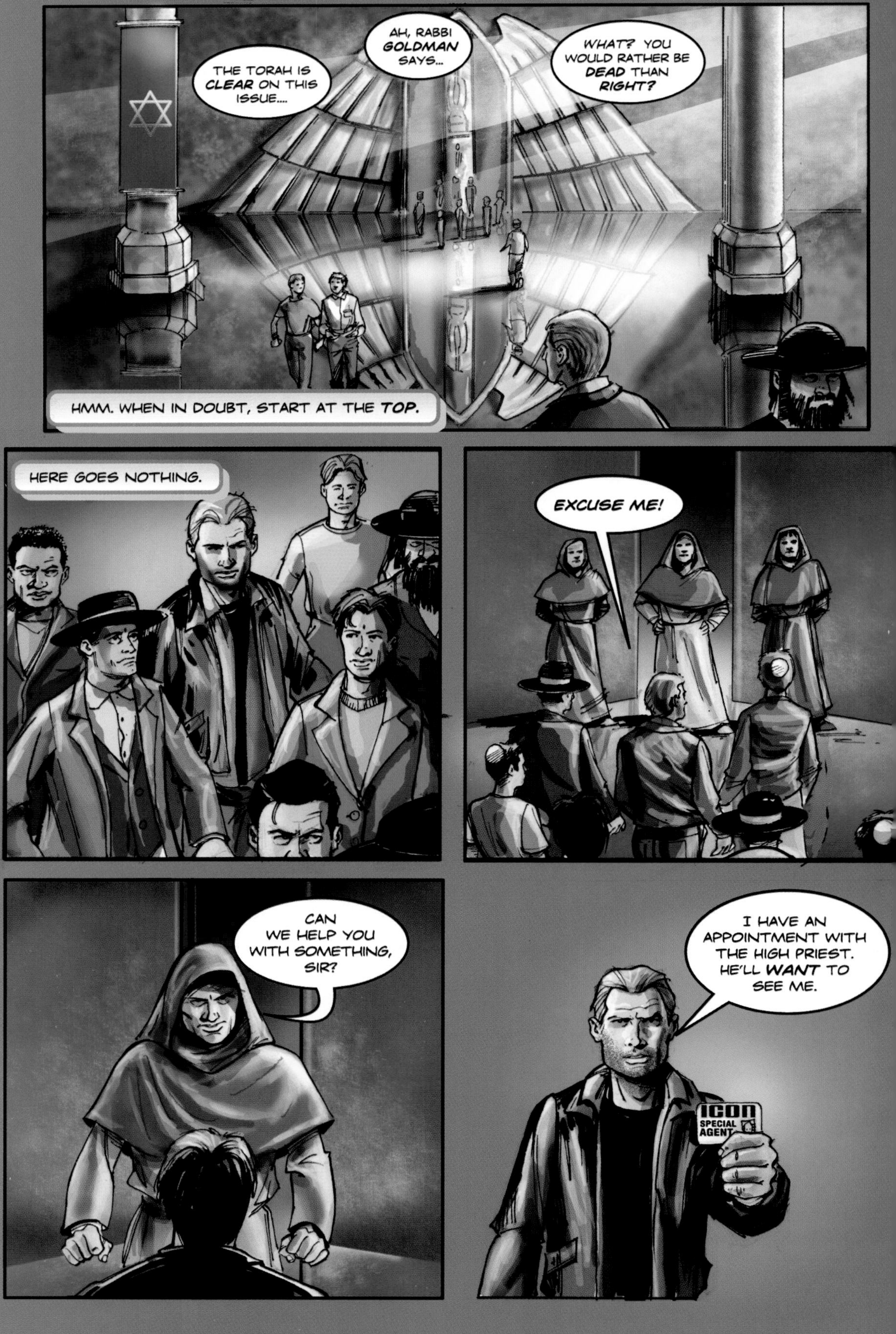
THE TORAH IS CLEAR ON THIS ISSUE....
AH, RABBI GOLDMAN SAYS...
WHAT? YOU WOULD RATHER BE DEAD THAN RIGHT?
HMM. WHEN IN DOUBT, START AT THE TOP.
HERE GOES NOTHING.
EXCUSE ME!
CAN WE HELP YOU WITH SOMETHING, SIR?
I HAVE AN APPOINTMENT WITH THE HIGH PRIEST. HE'LL WANT TO SEE ME.
ICON SPECIAL AGENT

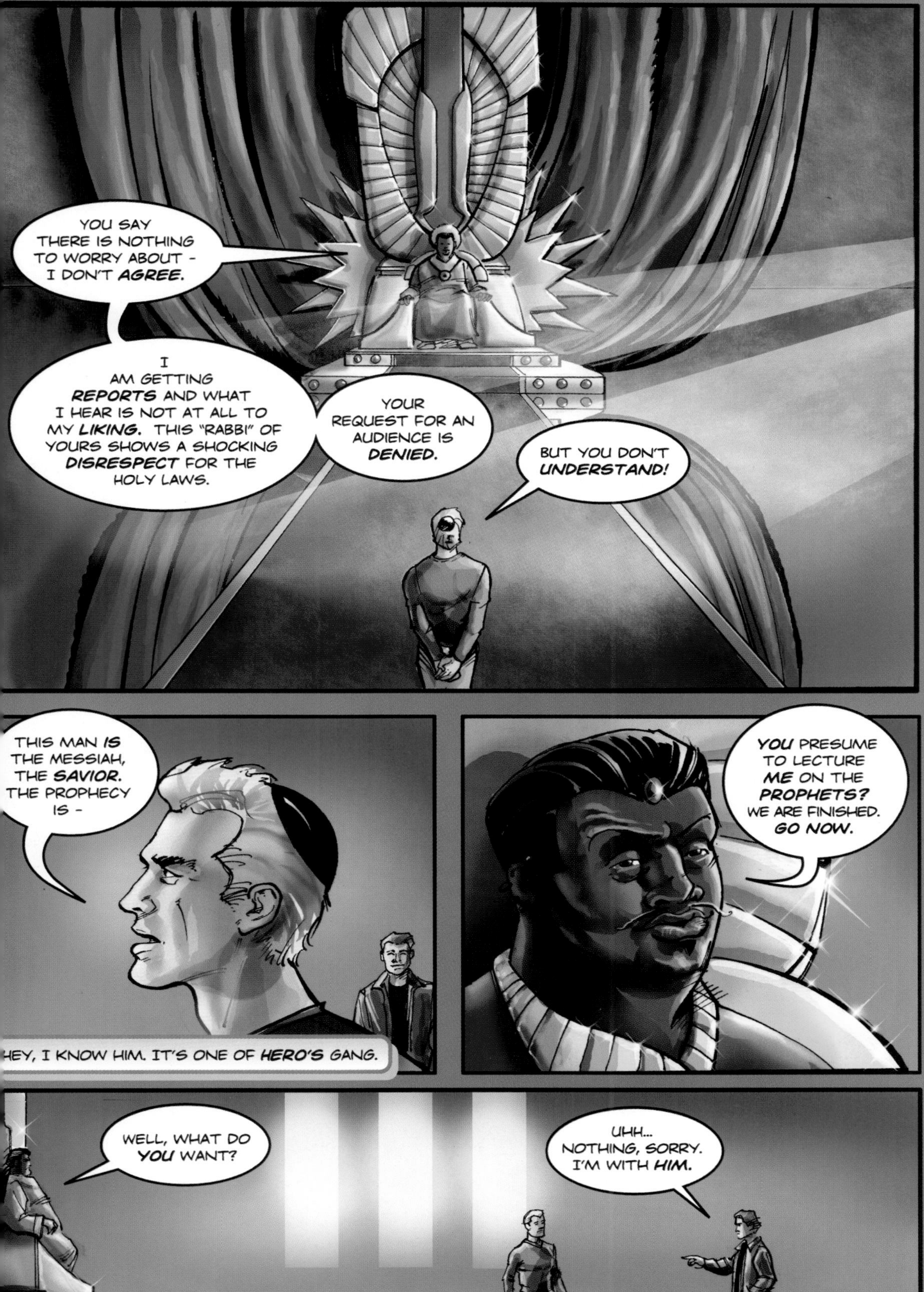
YOU SAY THERE IS NOTHING TO WORRY ABOUT - I DON'T AGREE.
I AM GETTING REPORTS AND WHAT I HEAR IS NOT AT ALL TO MY LIKING. THIS "RABBI" OF YOURS SHOWS A SHOCKING DISRESPECT FOR THE HOLY LAWS.
YOUR REQUEST FOR AN AUDIENCE IS DENIED.
BUT YOU DON'T UNDERSTAND!
THIS MAN IS THE MESSIAH, THE SAVIOR. THE PROPHECY IS -
HEY, I KNOW HIM. IT'S ONE OF HERO'S GANG.
YOU PRESUME TO LECTURE ME ON THE PROPHETS? WE ARE FINISHED. GO NOW.
WELL, WHAT DO YOU WANT?
UHH... NOTHING, SORRY. I'M WITH HIM.

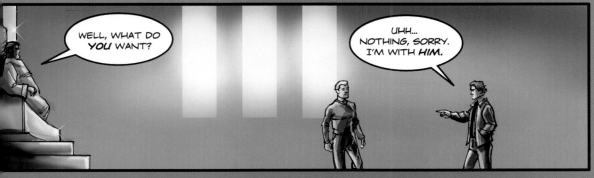

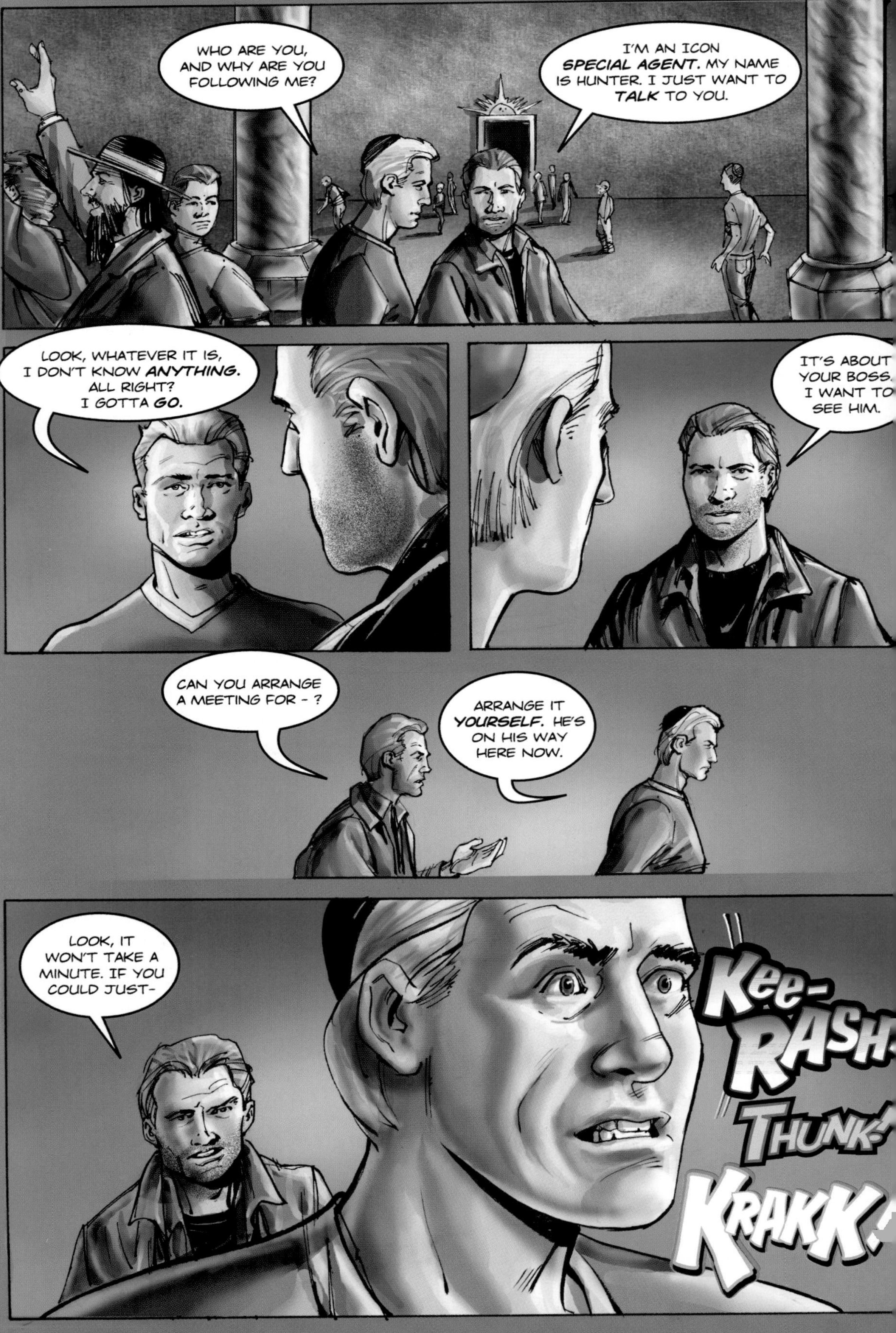

WHO ARE YOU, AND WHY ARE YOU FOLLOWING ME?
I'M AN ICON SPECIAL AGENT. MY NAME IS HUNTER. I JUST WANT TO TALK TO YOU.
LOOK, WHATEVER IT IS, I DON'T KNOW ANYTHING. ALL RIGHT? I GOTTA GO.
IT'S ABOUT YOUR BOSS. I WANT TO SEE HIM.
CAN YOU ARRANGE A MEETING FOR - ?
ARRANGE IT YOURSELF. HE'S ON HIS WAY HERE NOW.
LOOK, IT WON'T TAKE A MINUTE. IF YOU COULD JUST-
KEE-RASH
THUNK
KRAKK

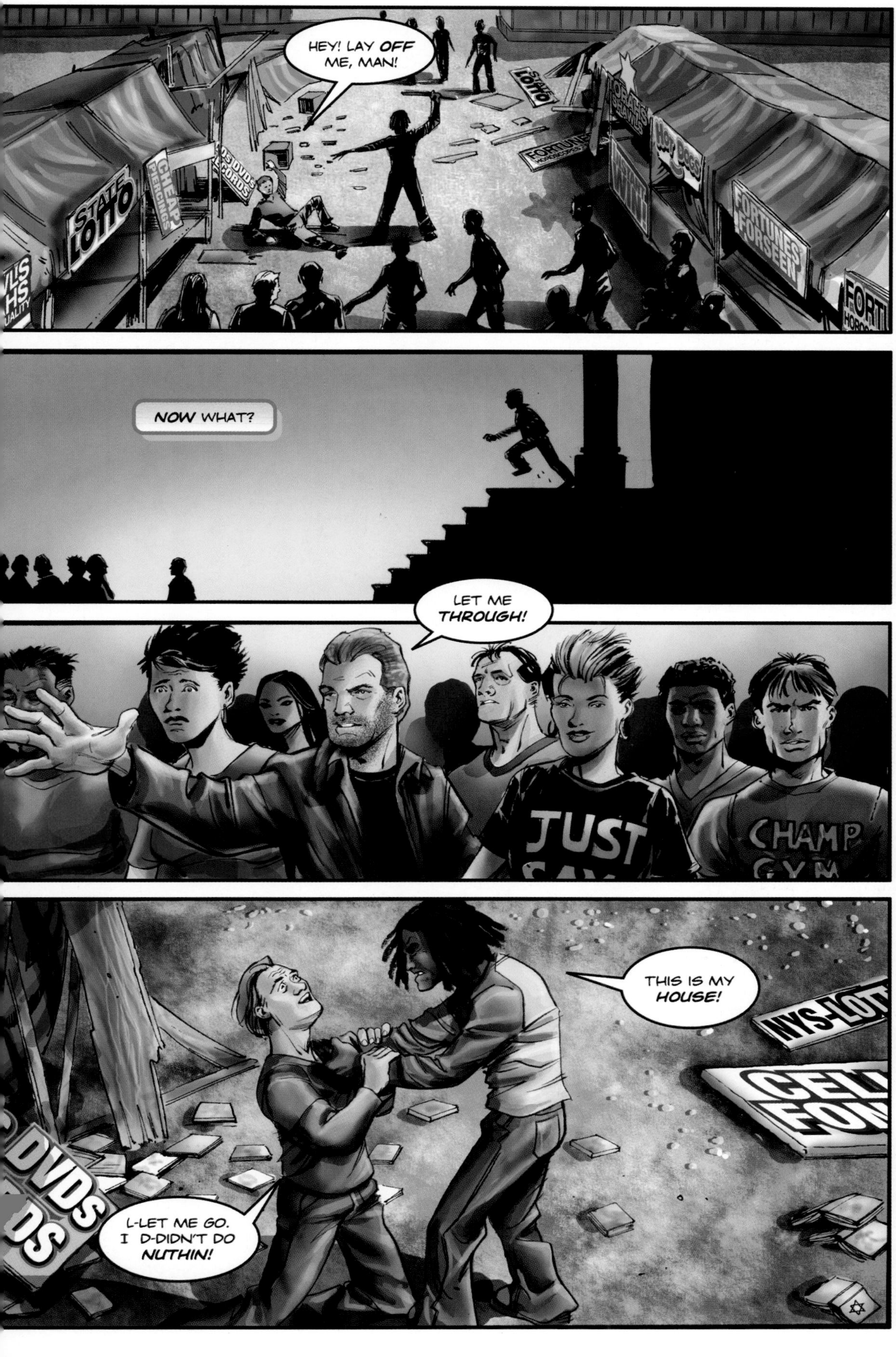
HEY! LAY OFF ME, MAN!
STATE LOTTO
CHEAP PIERCINGS
FORTUNES FORSEEN
HOT DOGS
NOW WHAT?
LET ME THROUGH!
JUST
CHAMP GYM
THIS IS MY HOUSE!
NYS-LOTT
DVDS
L-LET ME GO. I D-DIDN'T DO NUTHIN!

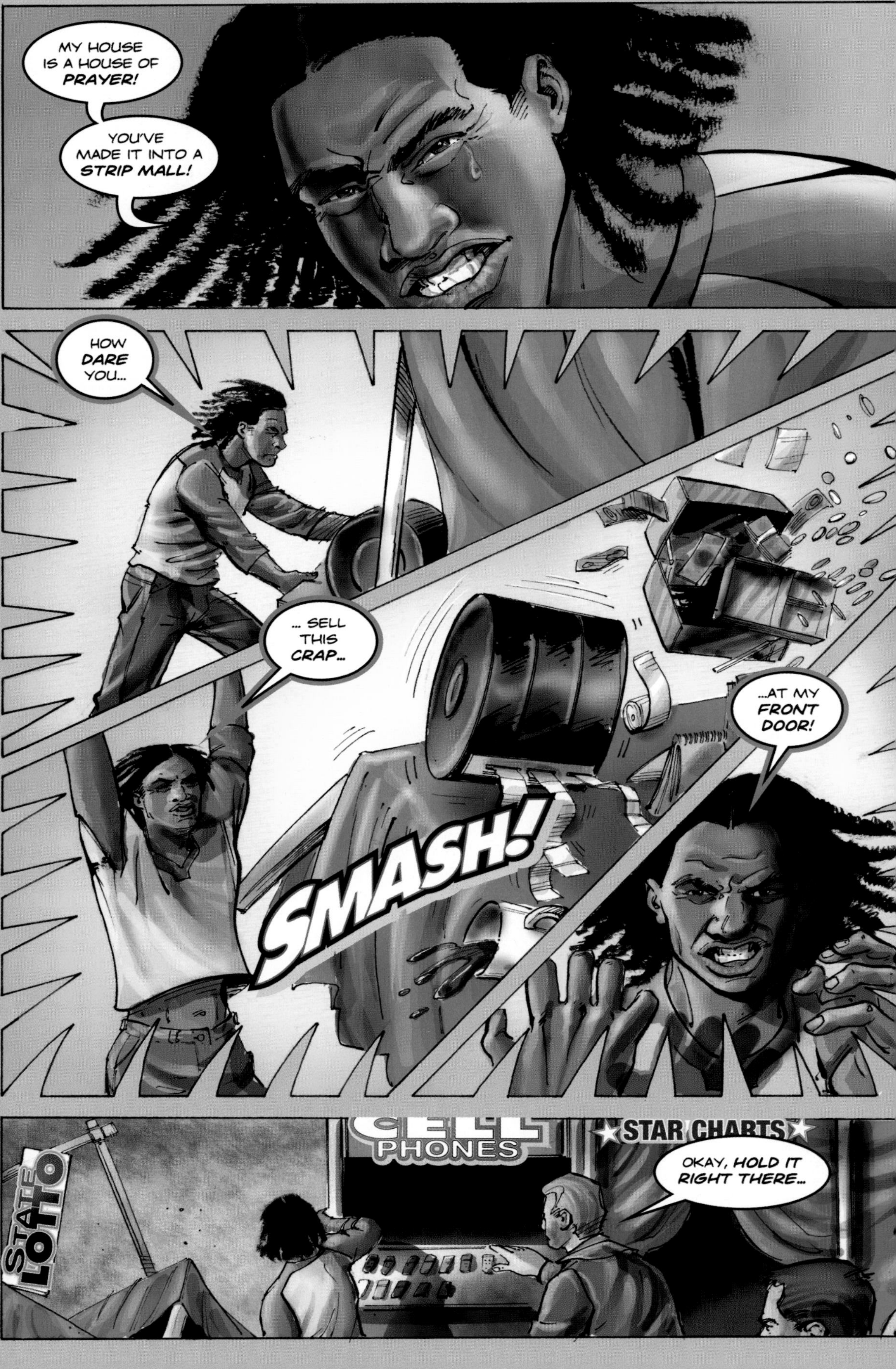

MY HOUSE IS A HOUSE OF PRAYER!
YOU'VE MADE IT INTO A STRIP MALL!
HOW DARE YOU...
... SELL THIS CRAP...
...AT MY FRONT DOOR!
SMASH!
STATE LOTTO
CELL PHONES
STAR CHARTS
OKAY, HOLD IT RIGHT THERE...

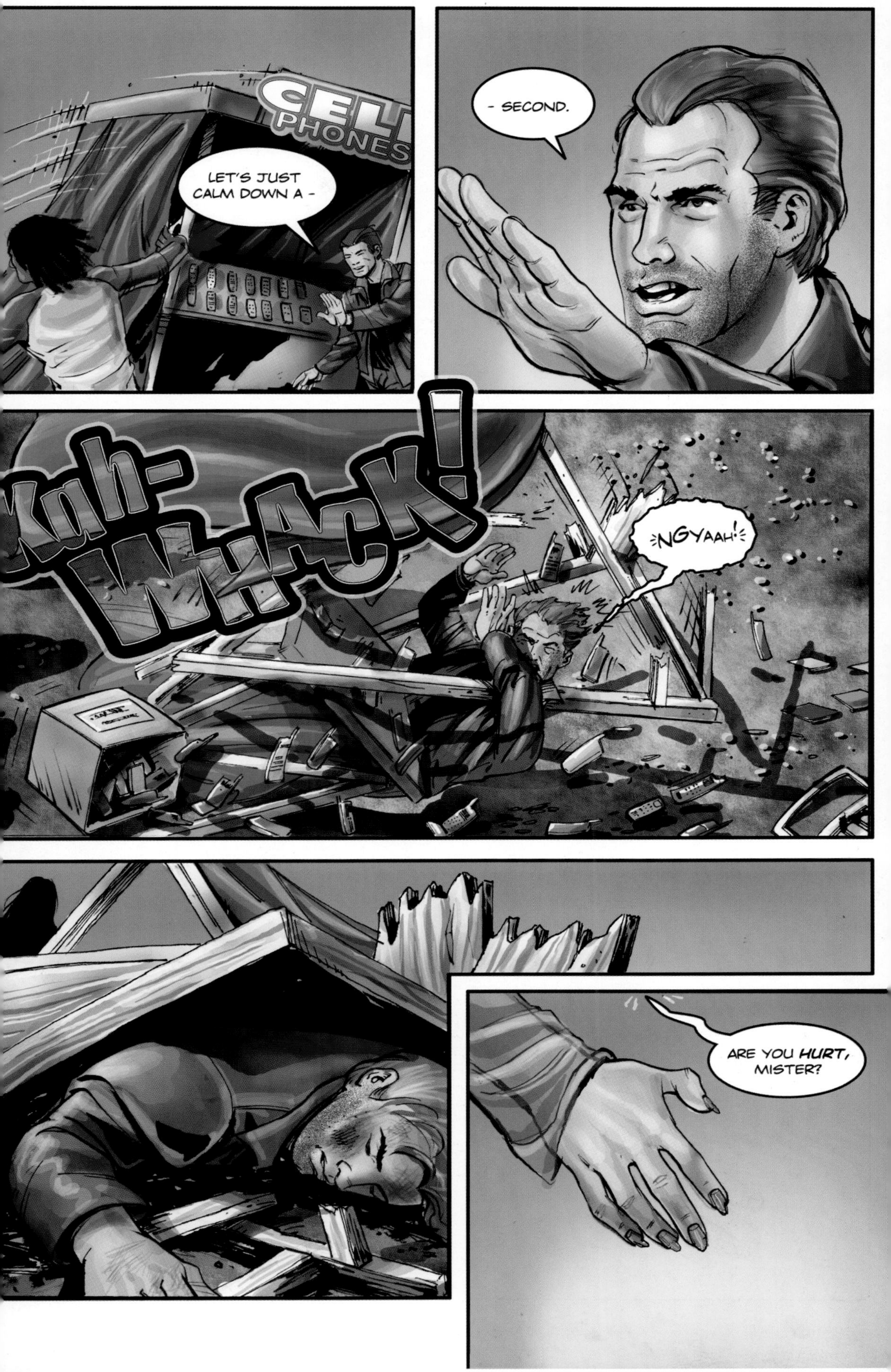
CELL PHONES
LET'S JUST CALM DOWN A -
- SECOND.
KAH-WHACK!
NGYAAH!
ARE YOU HURT, MISTER?

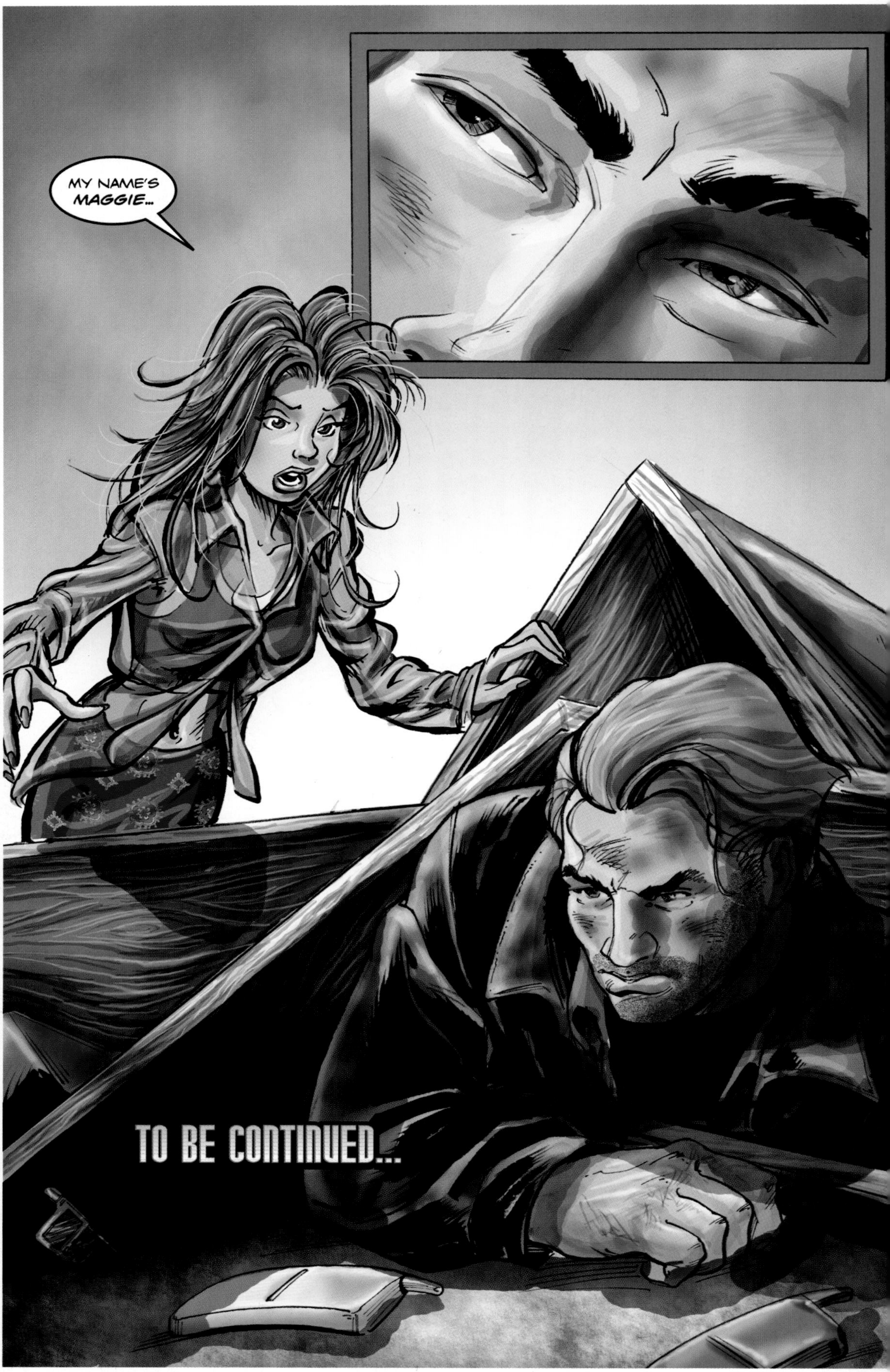
MY NAME'S MAGGIE...
TO BE CONTINUED...

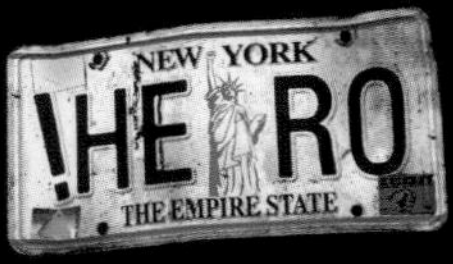
NEW YORK
!HE RO
THE EMPIRE STATE

THREE

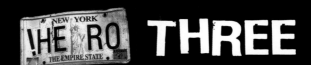

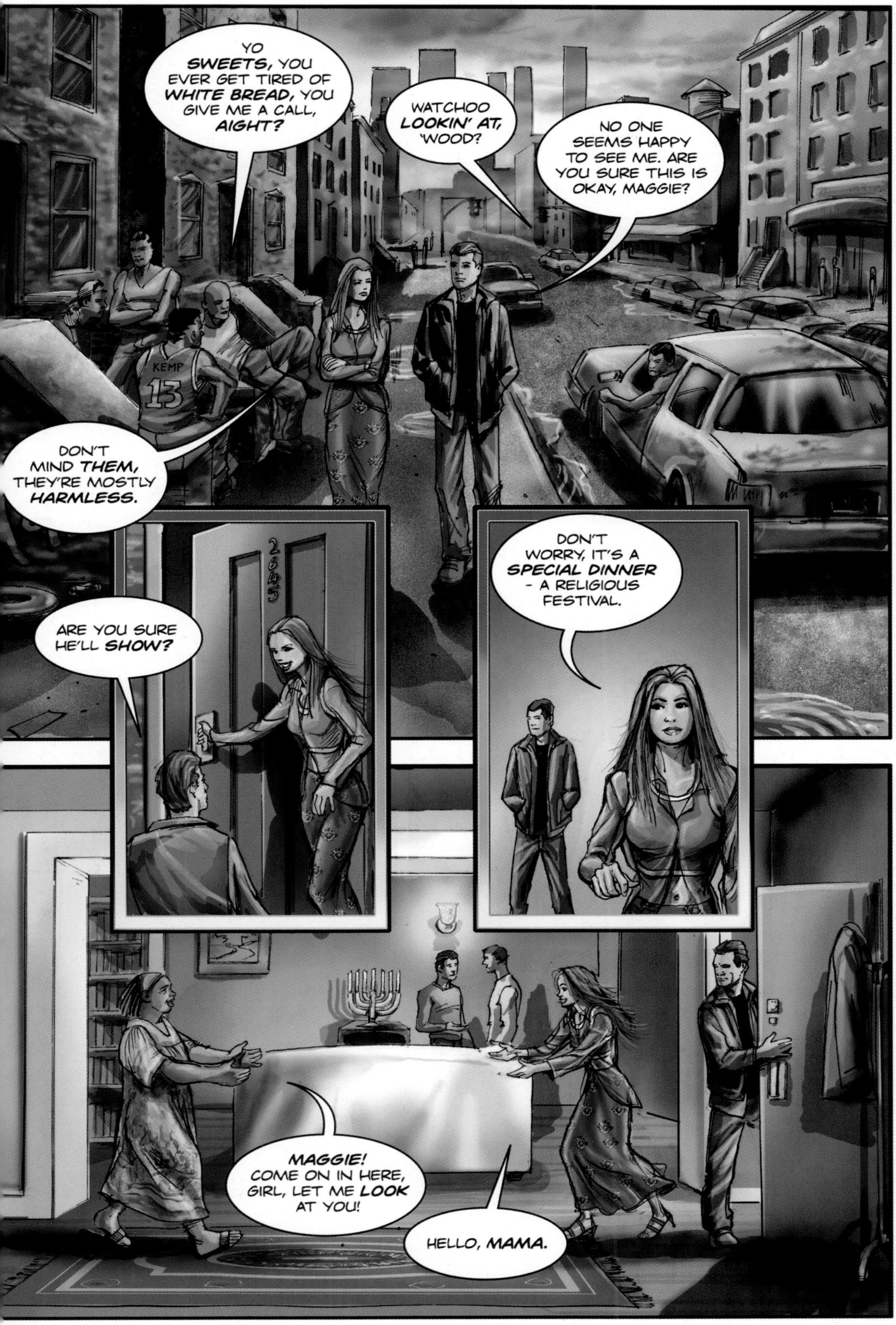
YO SWEETS, YOU EVER GET TIRED OF WHITE BREAD, YOU GIVE ME A CALL, AIGHT?
WATCHOO LOOKIN' AT, 'WOOD?
NO ONE SEEMS HAPPY TO SEE ME. ARE YOU SURE THIS IS OKAY, MAGGIE?
DON'T MIND THEM, THEY'RE MOSTLY HARMLESS.
KEMP 13
2645
ARE YOU SURE HE'LL SHOW?
DON'T WORRY, IT'S A SPECIAL DINNER - A RELIGIOUS FESTIVAL.
MAGGIE! COME ON IN HERE, GIRL, LET ME LOOK AT YOU!
HELLO, MAMA.

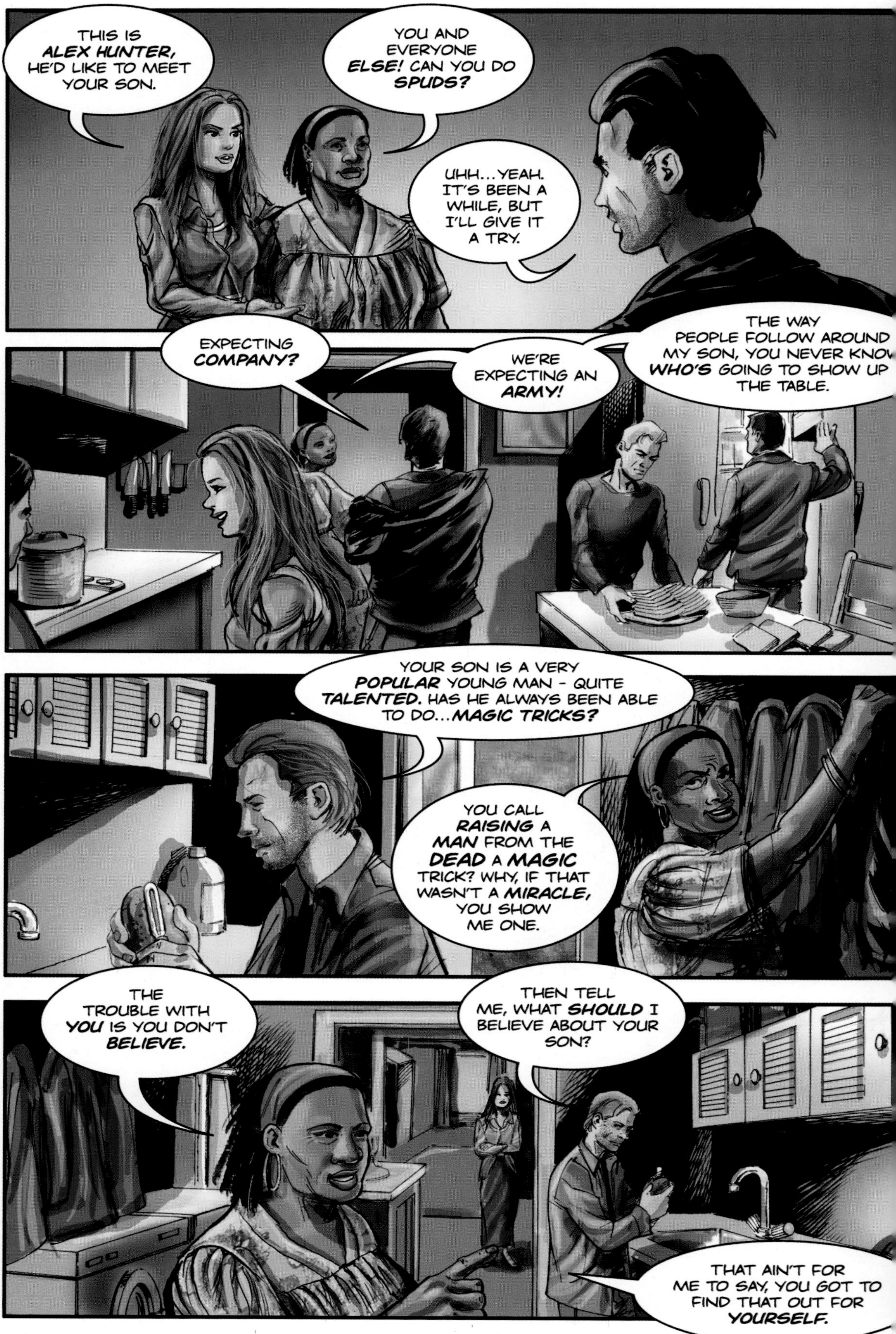

THIS IS ALEX HUNTER, HE'D LIKE TO MEET YOUR SON.
YOU AND EVERYONE ELSE! CAN YOU DO SPUDS?
UHH...YEAH. IT'S BEEN A WHILE, BUT I'LL GIVE IT A TRY.
EXPECTING COMPANY?
WE'RE EXPECTING AN ARMY!
THE WAY PEOPLE FOLLOW AROUND MY SON, YOU NEVER KNOW WHO'S GOING TO SHOW UP THE TABLE.
YOUR SON IS A VERY POPULAR YOUNG MAN - QUITE TALENTED. HAS HE ALWAYS BEEN ABLE TO DO...MAGIC TRICKS?
YOU CALL RAISING A MAN FROM THE DEAD A MAGIC TRICK? WHY, IF THAT WASN'T A MIRACLE, YOU SHOW ME ONE.
THE TROUBLE WITH YOU IS YOU DON'T BELIEVE.
THEN TELL ME, WHAT SHOULD I BELIEVE ABOUT YOUR SON?
THAT AIN'T FOR ME TO SAY, YOU GOT TO FIND THAT OUT FOR YOURSELF.

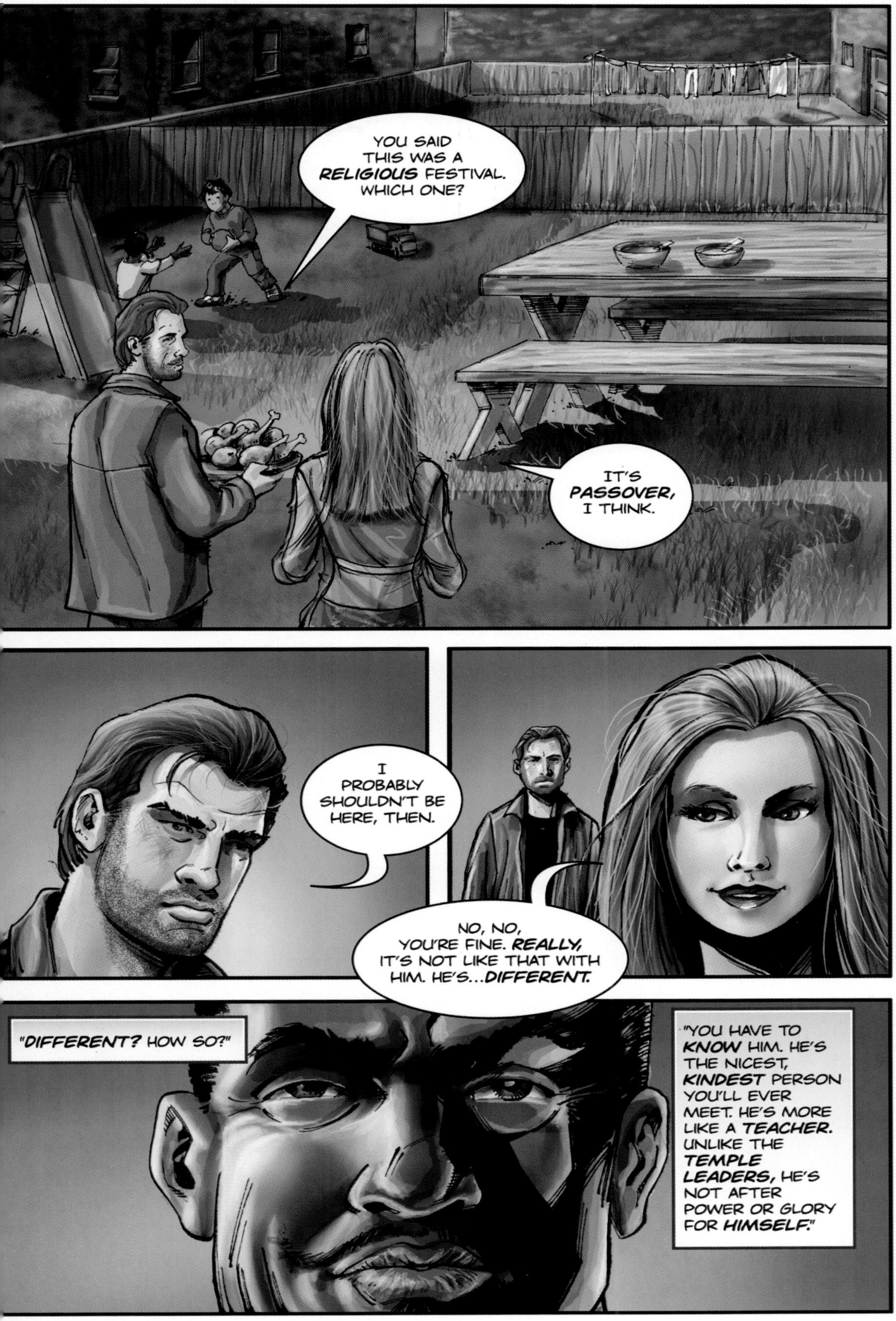
YOU SAID THIS WAS A **RELIGIOUS** FESTIVAL. WHICH ONE?
IT'S **PASSOVER,** I THINK.
I PROBABLY SHOULDN'T BE HERE, THEN.
NO, NO, YOU'RE FINE. ***REALLY,*** IT'S NOT LIKE THAT WITH HIM. HE'S...***DIFFERENT.***
"***DIFFERENT?*** HOW SO?"
"YOU HAVE TO ***KNOW*** HIM. HE'S THE NICEST, ***KINDEST*** PERSON YOU'LL EVER MEET. HE'S MORE LIKE A ***TEACHER.*** UNLIKE THE ***TEMPLE LEADERS,*** HE'S NOT AFTER POWER OR GLORY FOR ***HIMSELF.***"

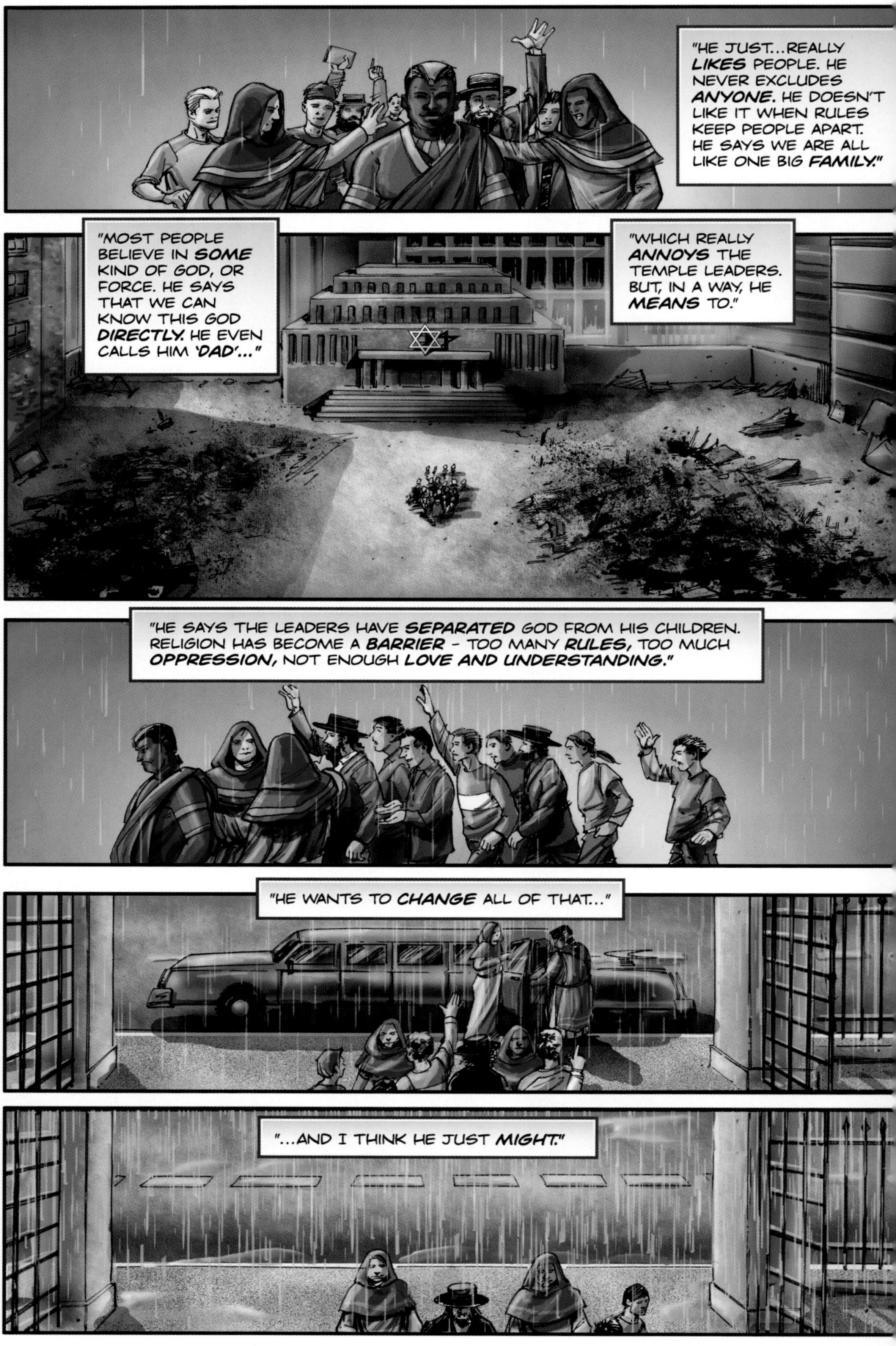
"HE JUST...REALLY LIKES PEOPLE. HE NEVER EXCLUDES ANYONE. HE DOESN'T LIKE IT WHEN RULES KEEP PEOPLE APART. HE SAYS WE ARE ALL LIKE ONE BIG FAMILY."
"MOST PEOPLE BELIEVE IN SOME KIND OF GOD, OR FORCE. HE SAYS THAT WE CAN KNOW THIS GOD DIRECTLY. HE EVEN CALLS HIM 'DAD'..."
"WHICH REALLY ANNOYS THE TEMPLE LEADERS. BUT, IN A WAY, HE MEANS TO."
"HE SAYS THE LEADERS HAVE SEPARATED GOD FROM HIS CHILDREN. RELIGION HAS BECOME A BARRIER - TOO MANY RULES, TOO MUCH OPPRESSION, NOT ENOUGH LOVE AND UNDERSTANDING."
"HE WANTS TO CHANGE ALL OF THAT..."
"...AND I THINK HE JUST MIGHT."

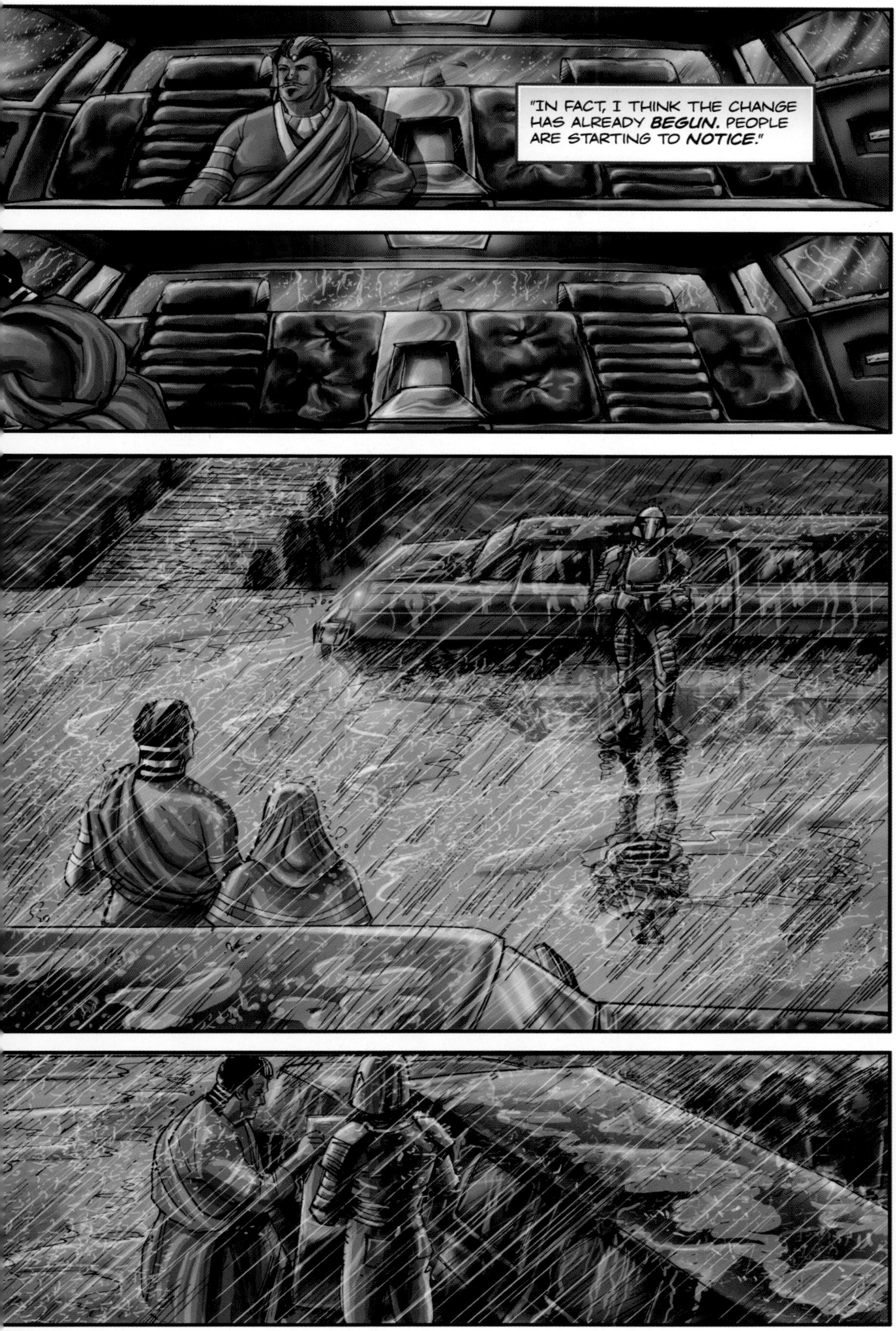
"IN FACT, I THINK THE CHANGE HAS ALREADY BEGUN. PEOPLE ARE STARTING TO NOTICE."

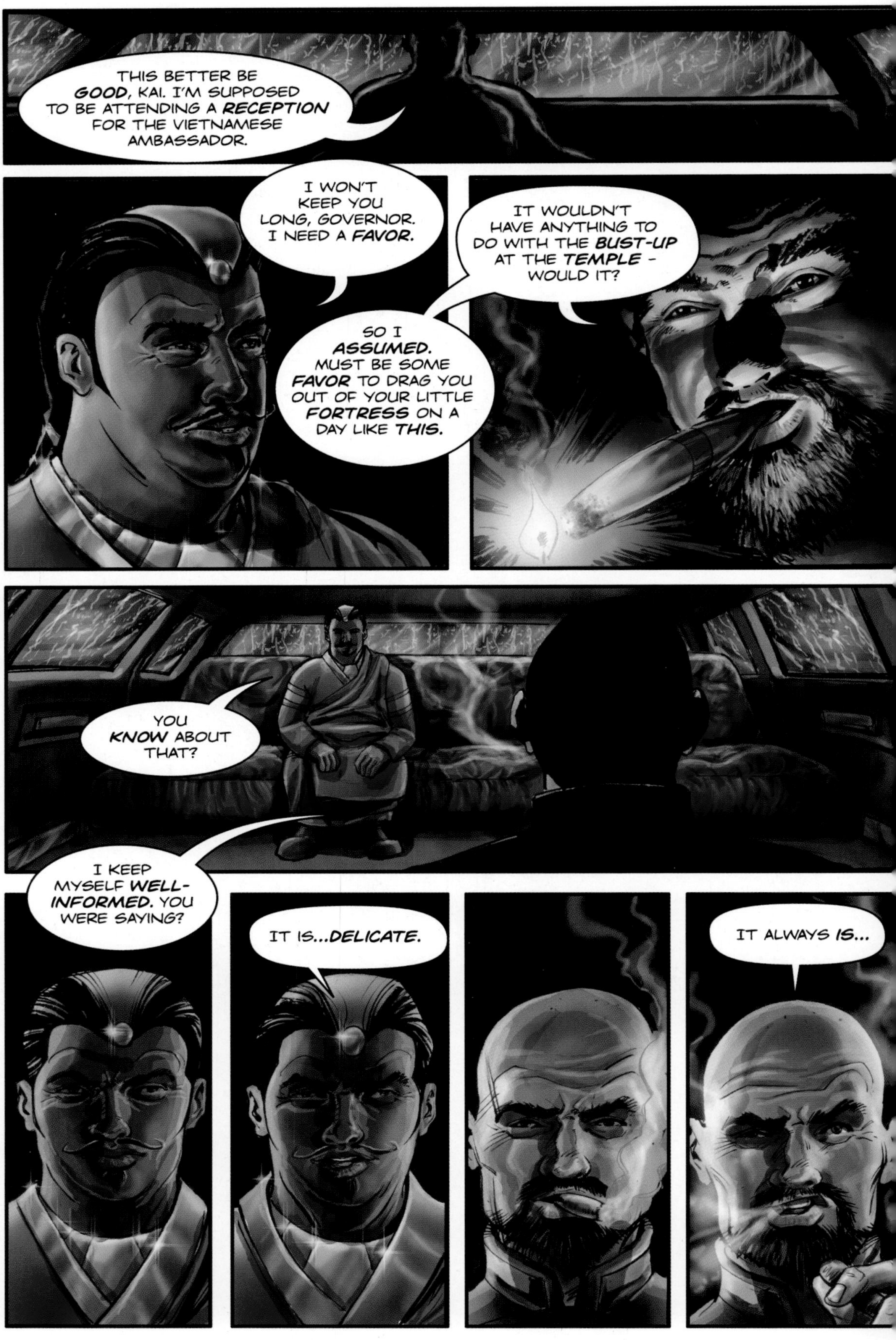

THIS BETTER BE GOOD, KAI. I'M SUPPOSED TO BE ATTENDING A RECEPTION FOR THE VIETNAMESE AMBASSADOR.
I WON'T KEEP YOU LONG, GOVERNOR. I NEED A FAVOR.
IT WOULDN'T HAVE ANYTHING TO DO WITH THE BUST-UP AT THE TEMPLE - WOULD IT?
SO I ASSUMED. MUST BE SOME FAVOR TO DRAG YOU OUT OF YOUR LITTLE FORTRESS ON A DAY LIKE THIS.
YOU KNOW ABOUT THAT?
I KEEP MYSELF WELL-INFORMED. YOU WERE SAYING?
IT IS...DELICATE.
IT ALWAYS IS...

THE PERSON RESPONSIBLE FOR THIS MORNING'S... *INCIDENT*...THIS TROUBLEMAKER...THIS SO-CALLED *HERO*. LET'S SAY I WANT HIM TAUGHT A PERMANENT *LESSON*.

IT COULD BE *DONE*, OF COURSE. BUT I HAVE TO ASK MYSELF – WHAT'S IN IT FOR *ME*?

OH, YES, *WELL*...THERE IS AN *ELECTION* SOON, IS THERE NOT? I'M SURE YOUR CAMPAIGN TREASURY COULD USE A SIZABLE *CONTRIBUTION*.

GO *ON*...

OF COURSE, NOT ONLY *THAT*, BUT I KNOW THE *RABBIS* WOULD BE ONLY TOO *HAPPY* TO MAKE SURE OUR PEOPLE *DELIVER* ON ELECTION DAY.

VERY WELL. CONSIDER YOUR PROBLEM *SOLVED*.

HOWEVER, I COULD NOT ALLOW THE TEMPLE TO SUFFER SO MUCH AS A *WHIFF* OF SUSPICION.

RELAX, YOUR HANDS WON'T GET *DIRTY*. I'LL SEE TO THAT.

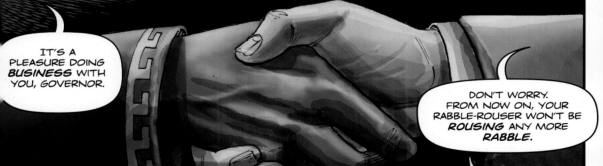

IT'S A PLEASURE DOING *BUSINESS* WITH YOU, GOVERNOR.

DON'T WORRY. FROM NOW ON, YOUR RABBLE-ROUSER WON'T BE *ROUSING* ANY MORE *RABBLE*.

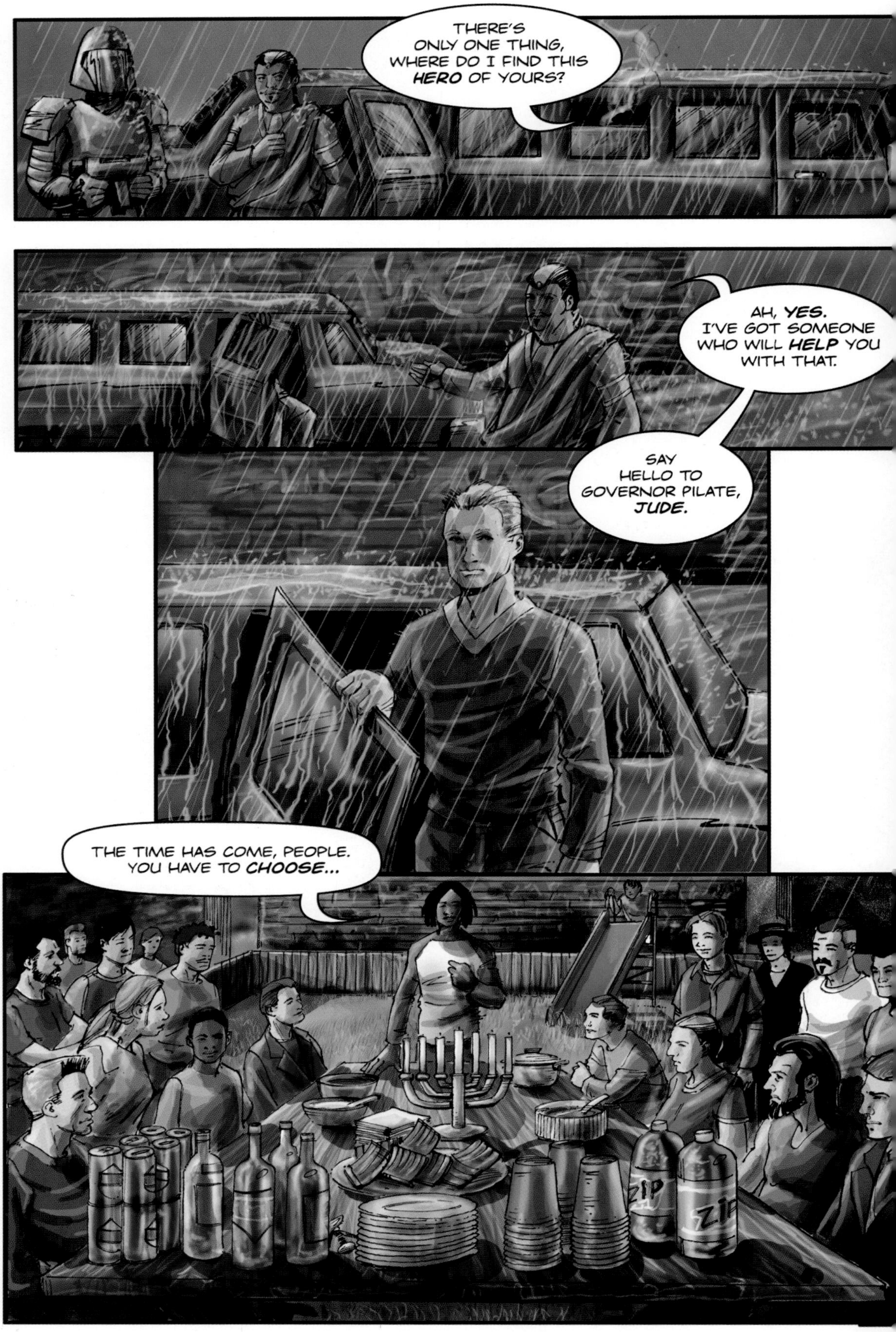
THERE'S ONLY ONE THING, WHERE DO I FIND THIS HERO OF YOURS?
AH, YES. I'VE GOT SOMEONE WHO WILL HELP YOU WITH THAT.
SAY HELLO TO GOVERNOR PILATE, JUDE.
THE TIME HAS COME, PEOPLE. YOU HAVE TO CHOOSE...
ZIP
ZIP

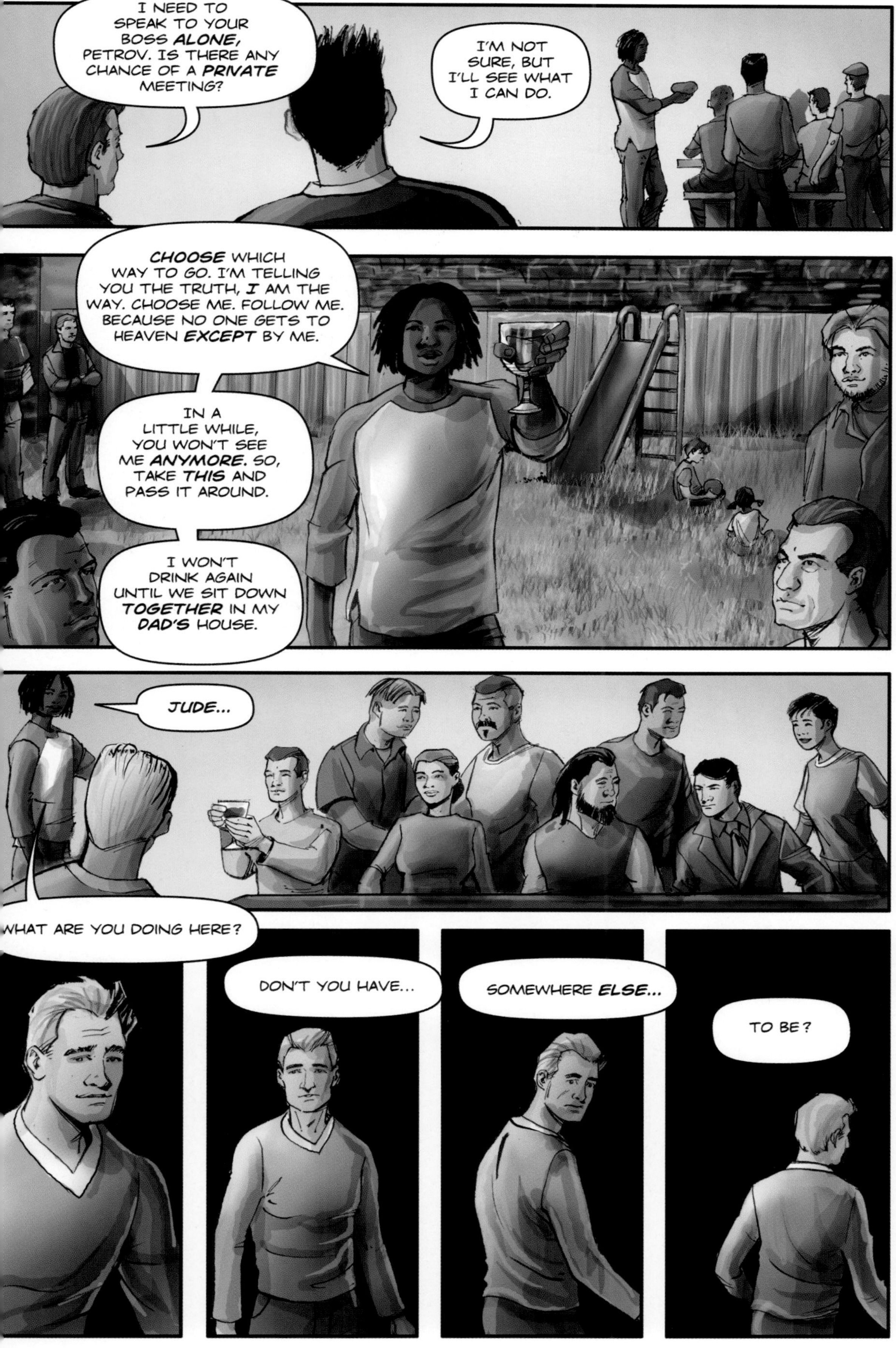
I NEED TO SPEAK TO YOUR BOSS ALONE, PETROV. IS THERE ANY CHANCE OF A PRIVATE MEETING?
I'M NOT SURE, BUT I'LL SEE WHAT I CAN DO.
CHOOSE WHICH WAY TO GO. I'M TELLING YOU THE TRUTH, I AM THE WAY. CHOOSE ME. FOLLOW ME. BECAUSE NO ONE GETS TO HEAVEN EXCEPT BY ME.
IN A LITTLE WHILE, YOU WON'T SEE ME ANYMORE. SO, TAKE THIS AND PASS IT AROUND.
I WON'T DRINK AGAIN UNTIL WE SIT DOWN TOGETHER IN MY DAD'S HOUSE.
JUDE...
WHAT ARE YOU DOING HERE?
DON'T YOU HAVE...
SOMEWHERE ELSE...
TO BE?

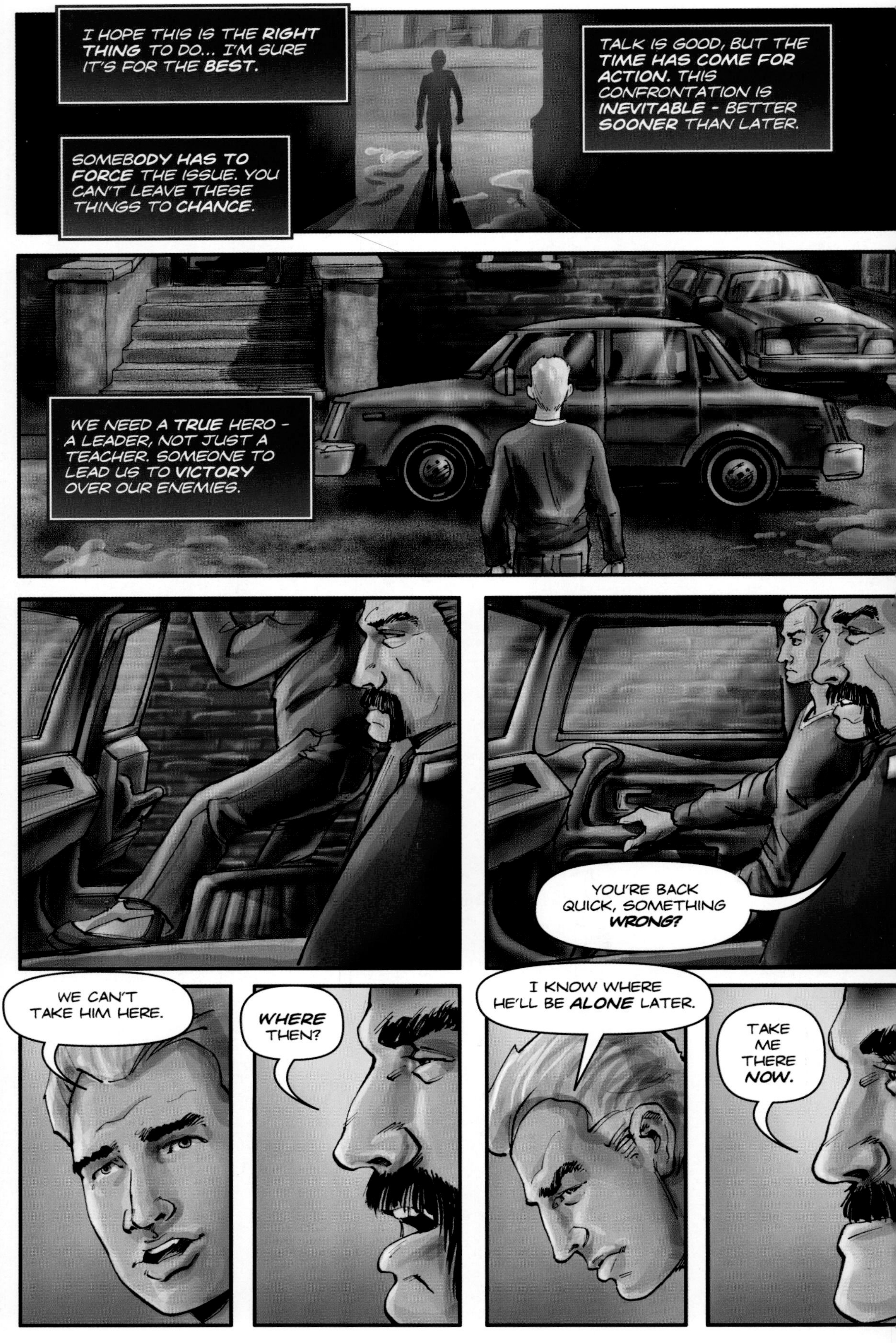
I HOPE THIS IS THE RIGHT THING TO DO... I'M SURE IT'S FOR THE BEST.
SOMEBODY HAS TO FORCE THE ISSUE. YOU CAN'T LEAVE THESE THINGS TO CHANCE.
TALK IS GOOD, BUT THE TIME HAS COME FOR ACTION. THIS CONFRONTATION IS INEVITABLE - BETTER SOONER THAN LATER.
WE NEED A TRUE HERO - A LEADER, NOT JUST A TEACHER. SOMEONE TO LEAD US TO VICTORY OVER OUR ENEMIES.
YOU'RE BACK QUICK, SOMETHING WRONG?
WE CAN'T TAKE HIM HERE.
WHERE THEN?
I KNOW WHERE HE'LL BE ALONE LATER.
TAKE ME THERE NOW.

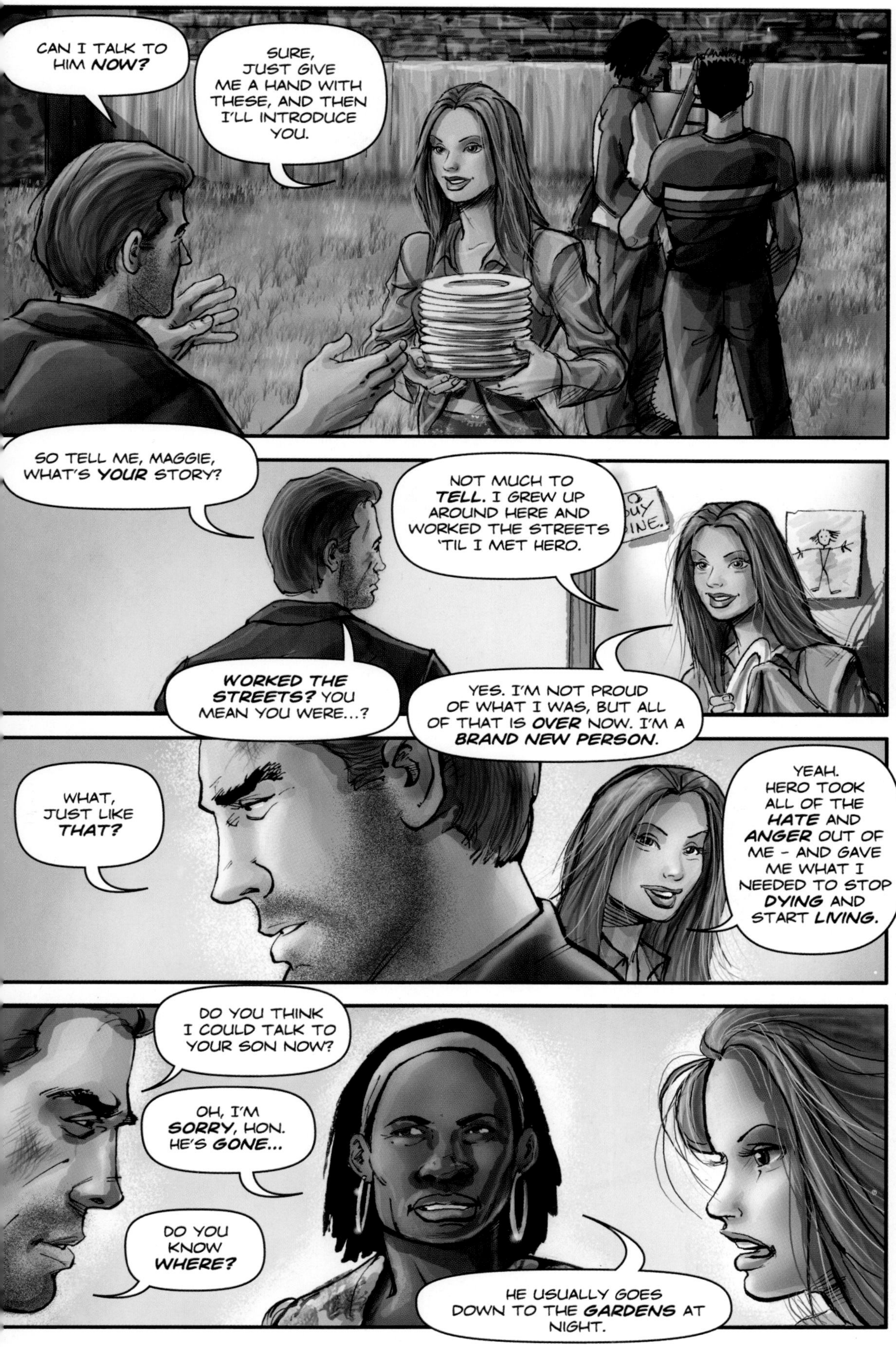
CAN I TALK TO HIM NOW?
SURE, JUST GIVE ME A HAND WITH THESE, AND THEN I'LL INTRODUCE YOU.
SO TELL ME, MAGGIE, WHAT'S YOUR STORY?
NOT MUCH TO TELL. I GREW UP AROUND HERE AND WORKED THE STREETS 'TIL I MET HERO.
WORKED THE STREETS? YOU MEAN YOU WERE...?
YES. I'M NOT PROUD OF WHAT I WAS, BUT ALL OF THAT IS OVER NOW. I'M A BRAND NEW PERSON.
WHAT, JUST LIKE THAT?
YEAH. HERO TOOK ALL OF THE HATE AND ANGER OUT OF ME - AND GAVE ME WHAT I NEEDED TO STOP DYING AND START LIVING.
DO YOU THINK I COULD TALK TO YOUR SON NOW?
OH, I'M SORRY, HON. HE'S GONE...
DO YOU KNOW WHERE?
HE USUALLY GOES DOWN TO THE GARDENS AT NIGHT.

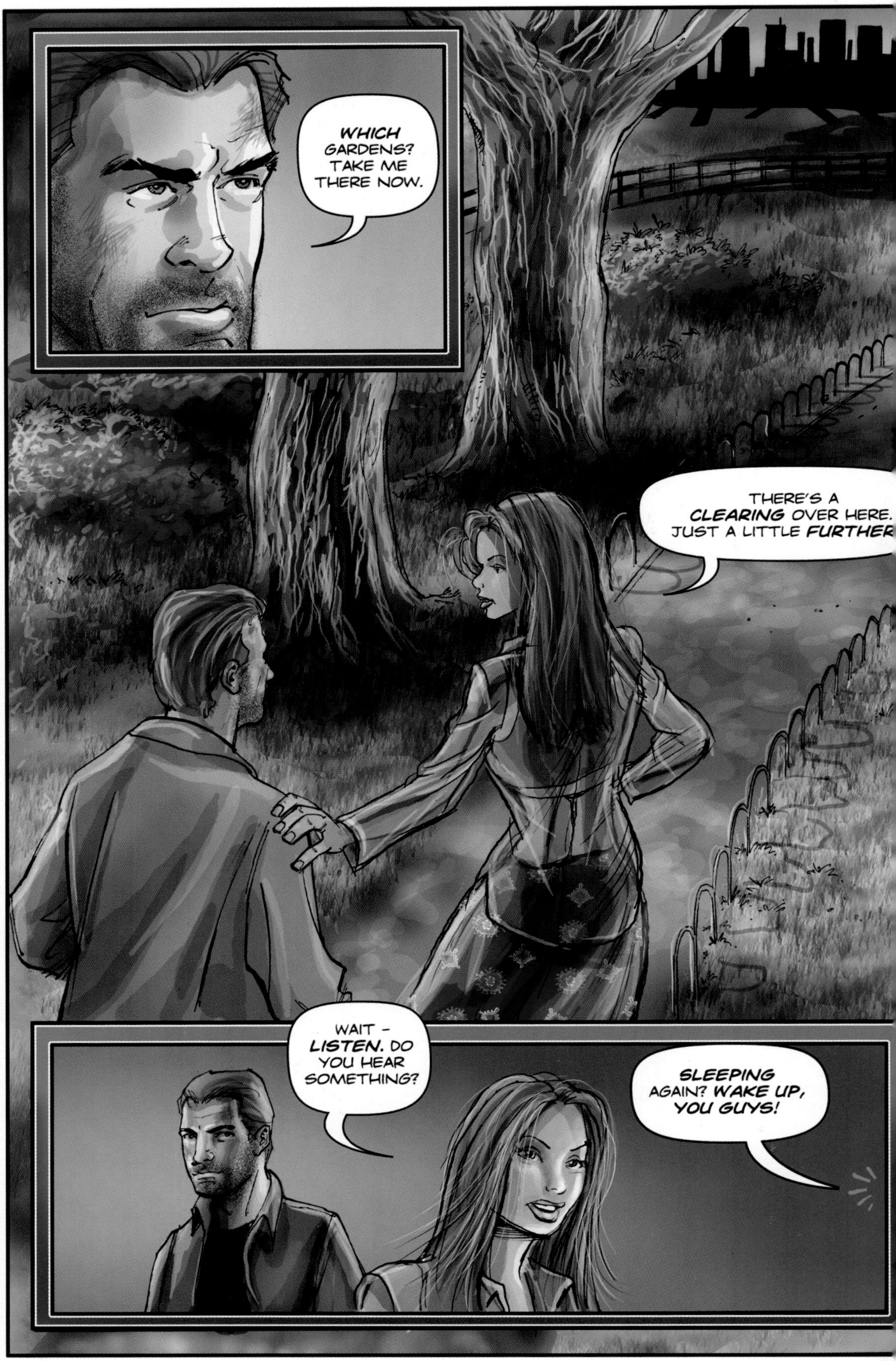
WHICH GARDENS? TAKE ME THERE NOW.
THERE'S A CLEARING OVER HERE. JUST A LITTLE FURTHER
WAIT - LISTEN. DO YOU HEAR SOMETHING?
SLEEPING AGAIN? WAKE UP, YOU GUYS!

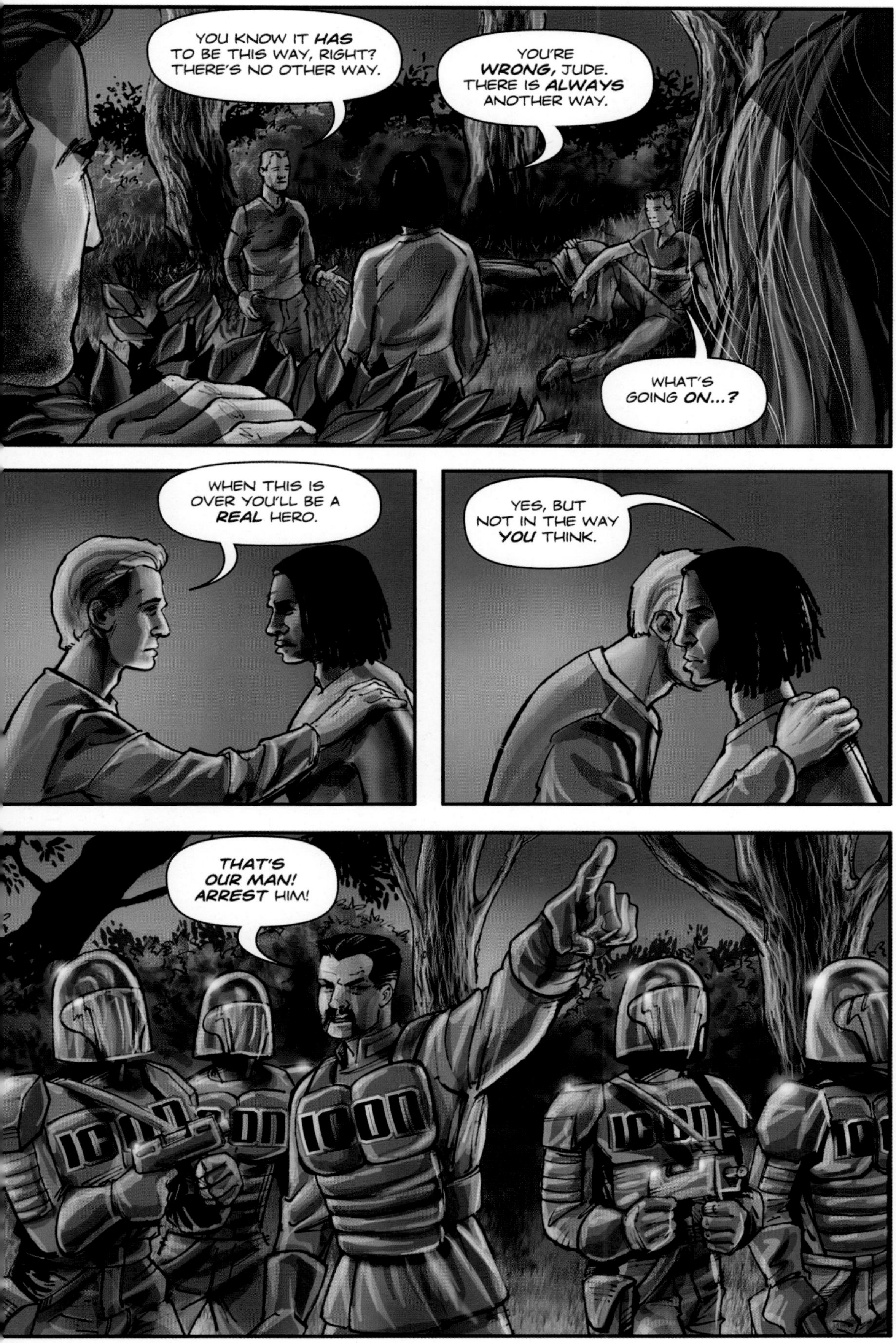
YOU KNOW IT HAS TO BE THIS WAY, RIGHT? THERE'S NO OTHER WAY.
YOU'RE WRONG, JUDE. THERE IS ALWAYS ANOTHER WAY.
WHAT'S GOING ON...?
WHEN THIS IS OVER YOU'LL BE A REAL HERO.
YES, BUT NOT IN THE WAY YOU THINK.
THAT'S OUR MAN! ARREST HIM!
ICON
ICON
ICON
ICON

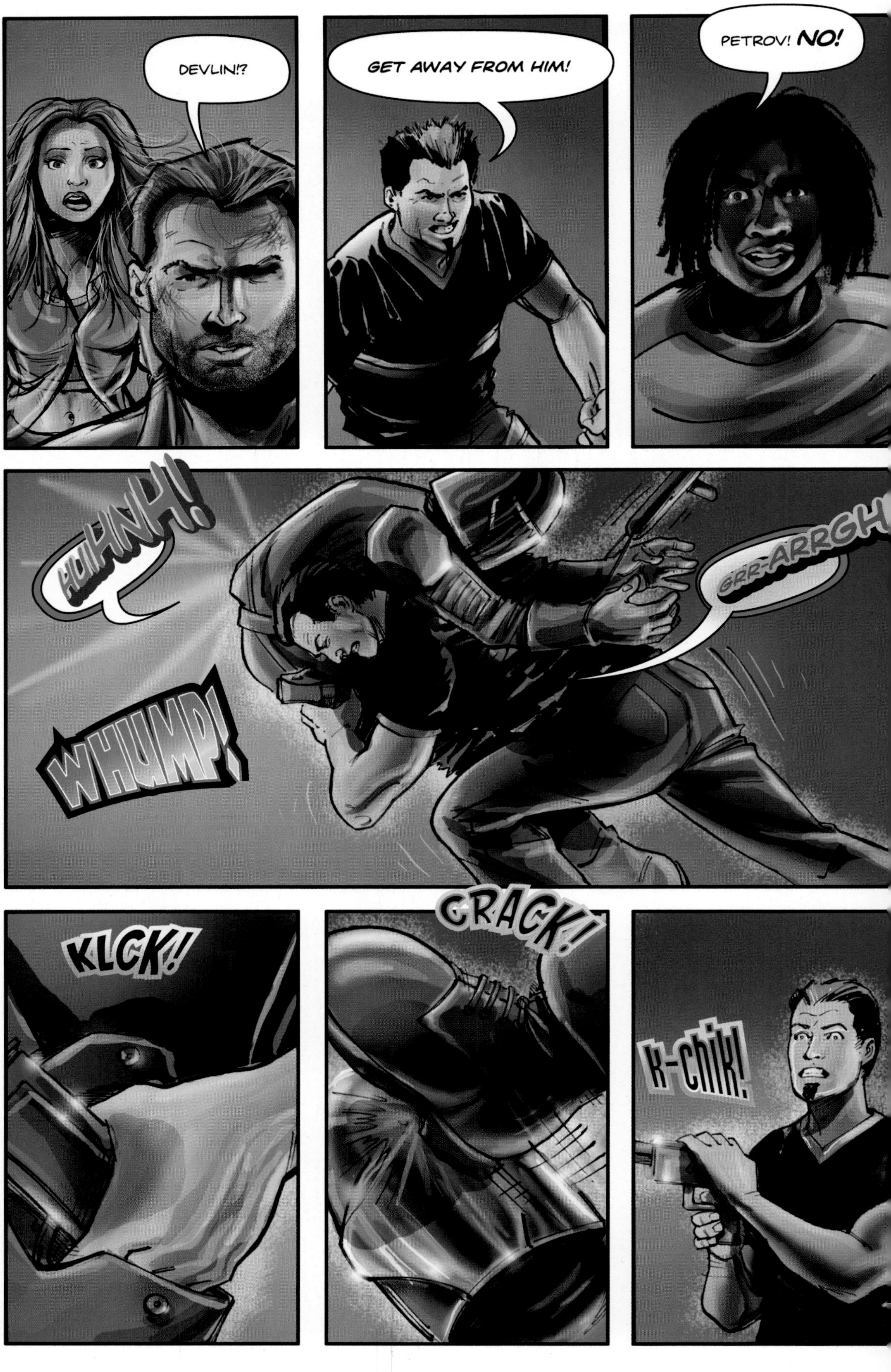
DEVLIN!?
GET AWAY FROM HIM!
PETROV! NO!
HUHNH!
GRR-ARRGH!
WHUMP!
KLCK!
CRACK!
K-CHIK!

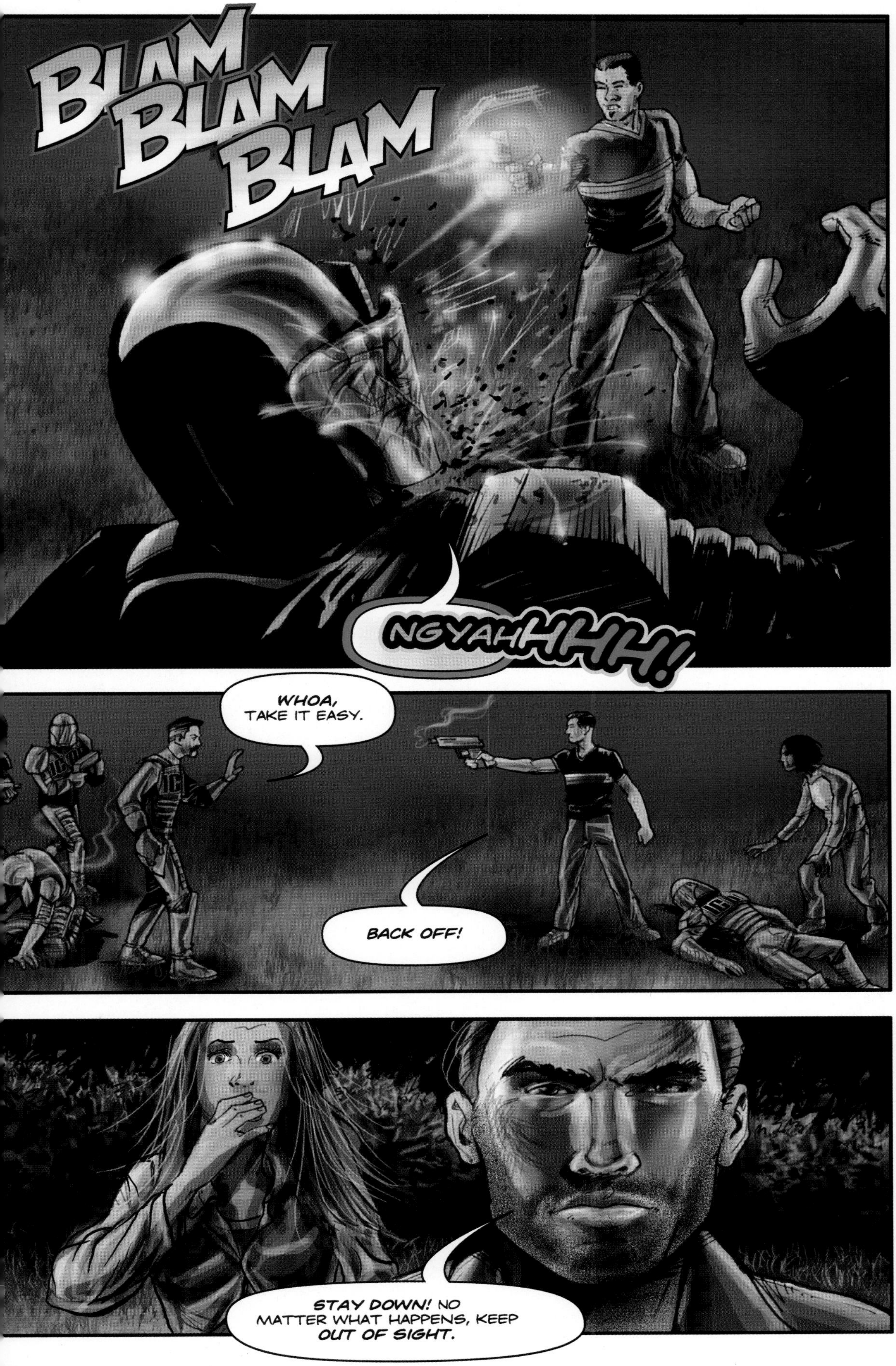
BLAM BLAM BLAM
NGYAHHHH!
WHOA, TAKE IT EASY.
BACK OFF!
STAY DOWN! NO MATTER WHAT HAPPENS, KEEP OUT OF SIGHT.

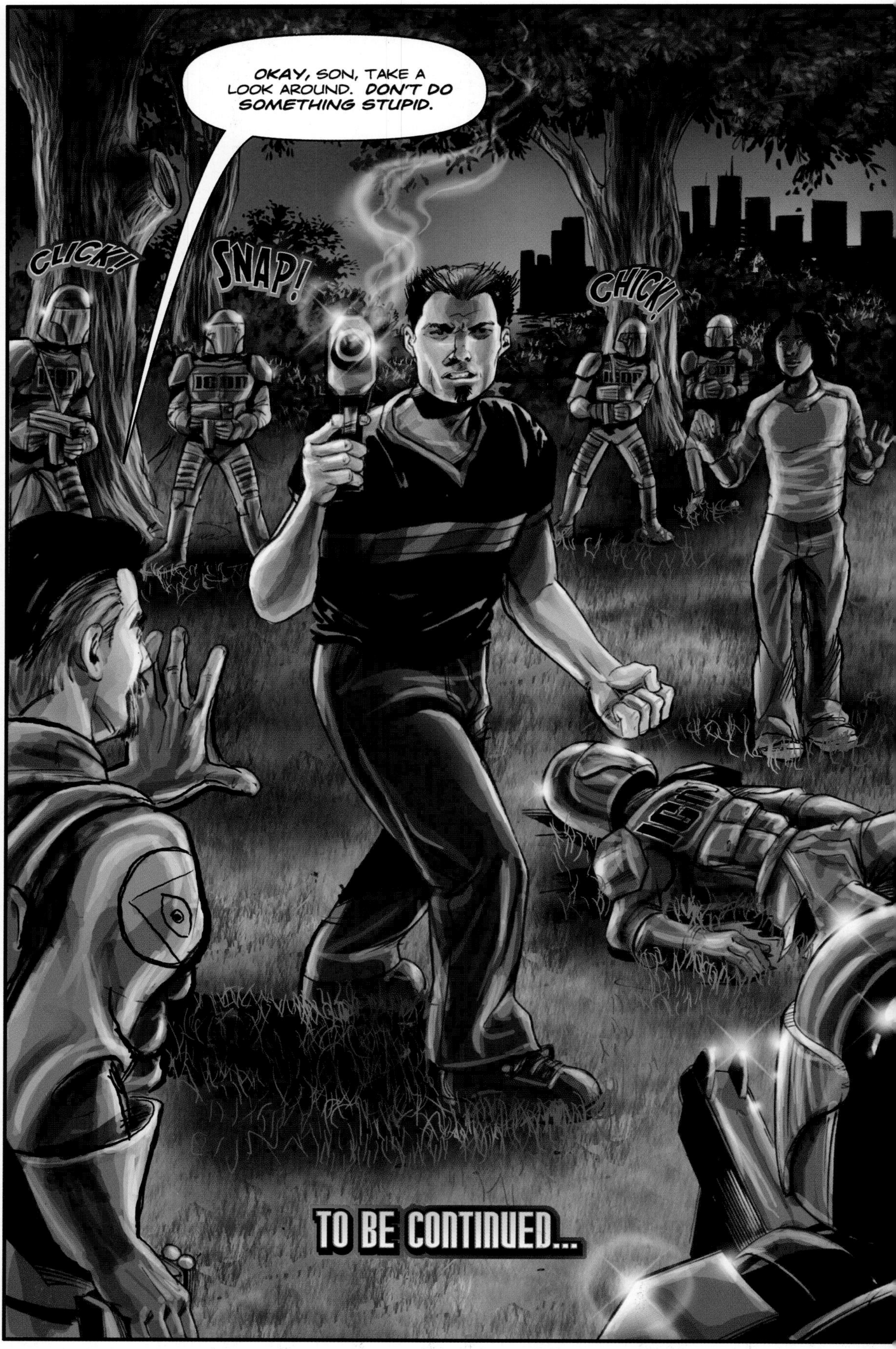
OKAY, SON, TAKE A LOOK AROUND. DON'T DO SOMETHING STUPID.
CLICK!!
SNAP!
CHICK!
TO BE CONTINUED...

!HERO FOUR

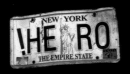

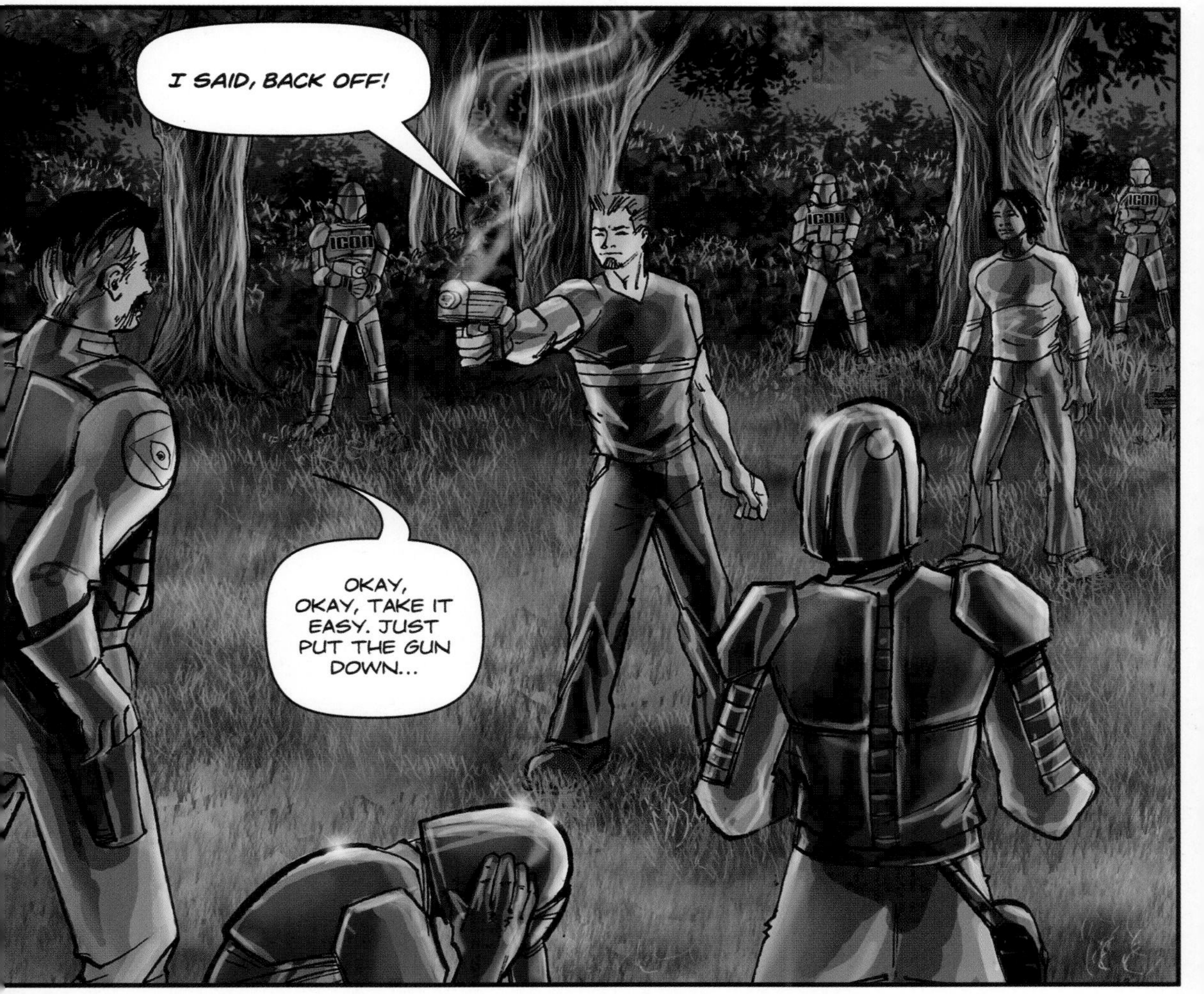
I SAID, BACK OFF!
OKAY, OKAY, TAKE IT EASY. JUST PUT THE GUN DOWN...

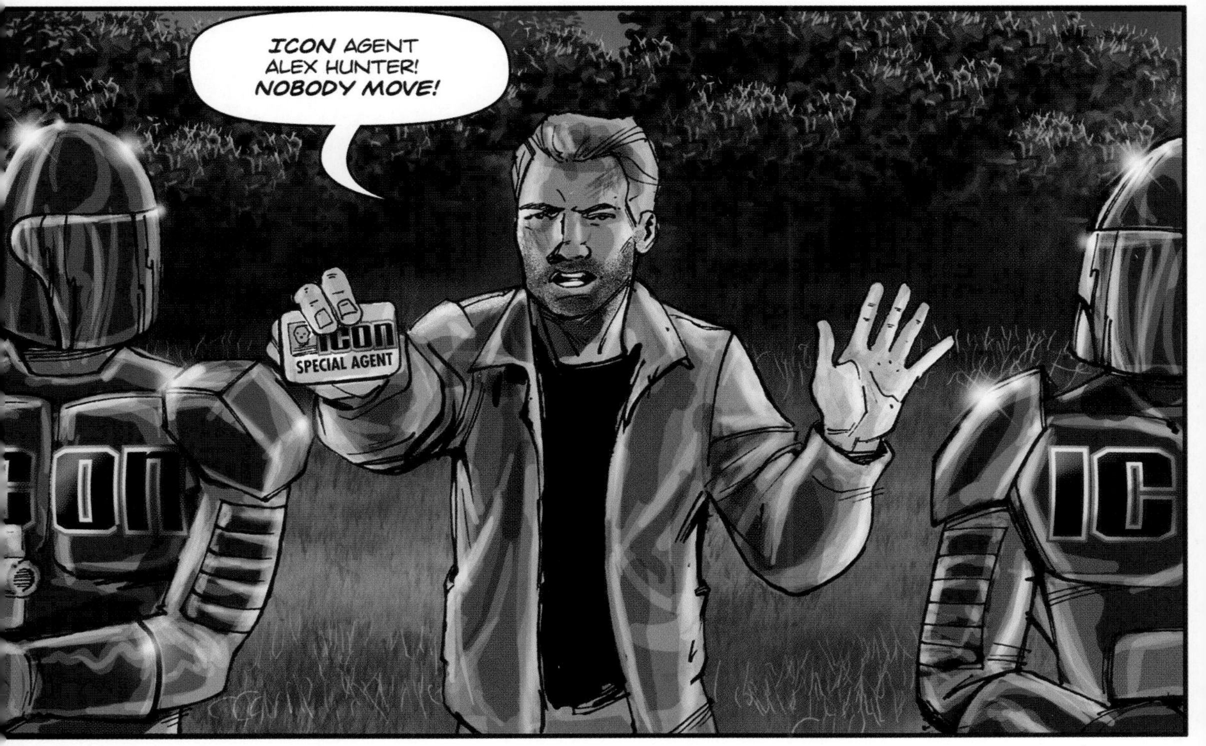
ICON AGENT ALEX HUNTER! NOBODY MOVE!
ICON
SPECIAL AGENT

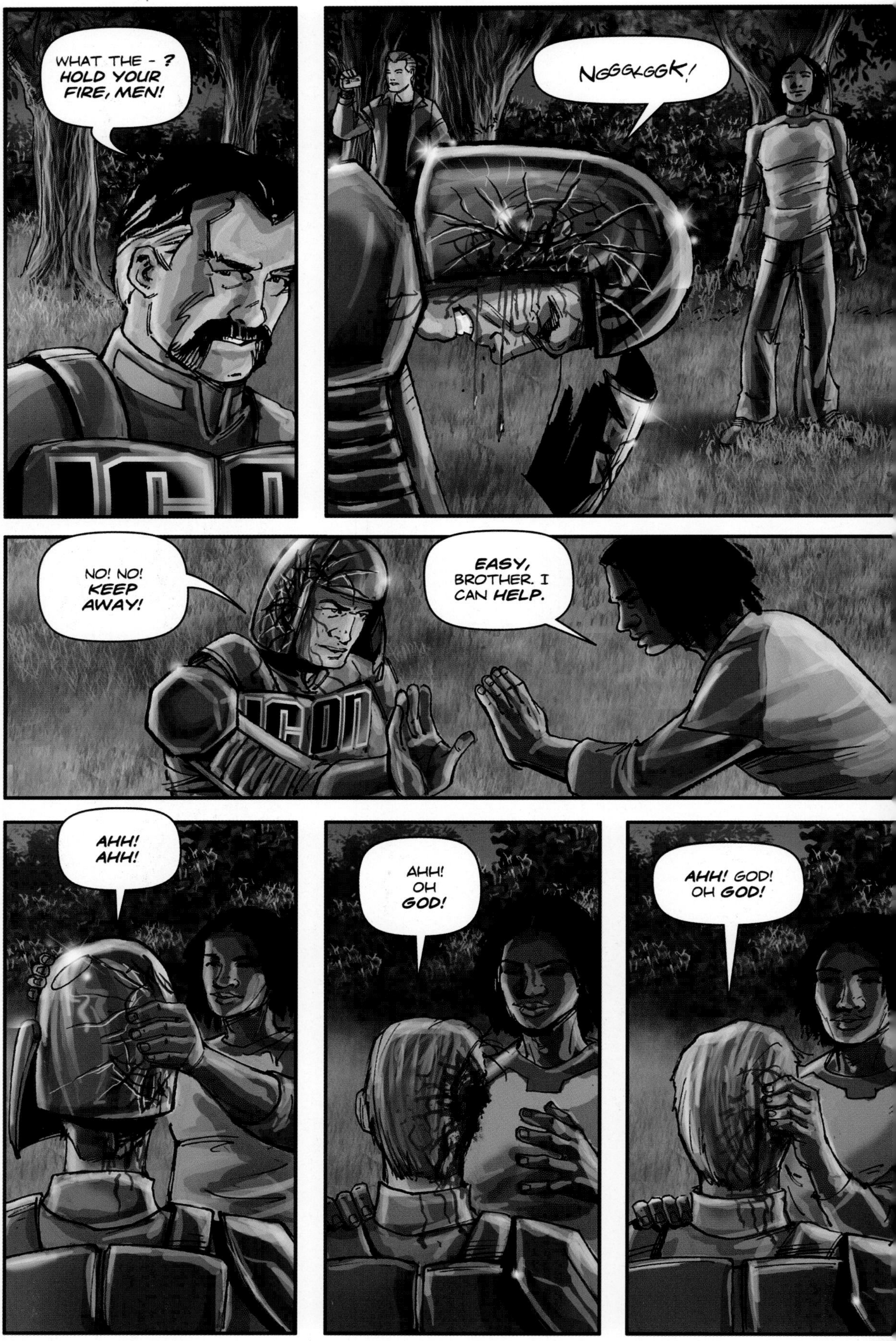
WHAT THE - ? HOLD YOUR FIRE, MEN!
NGGGKGGK!
NO! NO! KEEP AWAY!
EASY, BROTHER. I CAN HELP.
AHH! AHH!
AHH! OH GOD!
AHH! GOD! OH GOD!

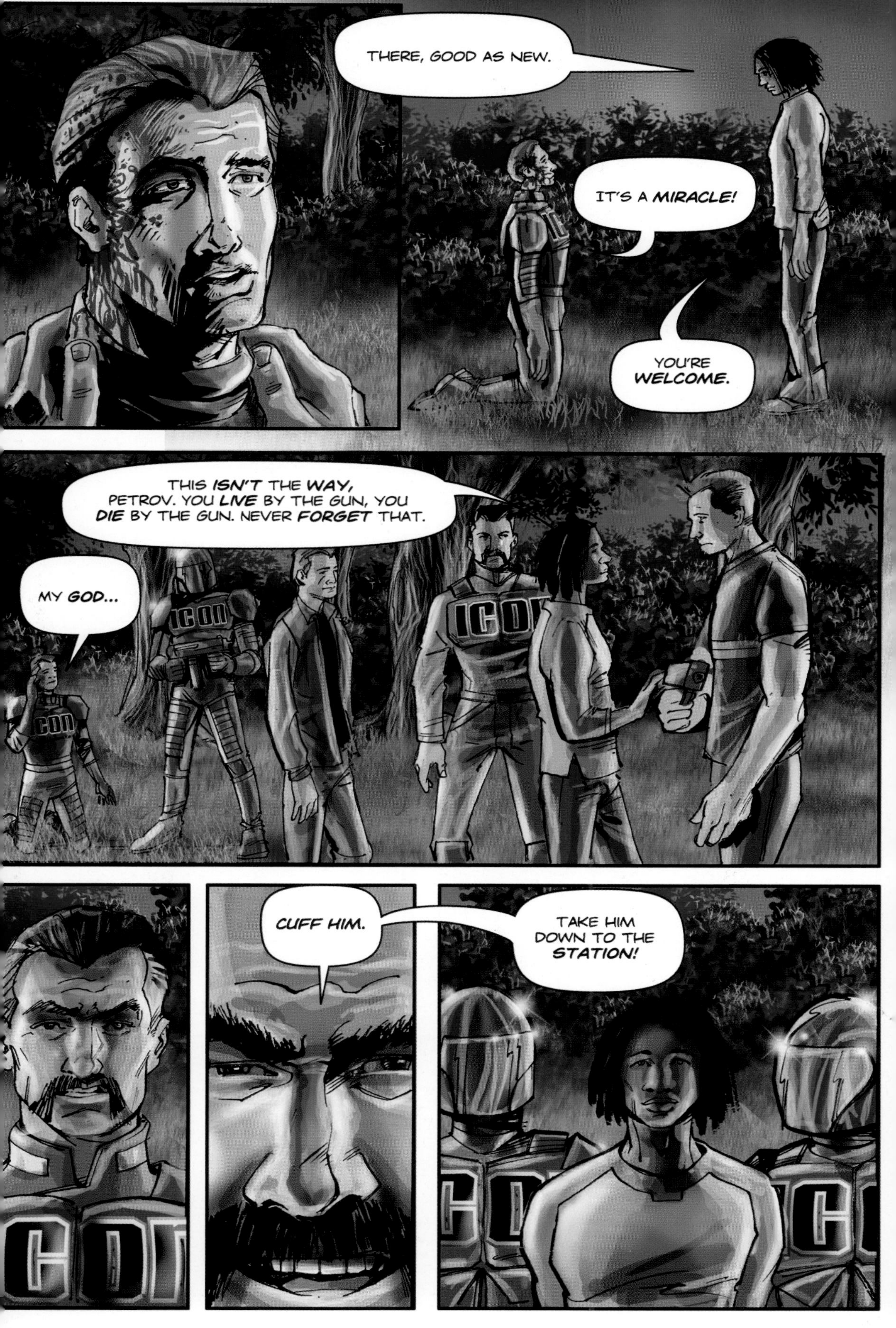
THERE, GOOD AS NEW.
IT'S A MIRACLE!
YOU'RE WELCOME.
THIS ISN'T THE WAY, PETROV. YOU LIVE BY THE GUN, YOU DIE BY THE GUN. NEVER FORGET THAT.
MY GOD...
ICON
CUFF HIM.
TAKE HIM DOWN TO THE STATION!

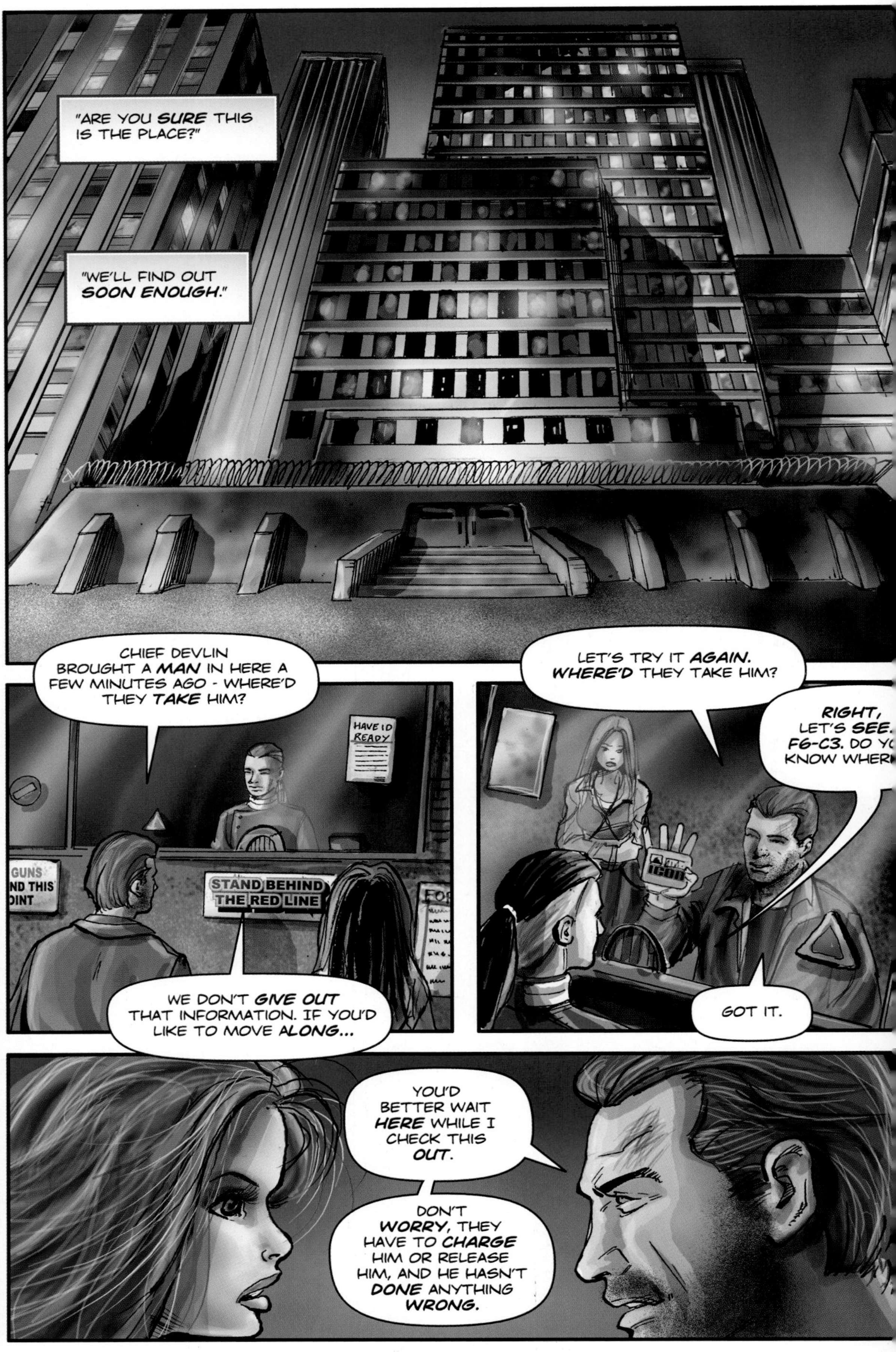
"ARE YOU SURE THIS IS THE PLACE?"
"WE'LL FIND OUT SOON ENOUGH."
CHIEF DEVLIN BROUGHT A MAN IN HERE A FEW MINUTES AGO - WHERE'D THEY TAKE HIM?
HAVE ID READY
STAND BEHIND THE RED LINE
WE DON'T GIVE OUT THAT INFORMATION. IF YOU'D LIKE TO MOVE ALONG...
LET'S TRY IT AGAIN. WHERE'D THEY TAKE HIM?
RIGHT, LET'S SEE. F6-C3.
GOT IT.
YOU'D BETTER WAIT HERE WHILE I CHECK THIS OUT.
DON'T WORRY, THEY HAVE TO CHARGE HIM OR RELEASE HIM, AND HE HASN'T DONE ANYTHING WRONG.

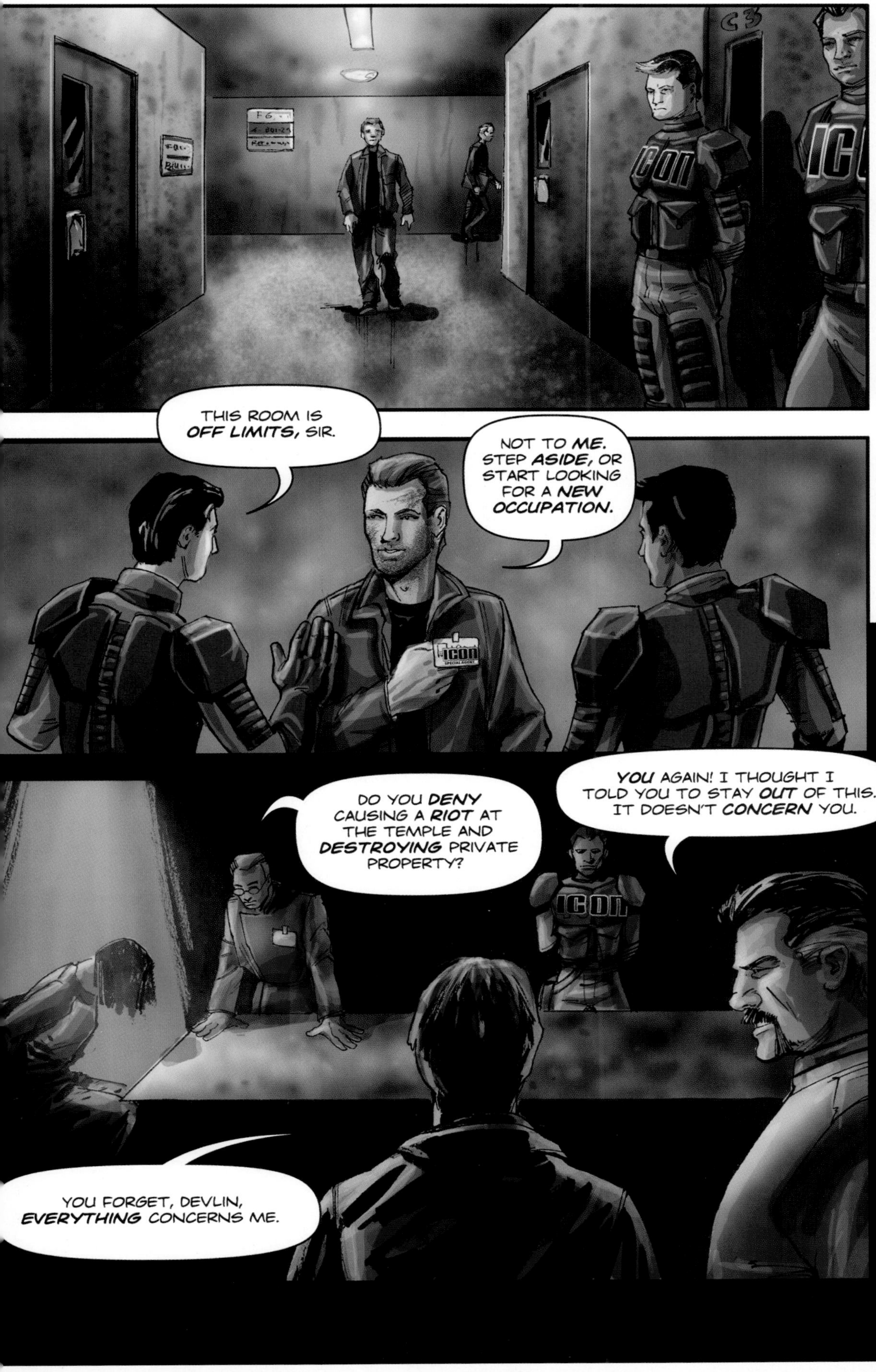
THIS ROOM IS OFF LIMITS, SIR.
NOT TO ME. STEP ASIDE, OR START LOOKING FOR A NEW OCCUPATION.
DO YOU DENY CAUSING A RIOT AT THE TEMPLE AND DESTROYING PRIVATE PROPERTY?
YOU AGAIN! I THOUGHT I TOLD YOU TO STAY OUT OF THIS. IT DOESN'T CONCERN YOU.
YOU FORGET, DEVLIN, EVERYTHING CONCERNS ME.

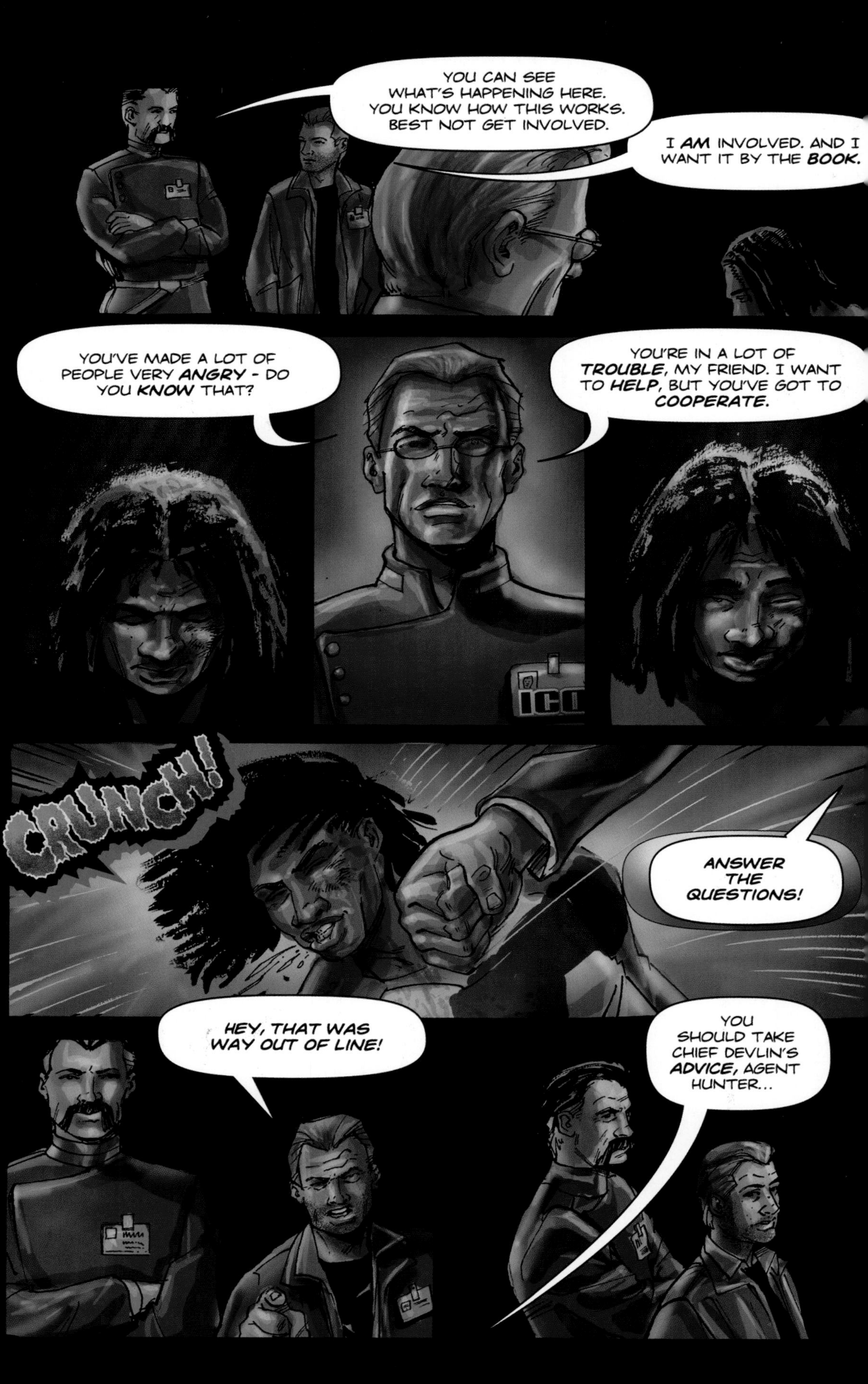
YOU CAN SEE WHAT'S HAPPENING HERE. YOU KNOW HOW THIS WORKS. BEST NOT GET INVOLVED.
I **AM** INVOLVED. AND I WANT IT BY THE **BOOK.**
YOU'VE MADE A LOT OF PEOPLE VERY **ANGRY** - DO YOU **KNOW** THAT?
YOU'RE IN A LOT OF **TROUBLE**, MY FRIEND. I WANT TO **HELP**, BUT YOU'VE GOT TO **COOPERATE.**
ICO
CRUNCH!
ANSWER THE QUESTIONS!
HEY, THAT WAS WAY OUT OF LINE!
YOU SHOULD TAKE CHIEF DEVLIN'S **ADVICE,** AGENT HUNTER...

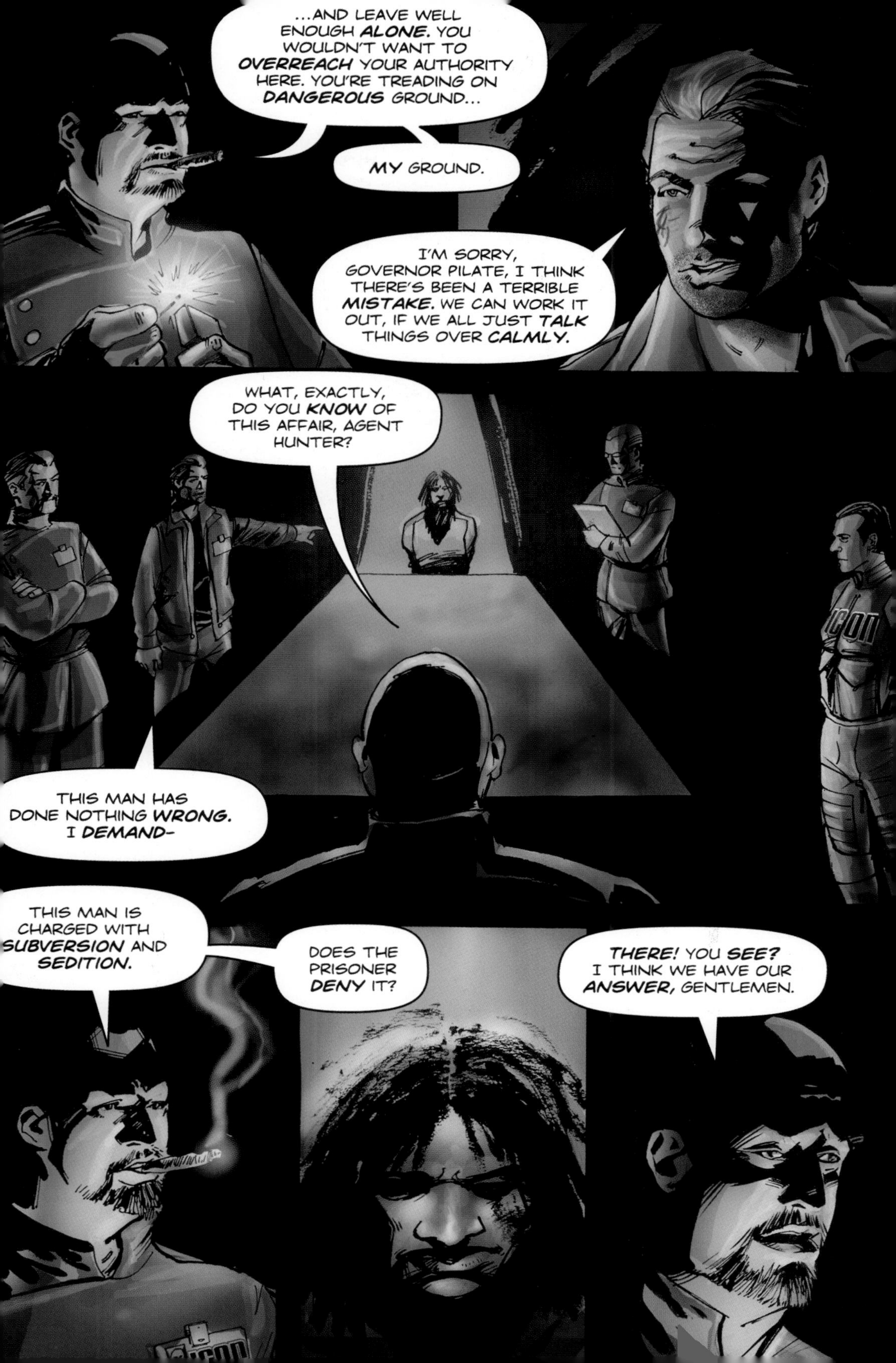
...AND LEAVE WELL ENOUGH ALONE. YOU WOULDN'T WANT TO OVERREACH YOUR AUTHORITY HERE. YOU'RE TREADING ON DANGEROUS GROUND...
MY GROUND.
I'M SORRY, GOVERNOR PILATE, I THINK THERE'S BEEN A TERRIBLE MISTAKE. WE CAN WORK IT OUT, IF WE ALL JUST TALK THINGS OVER CALMLY.
WHAT, EXACTLY, DO YOU KNOW OF THIS AFFAIR, AGENT HUNTER?
THIS MAN HAS DONE NOTHING WRONG. I DEMAND-
THIS MAN IS CHARGED WITH SUBVERSION AND SEDITION.
DOES THE PRISONER DENY IT?
THERE! YOU SEE? I THINK WE HAVE OUR ANSWER, GENTLEMEN.

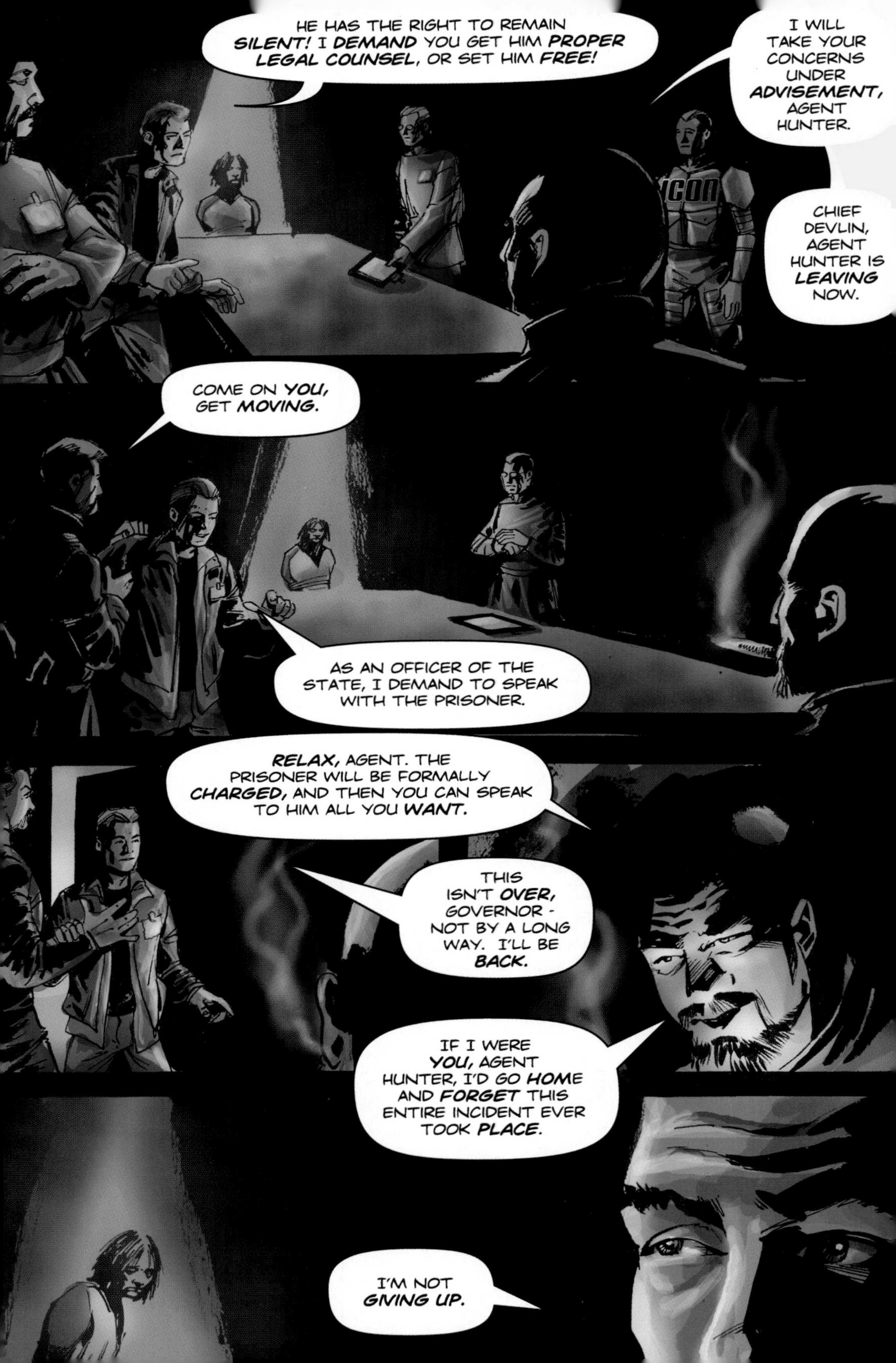
HE HAS THE RIGHT TO REMAIN SILENT! I DEMAND YOU GET HIM PROPER LEGAL COUNSEL, OR SET HIM FREE!
I WILL TAKE YOUR CONCERNS UNDER ADVISEMENT, AGENT HUNTER.
CHIEF DEVLIN, AGENT HUNTER IS LEAVING NOW.
ICON
COME ON YOU, GET MOVING.
AS AN OFFICER OF THE STATE, I DEMAND TO SPEAK WITH THE PRISONER.
RELAX, AGENT. THE PRISONER WILL BE FORMALLY CHARGED, AND THEN YOU CAN SPEAK TO HIM ALL YOU WANT.
THIS ISN'T OVER, GOVERNOR - NOT BY A LONG WAY. I'LL BE BACK.
IF I WERE YOU, AGENT HUNTER, I'D GO HOME AND FORGET THIS ENTIRE INCIDENT EVER TOOK PLACE.
I'M NOT GIVING UP.

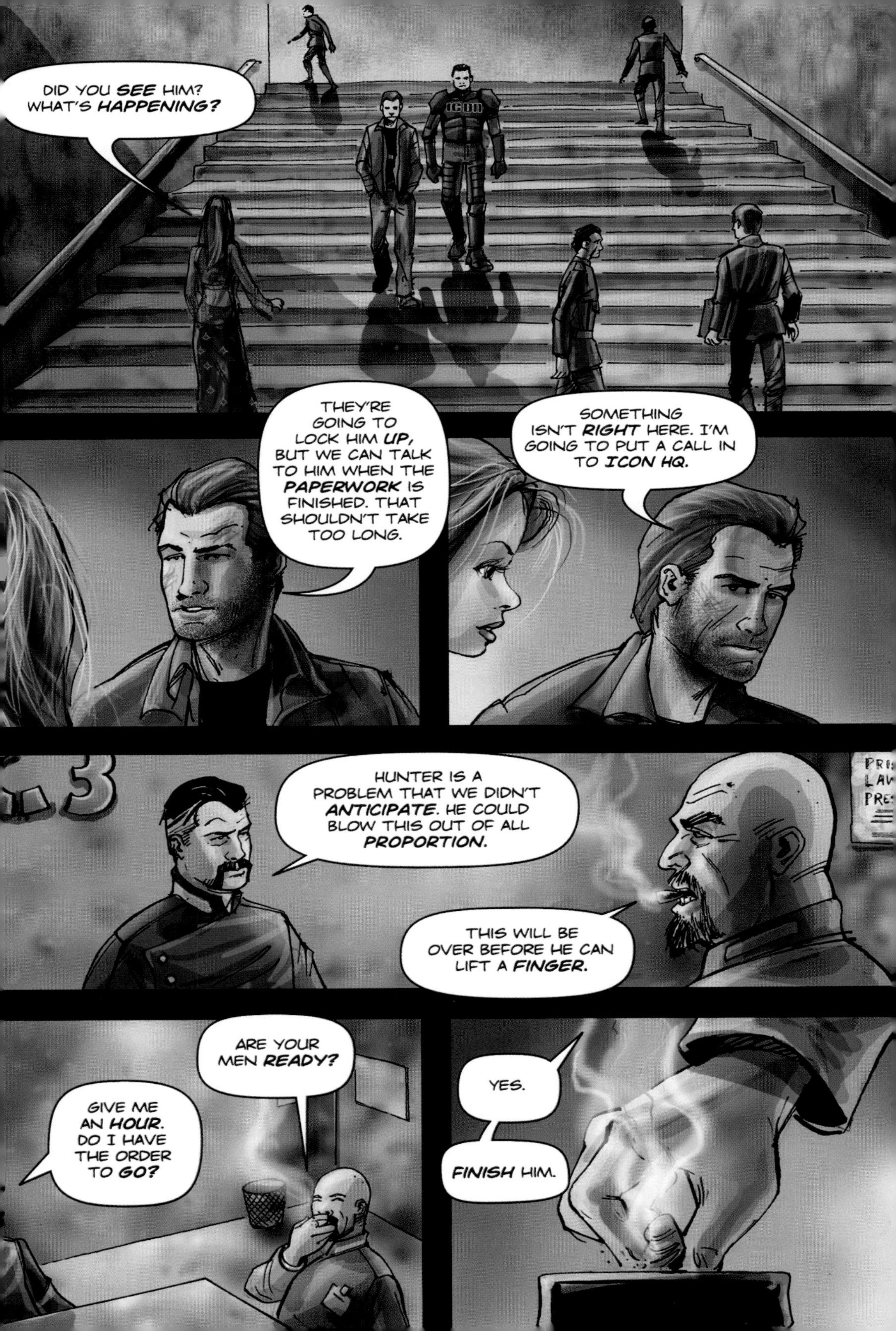
DID YOU SEE HIM? WHAT'S HAPPENING?
THEY'RE GOING TO LOCK HIM UP, BUT WE CAN TALK TO HIM WHEN THE PAPERWORK IS FINISHED. THAT SHOULDN'T TAKE TOO LONG.
SOMETHING ISN'T RIGHT HERE. I'M GOING TO PUT A CALL IN TO ICON HQ.
HUNTER IS A PROBLEM THAT WE DIDN'T ANTICIPATE. HE COULD BLOW THIS OUT OF ALL PROPORTION.
THIS WILL BE OVER BEFORE HE CAN LIFT A FINGER.
ARE YOUR MEN READY?
GIVE ME AN HOUR. DO I HAVE THE ORDER TO GO?
YES.
FINISH HIM.

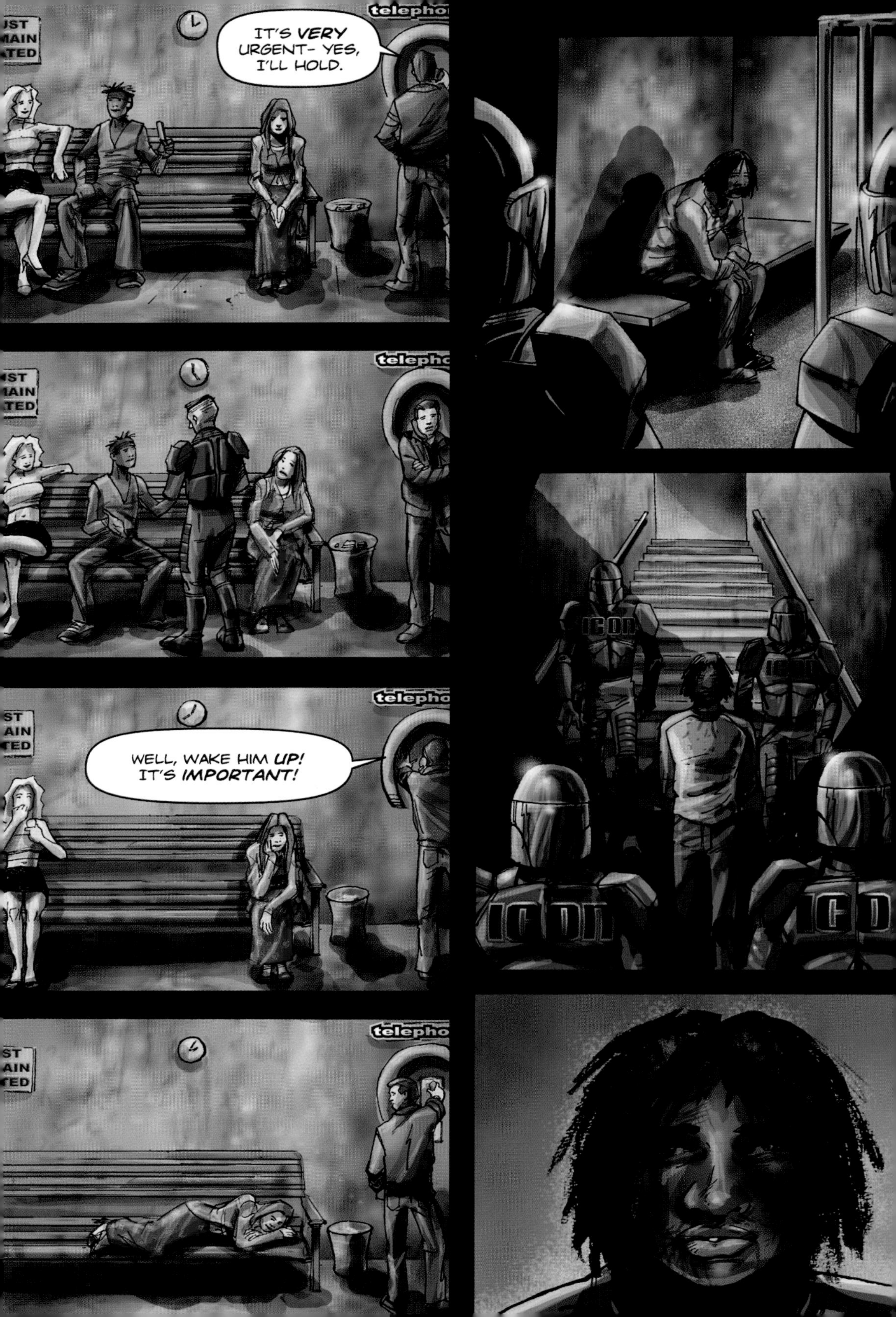
IT'S VERY URGENT- YES, I'LL HOLD.
WELL, WAKE HIM UP! IT'S IMPORTANT!

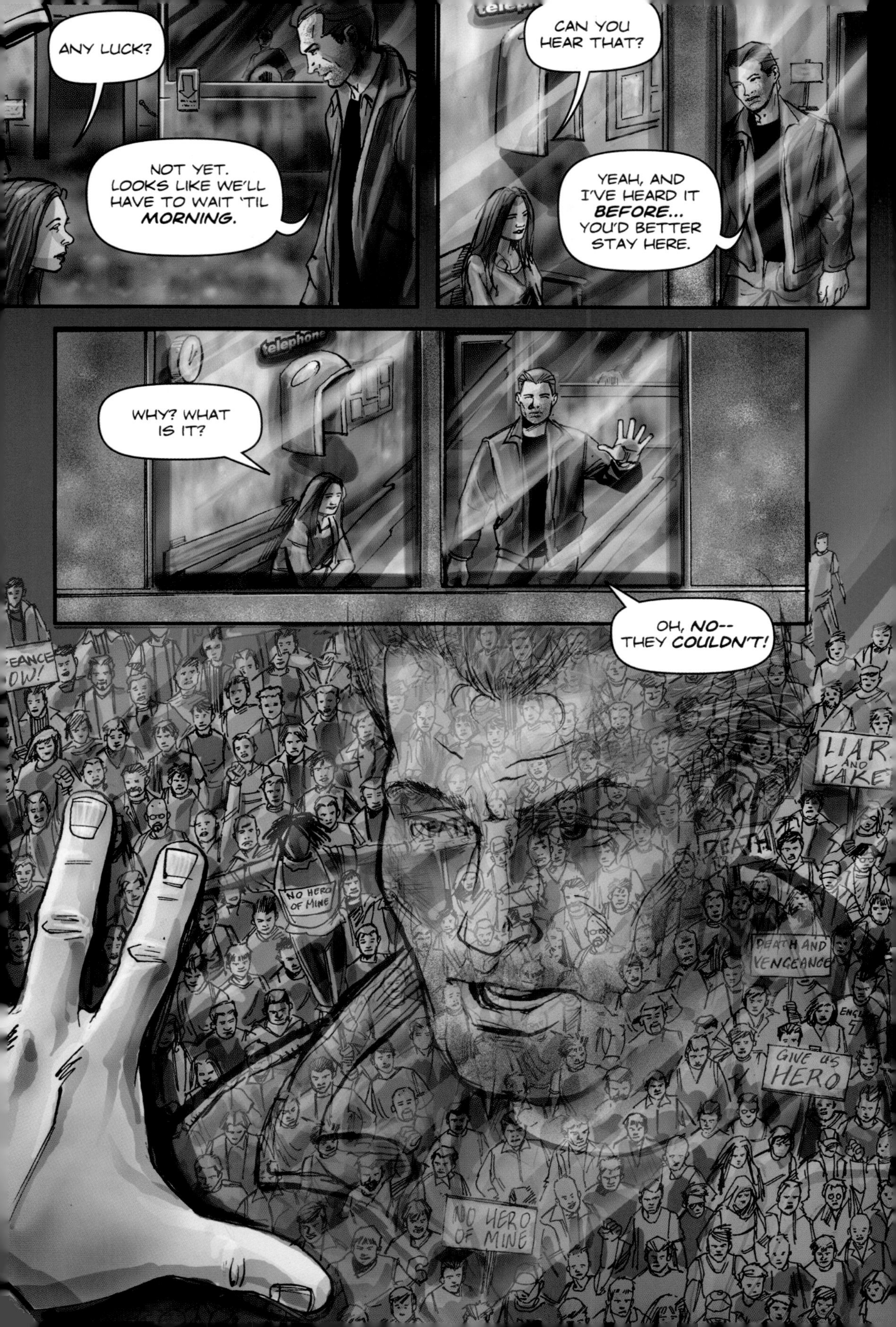
ANY LUCK?
NOT YET. LOOKS LIKE WE'LL HAVE TO WAIT 'TIL **MORNING.**
CAN YOU HEAR THAT?
YEAH, AND I'VE HEARD IT ***BEFORE...*** YOU'D BETTER STAY HERE.
telephone
WHY? WHAT IS IT?
OH, ***NO--*** THEY ***COULDN'T!***
LIAR AND FAKE
NO HERO OF MINE
DEATH
DEATH AND VENGEANCE
GIVE US HERO
NO HERO OF MINE

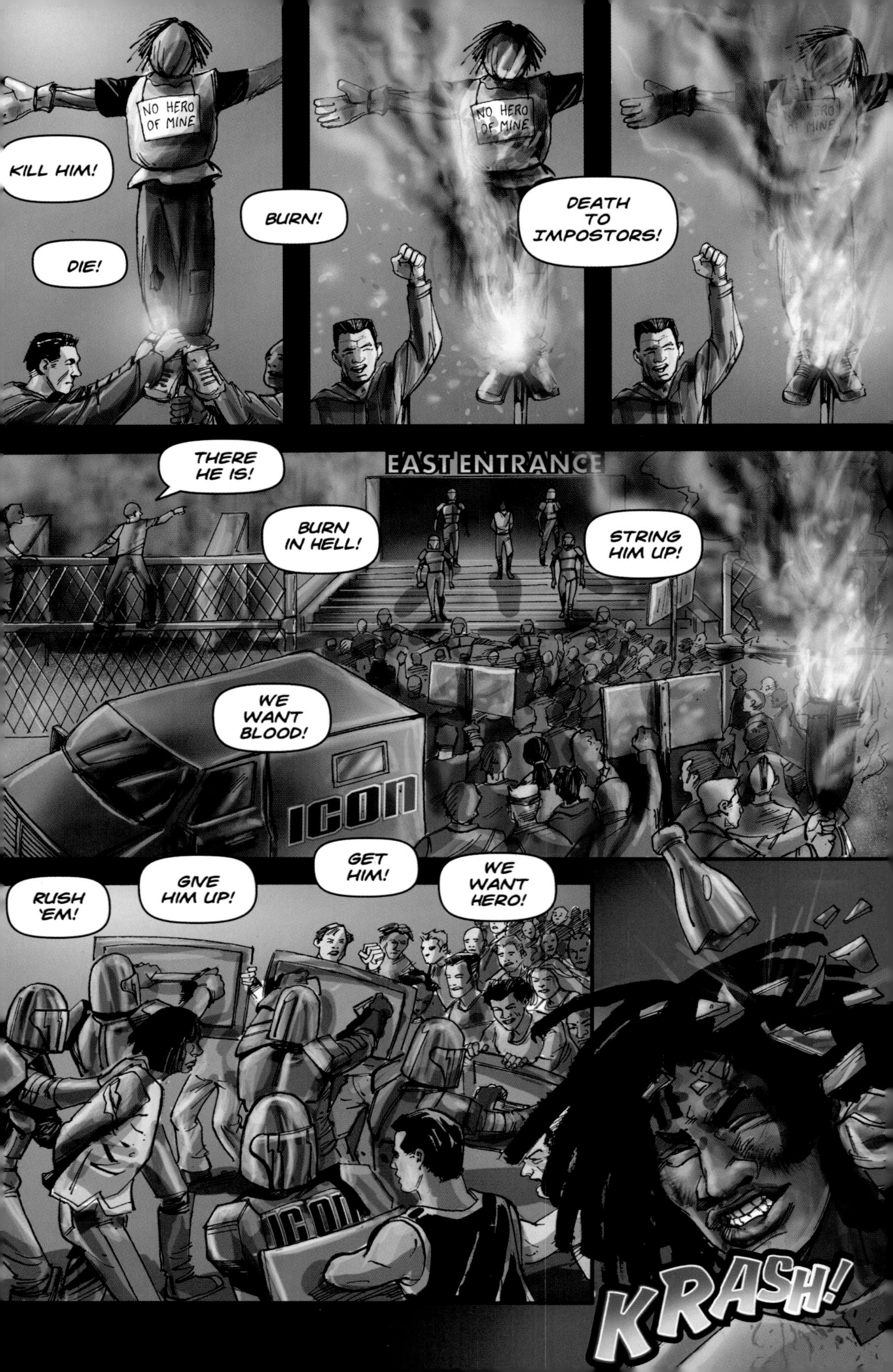
NO HERO OF MINE
KILL HIM!
DIE!
BURN!
NO HERO OF MINE
DEATH TO IMPOSTORS!
THERE HE IS!
EAST ENTRANCE
BURN IN HELL!
STRING HIM UP!
WE WANT BLOOD!
ICON
RUSH 'EM!
GIVE HIM UP!
GET HIM!
WE WANT HERO!
ICON
KRASH!

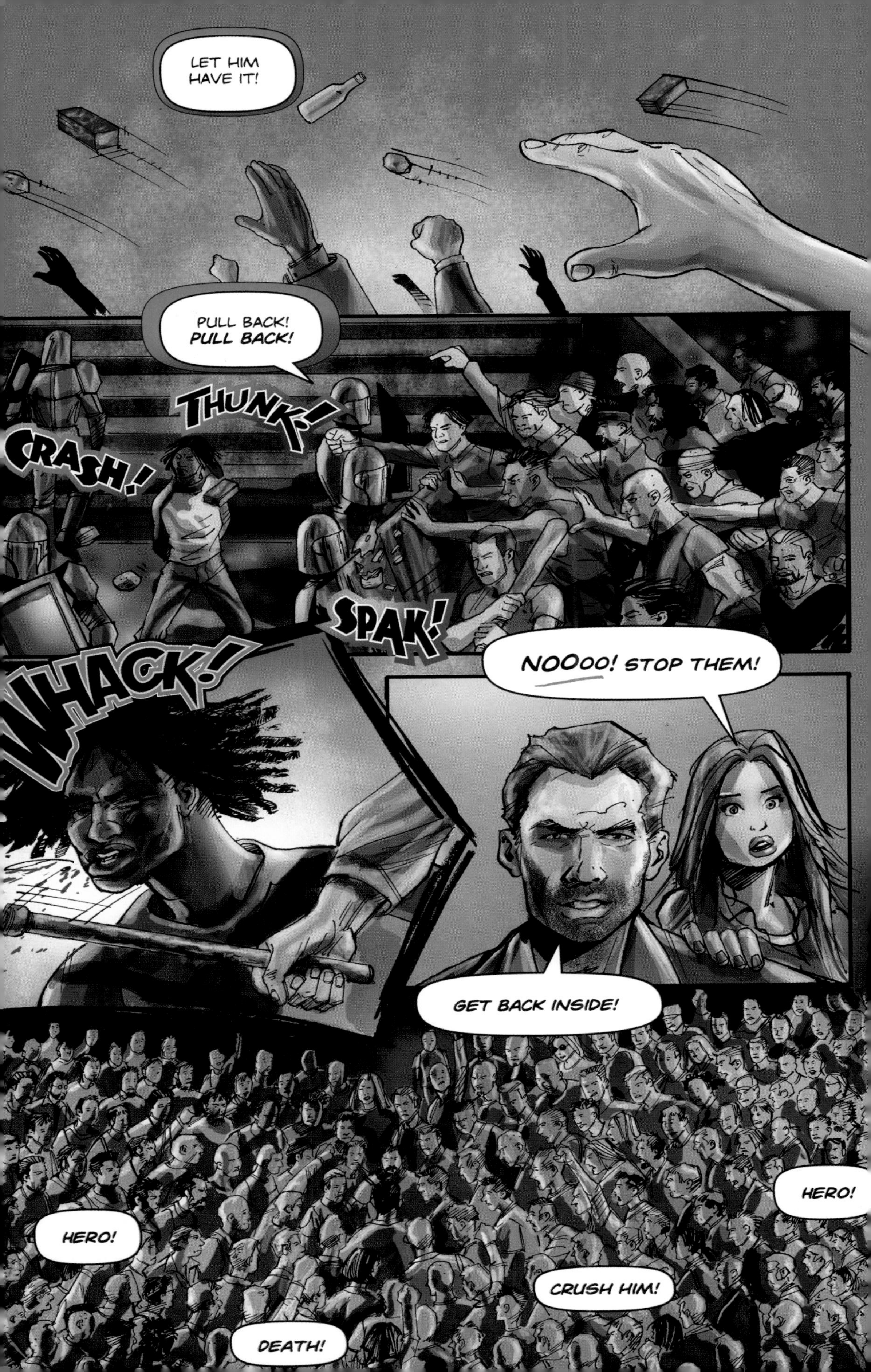
LET HIM HAVE IT!
PULL BACK! PULL BACK!
THUNK!
CRASH!
SPAK!
WHACK!
NOOoo! STOP THEM!
GET BACK INSIDE!
HERO!
HERO!
CRUSH HIM!
DEATH!

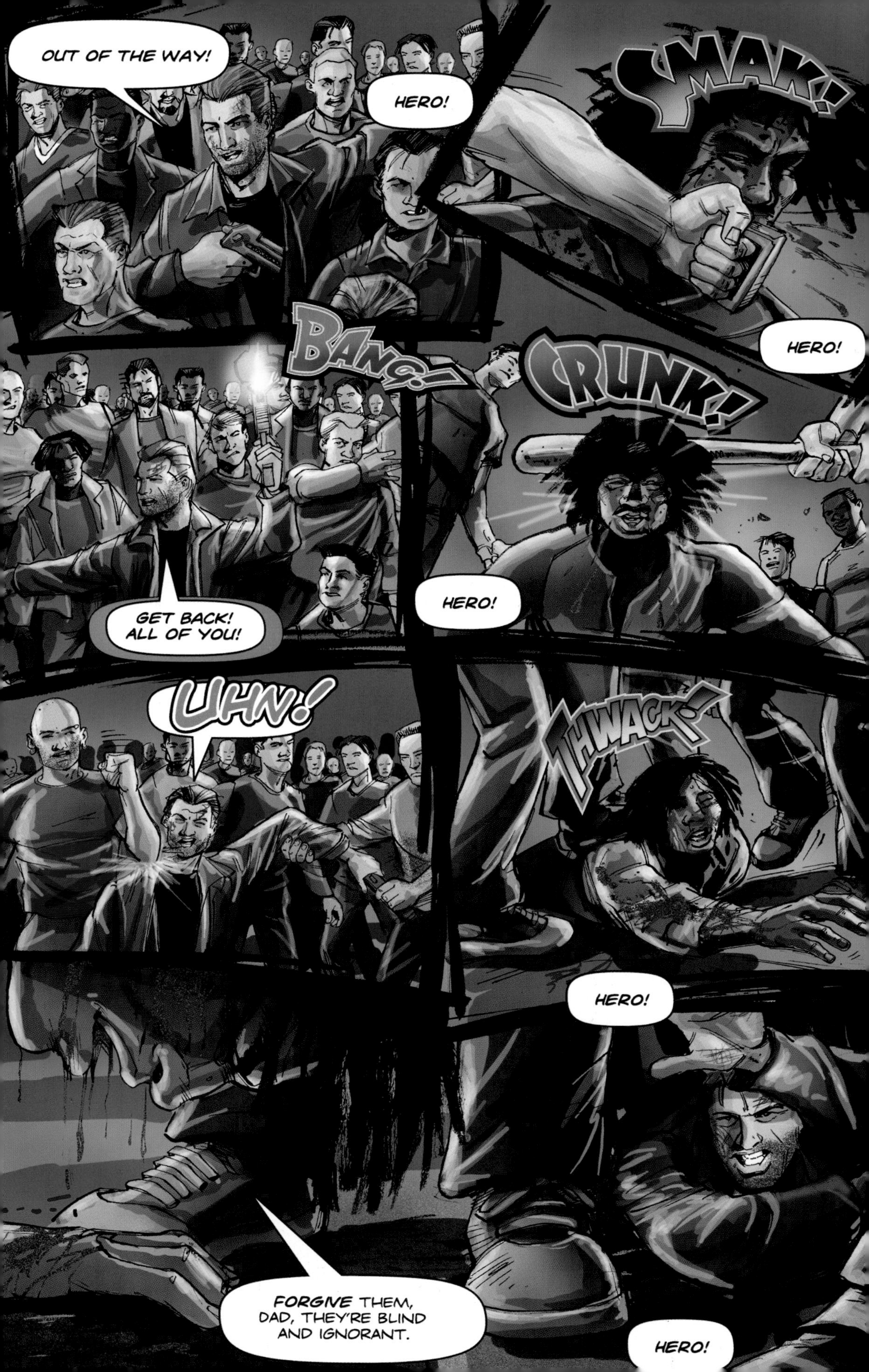
OUT OF THE WAY!
HERO!
SMAK!
HERO!
BANG!
CRUNK!
GET BACK! ALL OF YOU!
HERO!
UHN!
THWACK!
HERO!
FORGIVE THEM, DAD, THEY'RE BLIND AND IGNORANT.
HERO!

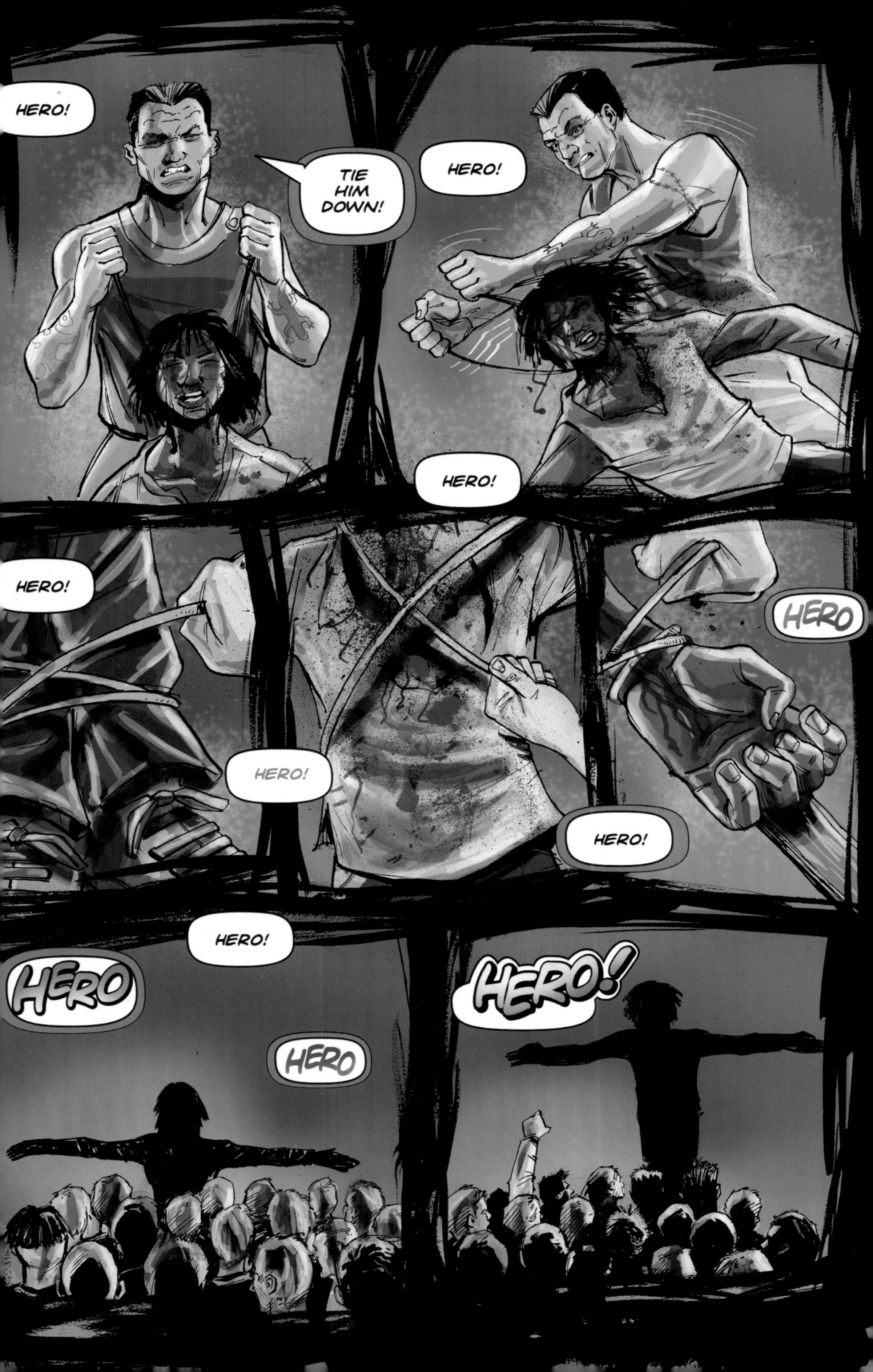
HERO!
TIE HIM DOWN!
HERO!
HERO!
HERO!
HERO
HERO!
HERO!
HERO!
HERO
HERO
HERO!

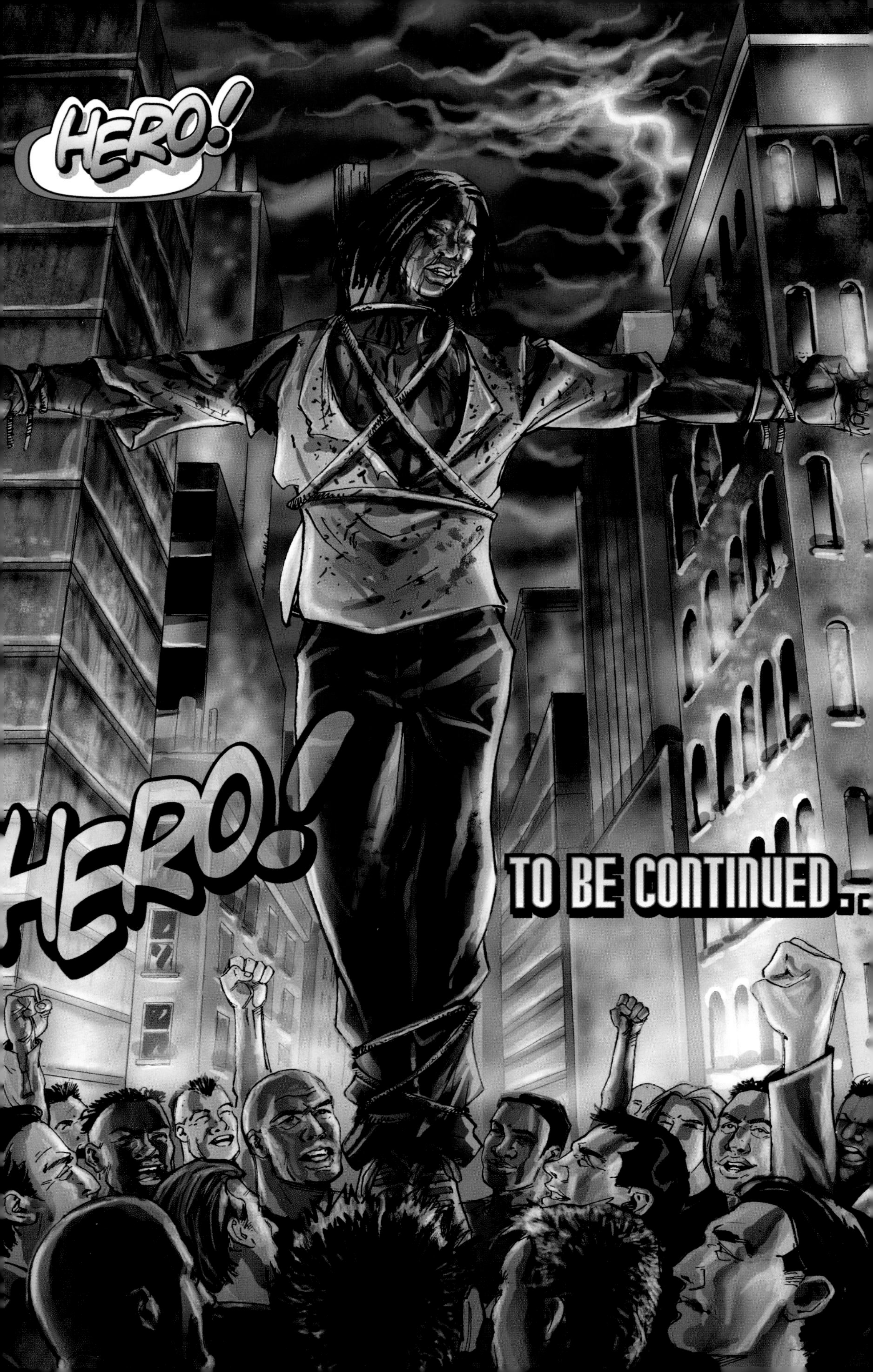
HERO!
HERO!
TO BE CONTINUED...

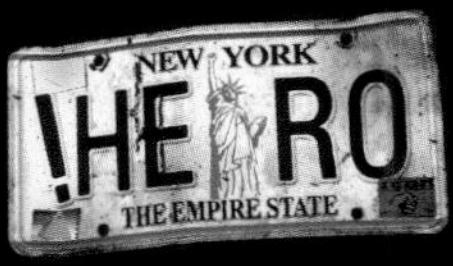
NEW YORK
!HERO
THE EMPIRE STATE

FIVE

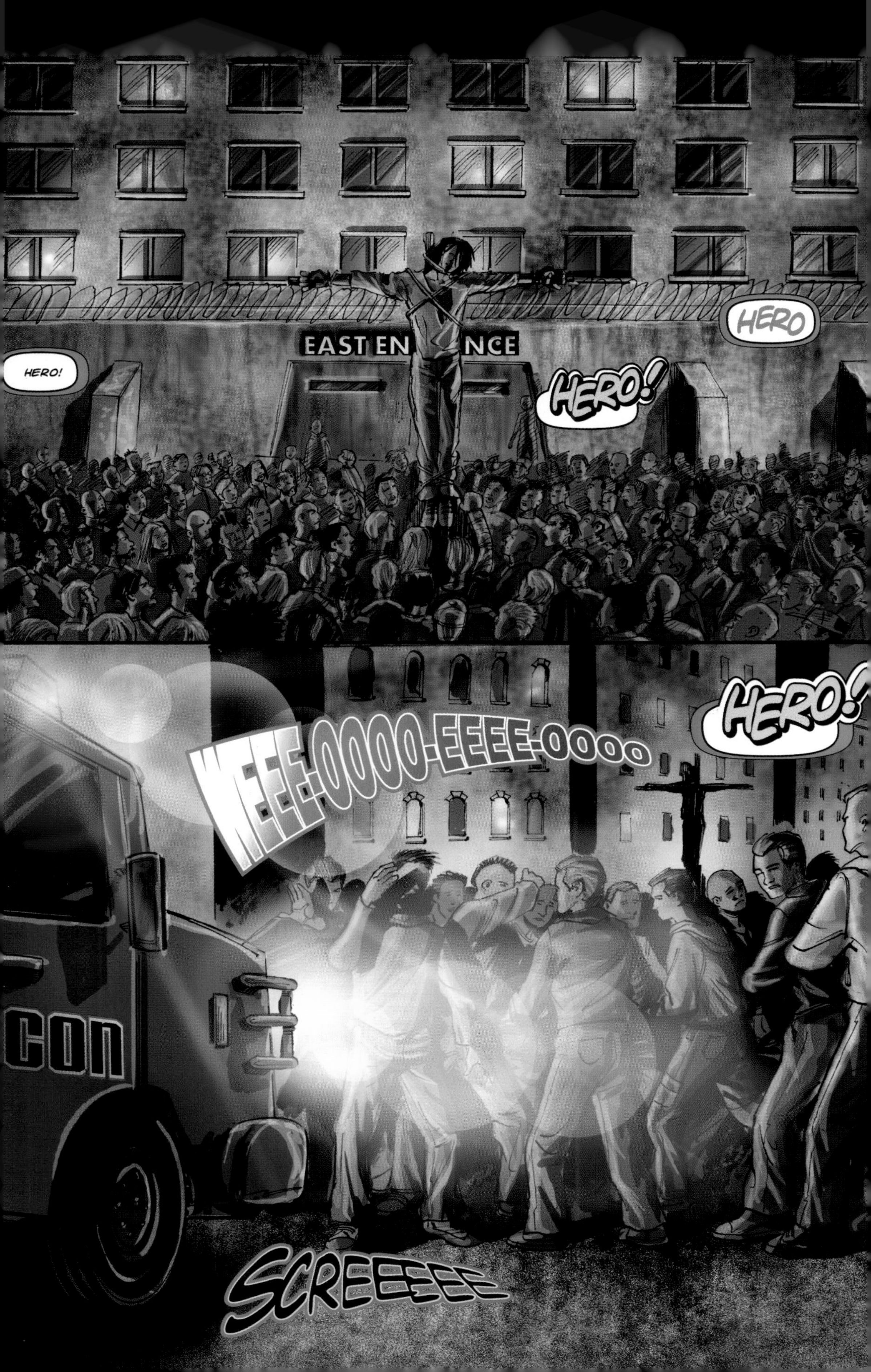
EAST EN NCE
HERO!
HERO!
HERO
HERO!
WEEE-OOOO-EEEE-OOOO
CON
SCREEEEEE

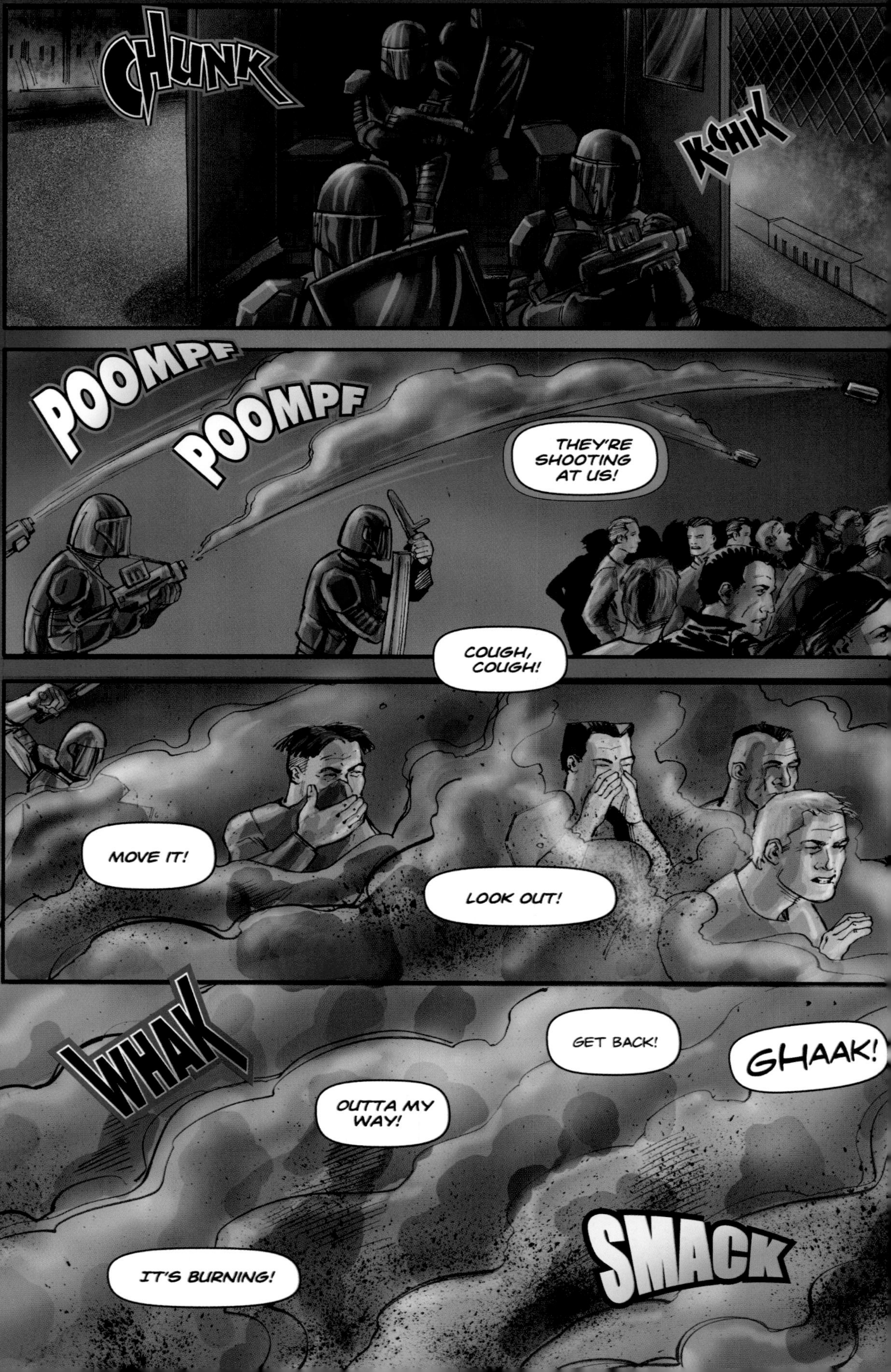
CHUNK
K-CHIK
POOMPF
POOMPF
THEY'RE SHOOTING AT US!
COUGH, COUGH!
MOVE IT!
LOOK OUT!
WHAK
GET BACK!
GHAAK!
OUTTA MY WAY!
SMACK
IT'S BURNING!

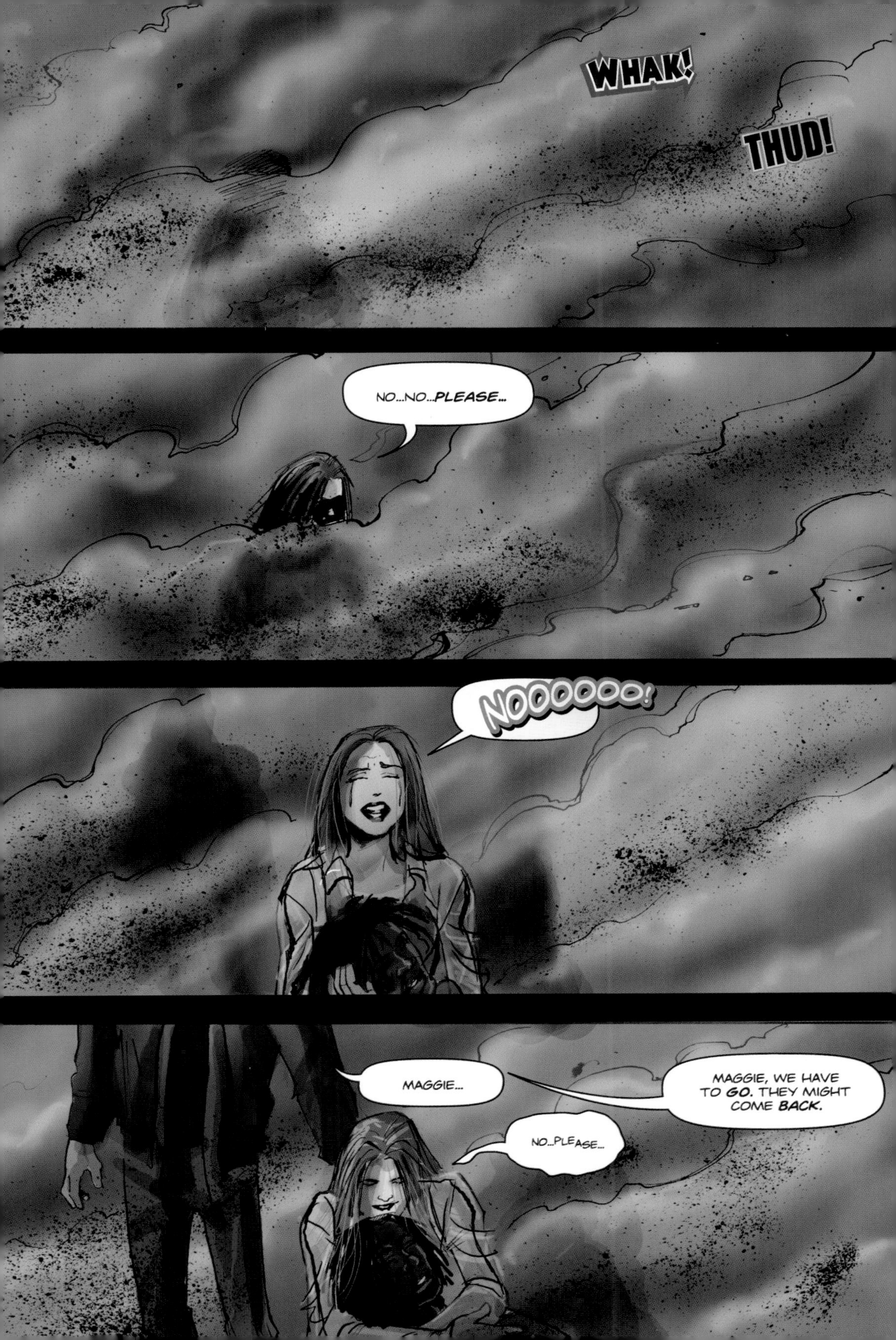
WHAK!
THUD!
NO...NO...PLEASE...
NOOOOOOO!
MAGGIE...
MAGGIE, WE HAVE TO GO. THEY MIGHT COME BACK.
NO...PLEASE...

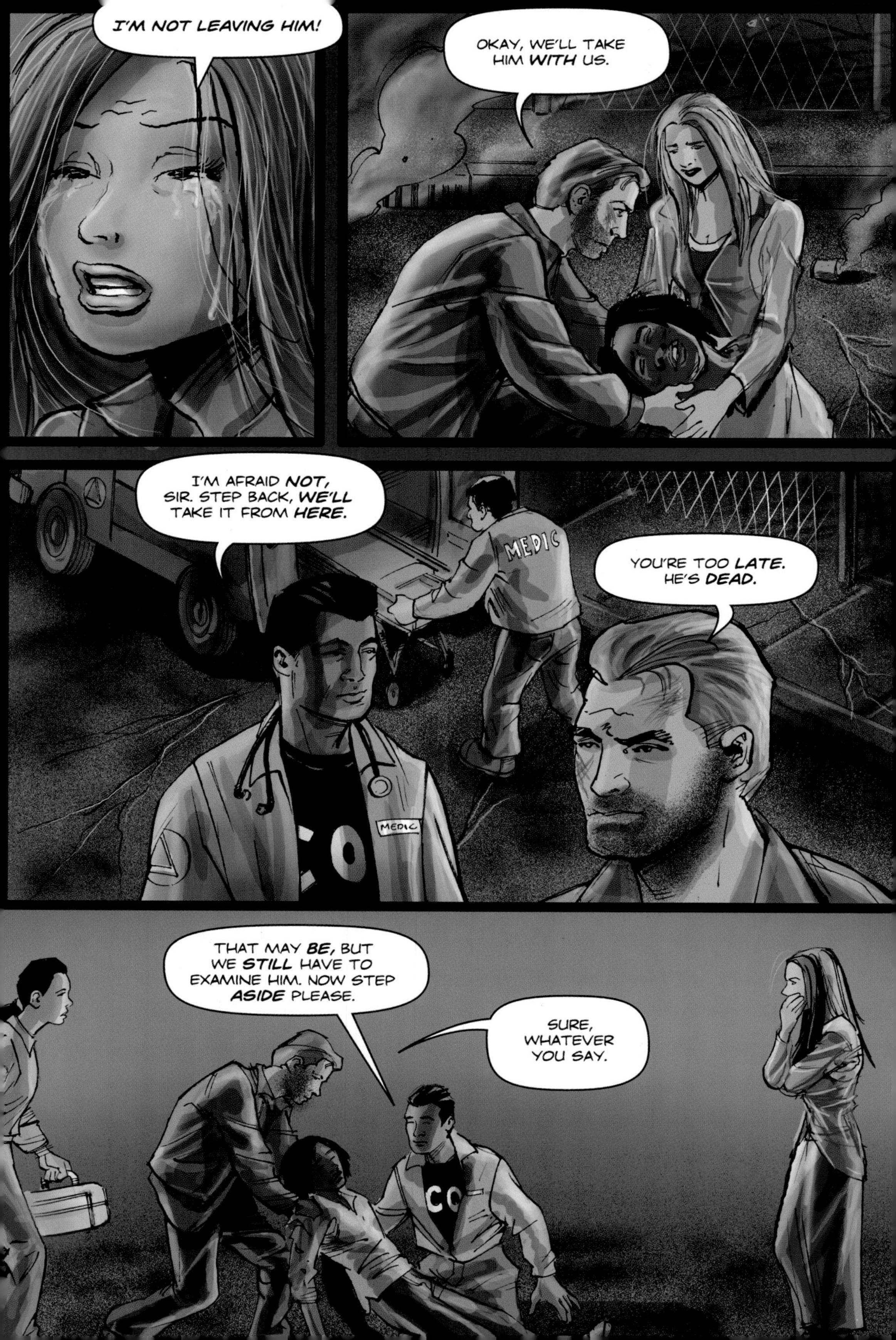
I'M NOT LEAVING HIM!
OKAY, WE'LL TAKE HIM WITH US.
I'M AFRAID NOT, SIR. STEP BACK, WE'LL TAKE IT FROM HERE.
MEDIC
YOU'RE TOO LATE. HE'S DEAD.
MEDIC
THAT MAY BE, BUT WE STILL HAVE TO EXAMINE HIM. NOW STEP ASIDE PLEASE.
SURE, WHATEVER YOU SAY.

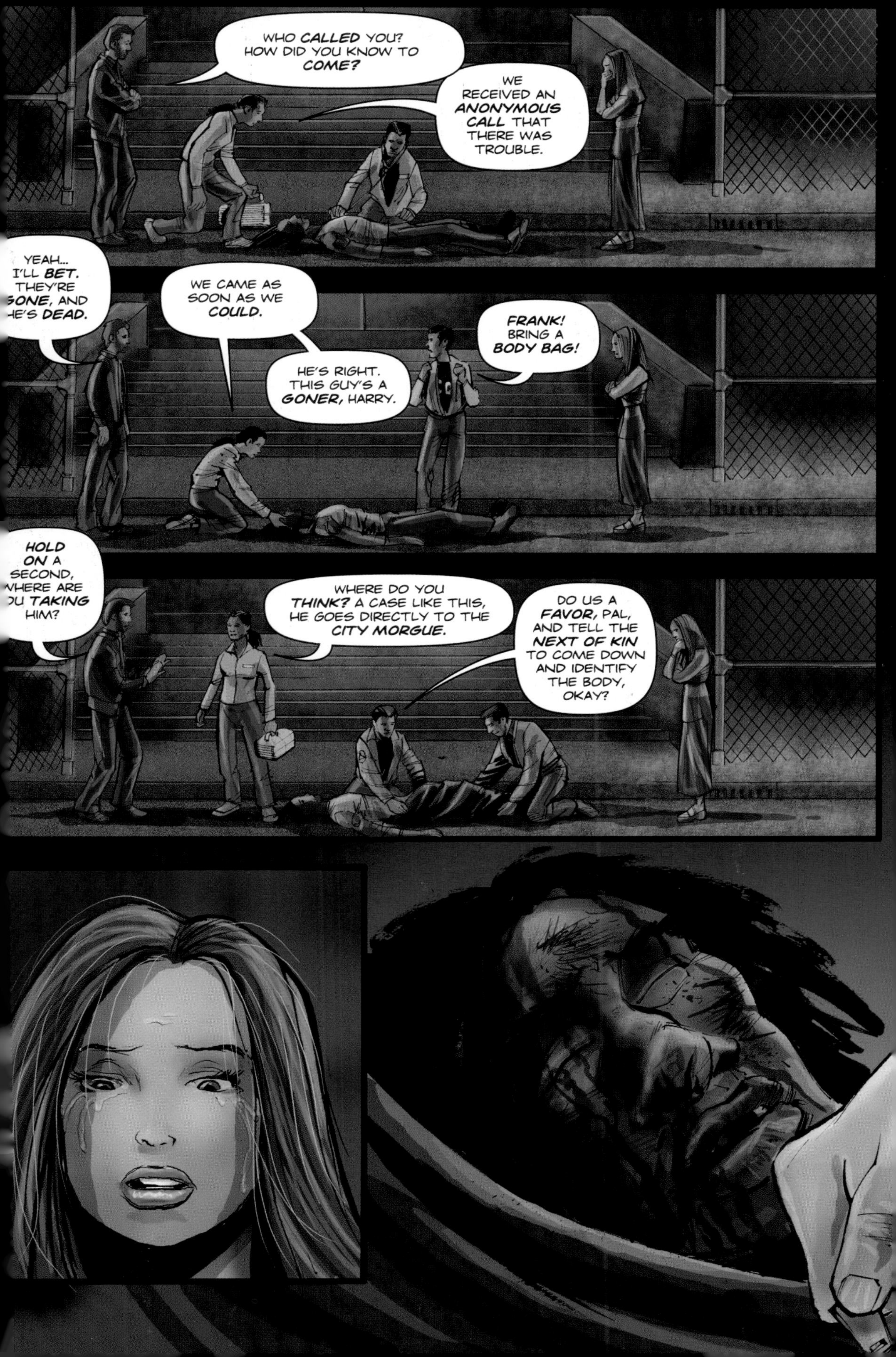
WHO CALLED YOU? HOW DID YOU KNOW TO COME?
WE RECEIVED AN ANONYMOUS CALL THAT THERE WAS TROUBLE.
YEAH... I'LL BET. THEY'RE ONE, AND E'S DEAD.
WE CAME AS SOON AS WE COULD.
HE'S RIGHT. THIS GUY'S A GONER, HARRY.
FRANK! BRING A BODY BAG!
HOLD ON A SECOND, HERE ARE U TAKING HIM?
WHERE DO YOU THINK? A CASE LIKE THIS, HE GOES DIRECTLY TO THE CITY MORGUE.
DO US A FAVOR, PAL, AND TELL THE NEXT OF KIN TO COME DOWN AND IDENTIFY THE BODY, OKAY?

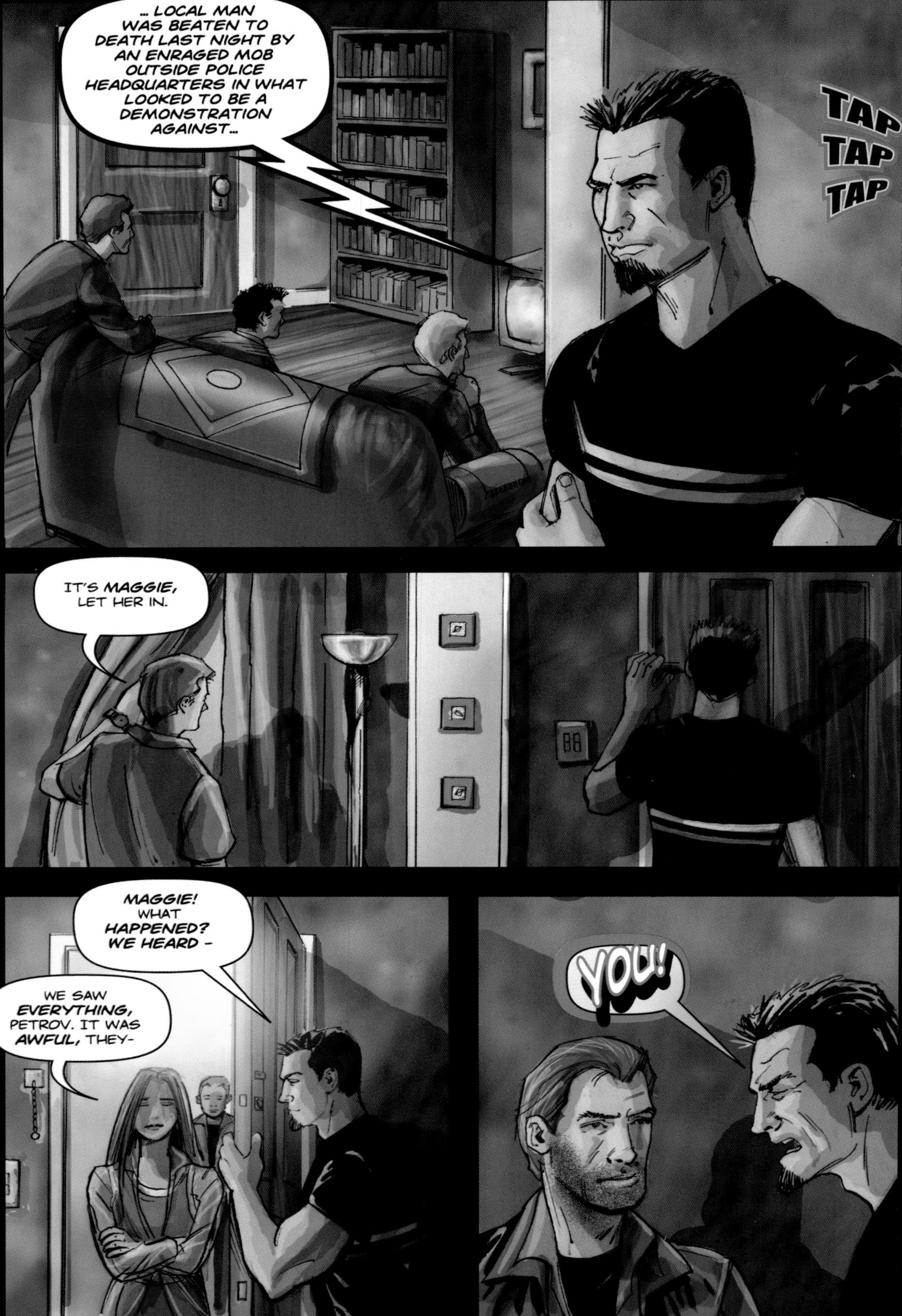

... LOCAL MAN WAS BEATEN TO DEATH LAST NIGHT BY AN ENRAGED MOB OUTSIDE POLICE HEADQUARTERS IN WHAT LOOKED TO BE A DEMONSTRATION AGAINST...
TAP TAP TAP
IT'S MAGGIE, LET HER IN.
MAGGIE! WHAT HAPPENED? WE HEARD –
WE SAW EVERYTHING, PETROV. IT WAS AWFUL, THEY-
YOU!

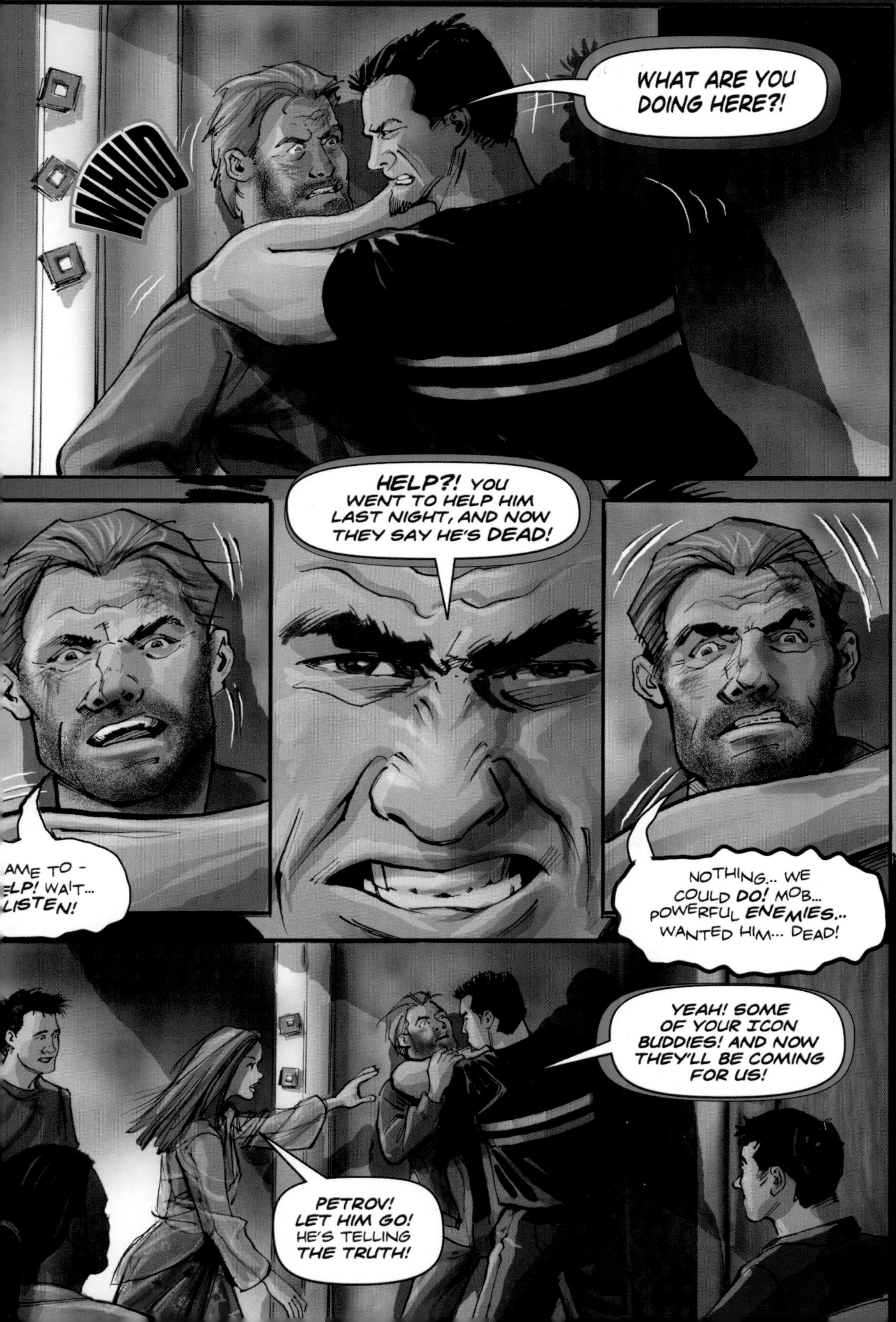
WHUD
WHAT ARE YOU DOING HERE?!
AME TO -
ELP! WAIT... LISTEN!
HELP?! YOU WENT TO HELP HIM LAST NIGHT, AND NOW THEY SAY HE'S DEAD!
NOTHING... WE COULD DO! MOB... POWERFUL ENEMIES... WANTED HIM... DEAD!
YEAH! SOME OF YOUR ICON BUDDIES! AND NOW THEY'LL BE COMING FOR US!
PETROV! LET HIM GO! HE'S TELLING THE TRUTH!

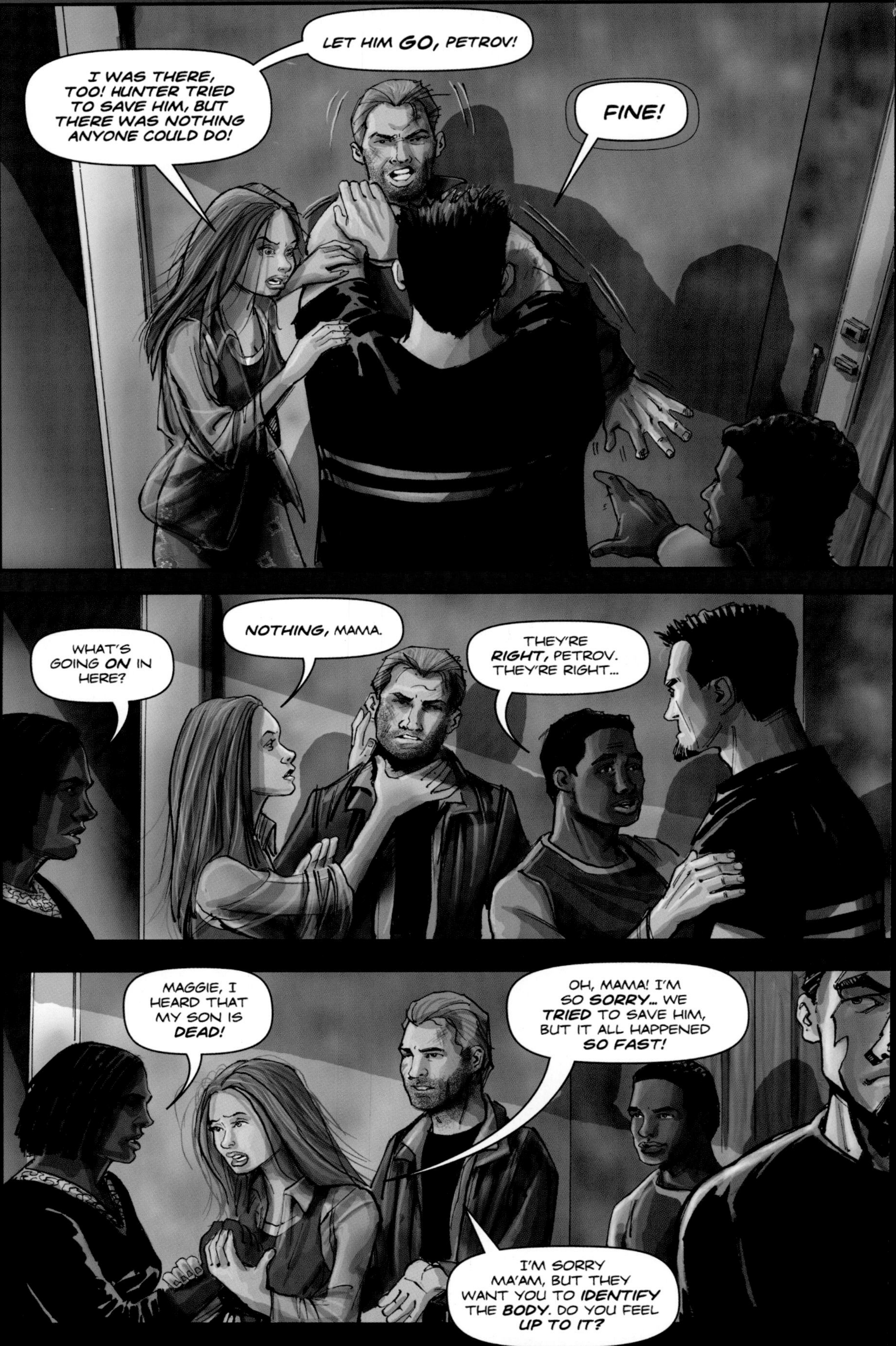
I WAS THERE, TOO! HUNTER TRIED TO SAVE HIM, BUT THERE WAS NOTHING ANYONE COULD DO!
LET HIM GO, PETROV!
FINE!
WHAT'S GOING ON IN HERE?
NOTHING, MAMA.
THEY'RE RIGHT, PETROV. THEY'RE RIGHT...
MAGGIE, I HEARD THAT MY SON IS DEAD!
OH, MAMA! I'M SO SORRY... WE TRIED TO SAVE HIM, BUT IT ALL HAPPENED SO FAST!
I'M SORRY MA'AM, BUT THEY WANT YOU TO IDENTIFY THE BODY. DO YOU FEEL UP TO IT?

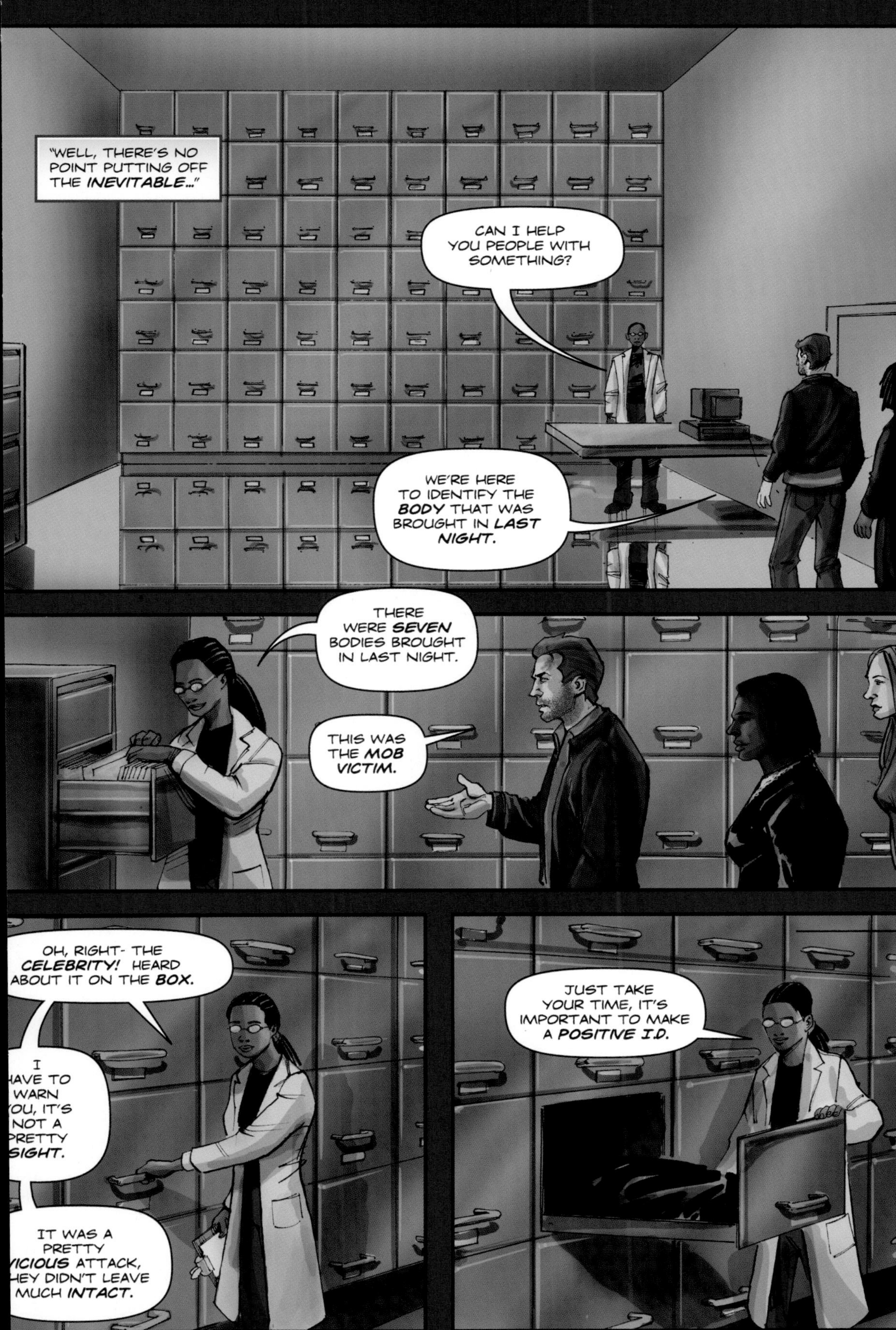
"WELL, THERE'S NO POINT PUTTING OFF THE INEVITABLE..."
CAN I HELP YOU PEOPLE WITH SOMETHING?
WE'RE HERE TO IDENTIFY THE BODY THAT WAS BROUGHT IN LAST NIGHT.
THERE WERE SEVEN BODIES BROUGHT IN LAST NIGHT.
THIS WAS THE MOB VICTIM.
OH, RIGHT- THE CELEBRITY! HEARD ABOUT IT ON THE BOX.
I HAVE TO WARN YOU, IT'S NOT A PRETTY SIGHT.
IT WAS A PRETTY VICIOUS ATTACK, THEY DIDN'T LEAVE MUCH INTACT.
JUST TAKE YOUR TIME, IT'S IMPORTANT TO MAKE A POSITIVE I.D.

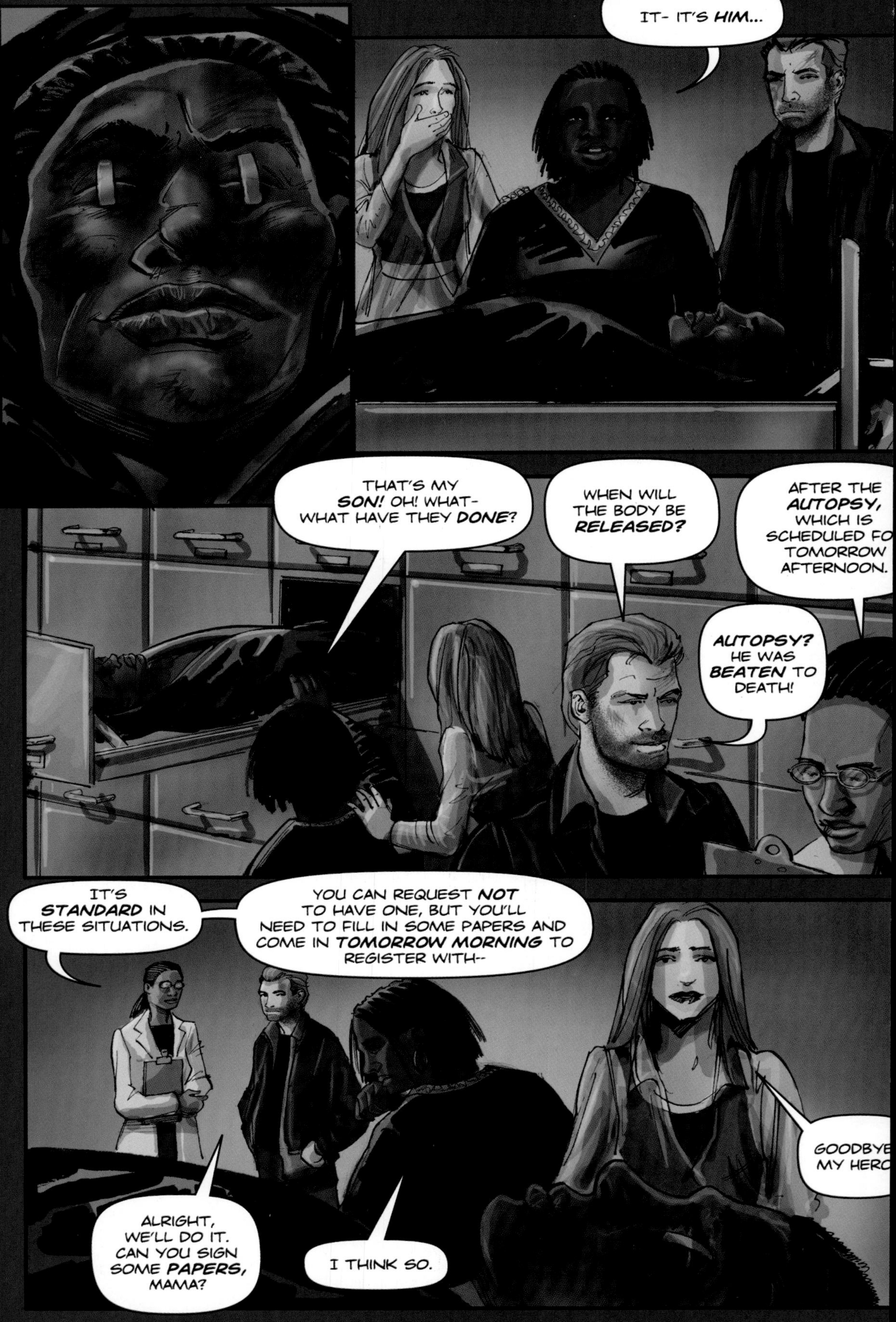
IT- IT'S **HIM...**
THAT'S MY **SON!** OH! WHAT- WHAT HAVE THEY **DONE**?
WHEN WILL THE BODY BE **RELEASED?**
AFTER THE **AUTOPSY,** WHICH IS SCHEDULED FO TOMORROW AFTERNOON.
AUTOPSY? HE WAS **BEATEN** TO DEATH!
IT'S **STANDARD** IN THESE SITUATIONS.
YOU CAN REQUEST **NOT** TO HAVE ONE, BUT YOU'LL NEED TO FILL IN SOME PAPERS AND COME IN **TOMORROW MORNING** TO REGISTER WITH--
GOODBYE MY HERO
ALRIGHT, WE'LL DO IT. CAN YOU SIGN SOME **PAPERS,** MAMA?
I THINK SO.

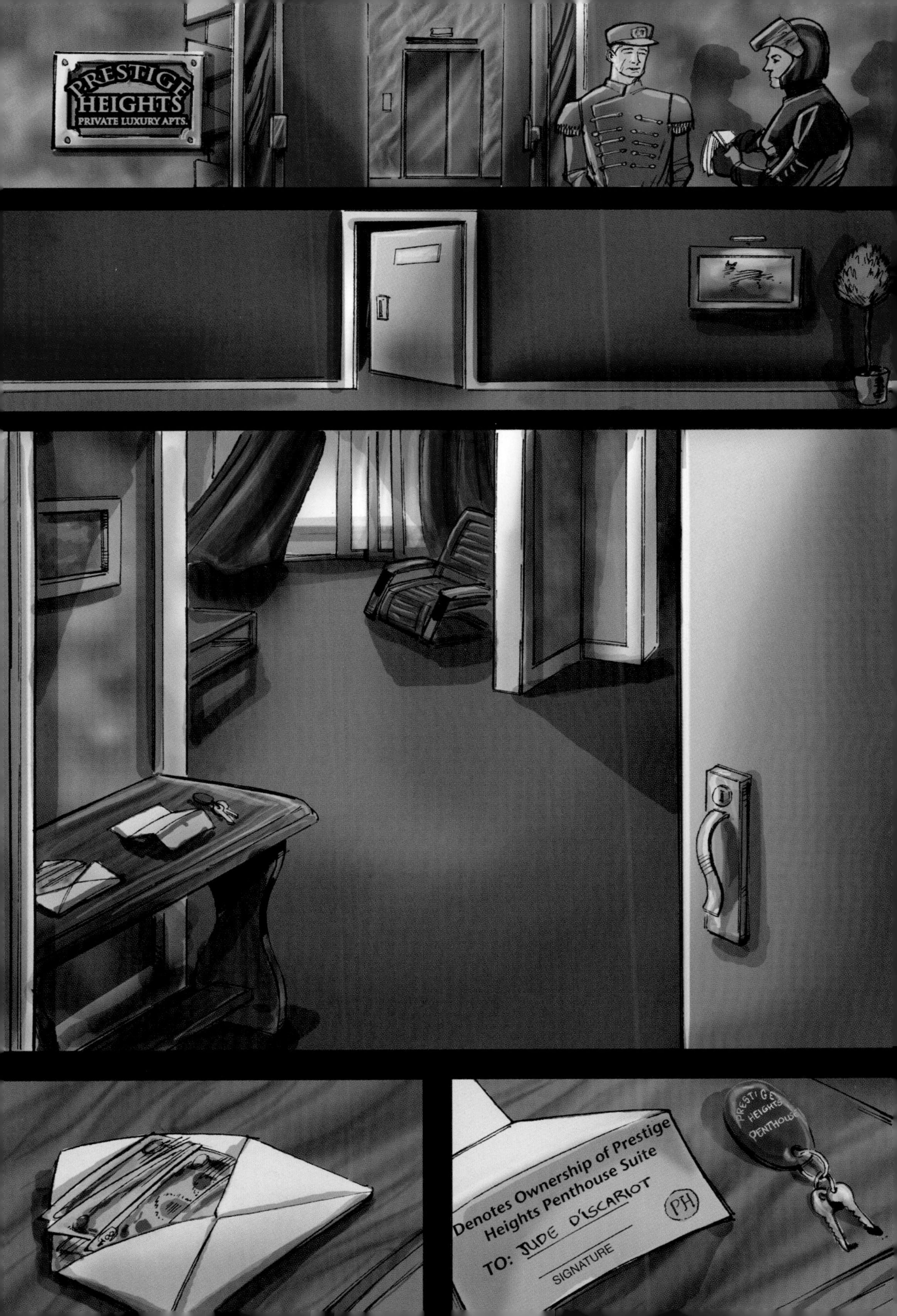
PRESTIGE HEIGHTS
PRIVATE LUXURY APTS.
PRESTIGE HEIGHTS PENTHOUSE
Denotes Ownership of Prestige Heights Penthouse Suite
PH
TO: JUDE D'ISCARIOT
SIGNATURE

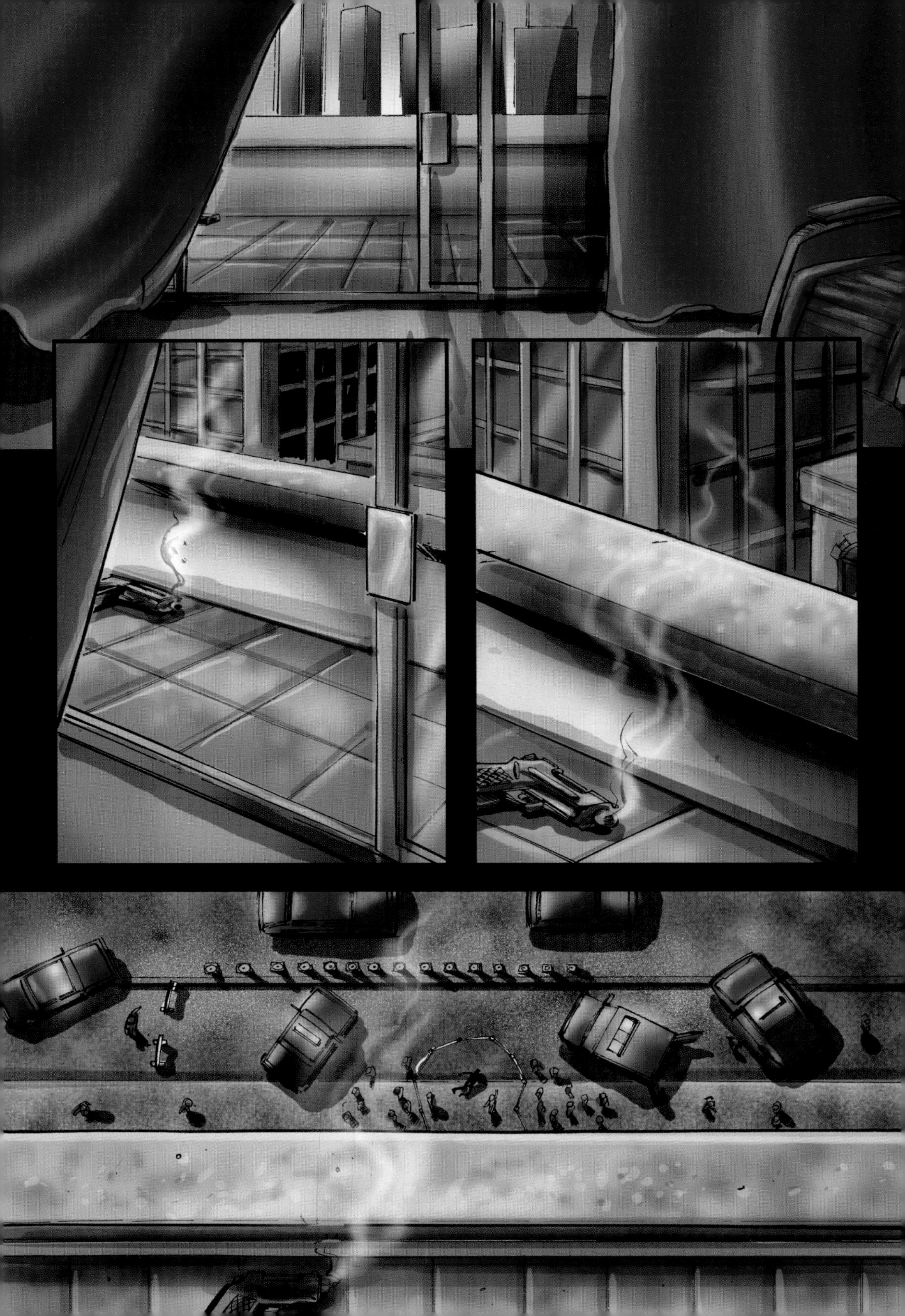

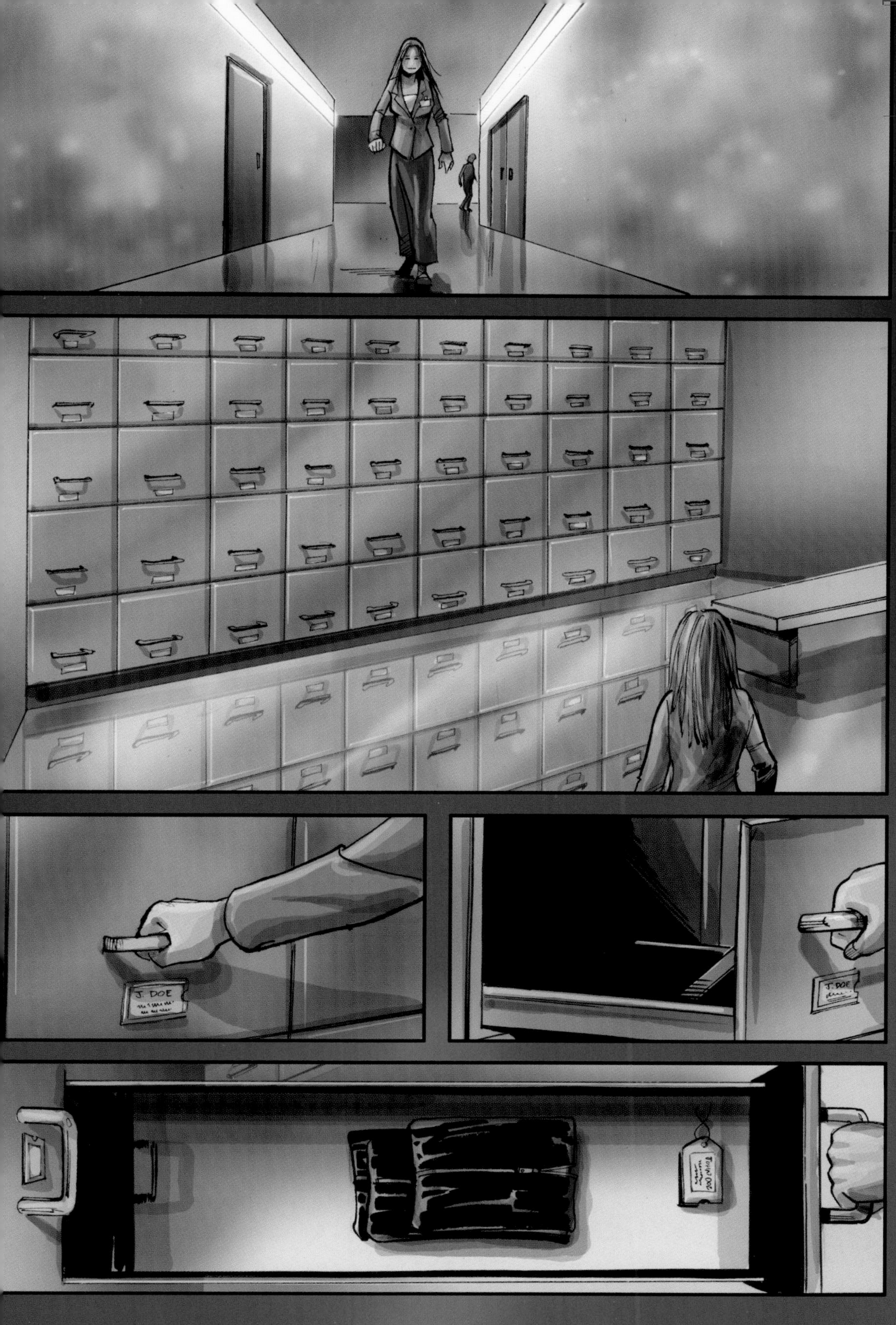
J. DOE
J. DOE

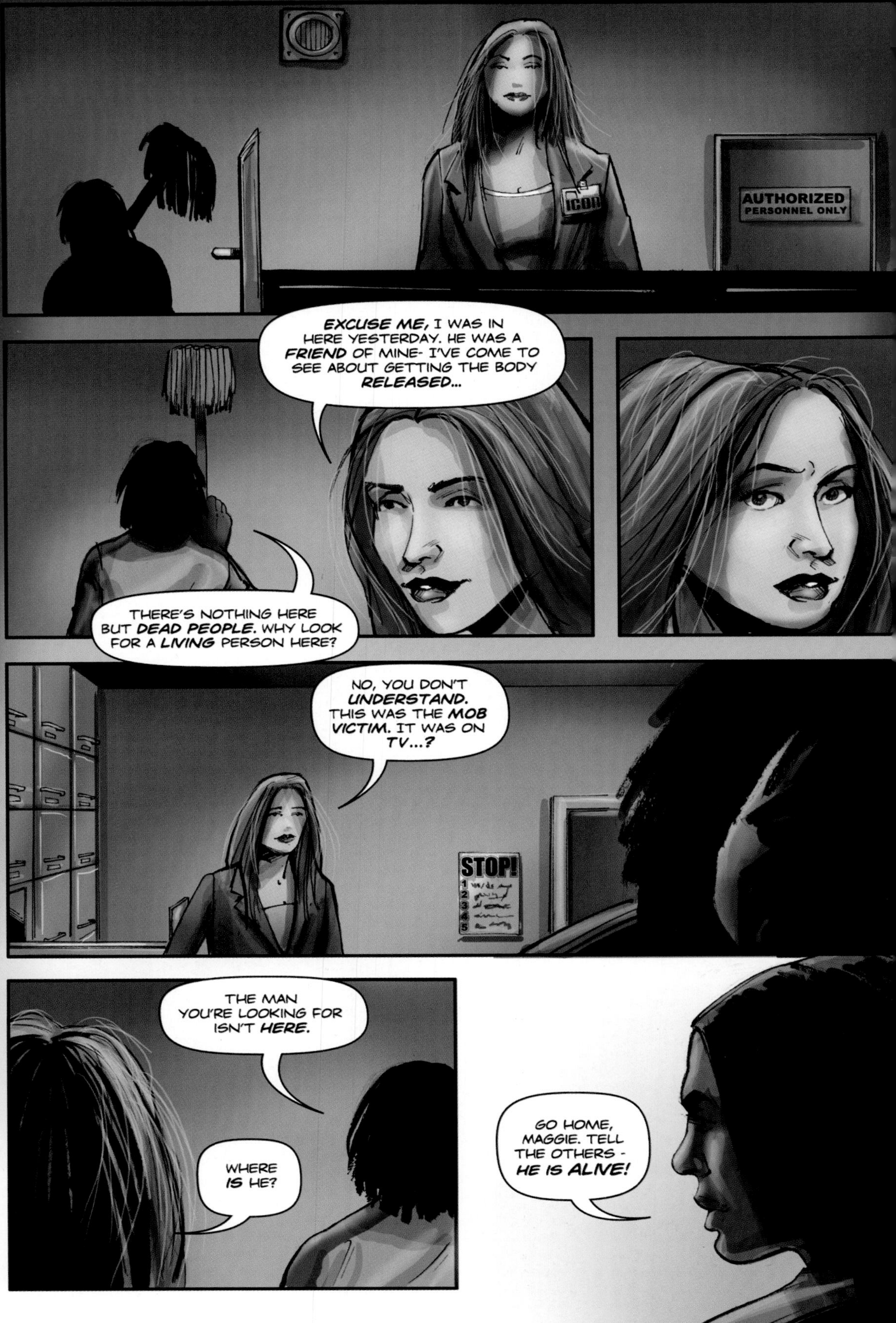
AUTHORIZED PERSONNEL ONLY
EXCUSE ME, I WAS IN HERE YESTERDAY. HE WAS A FRIEND OF MINE- I'VE COME TO SEE ABOUT GETTING THE BODY RELEASED...
THERE'S NOTHING HERE BUT DEAD PEOPLE. WHY LOOK FOR A LIVING PERSON HERE?
NO, YOU DON'T UNDERSTAND. THIS WAS THE MOB VICTIM. IT WAS ON TV...?
STOP!
THE MAN YOU'RE LOOKING FOR ISN'T HERE.
WHERE IS HE?
GO HOME, MAGGIE. TELL THE OTHERS - HE IS ALIVE!

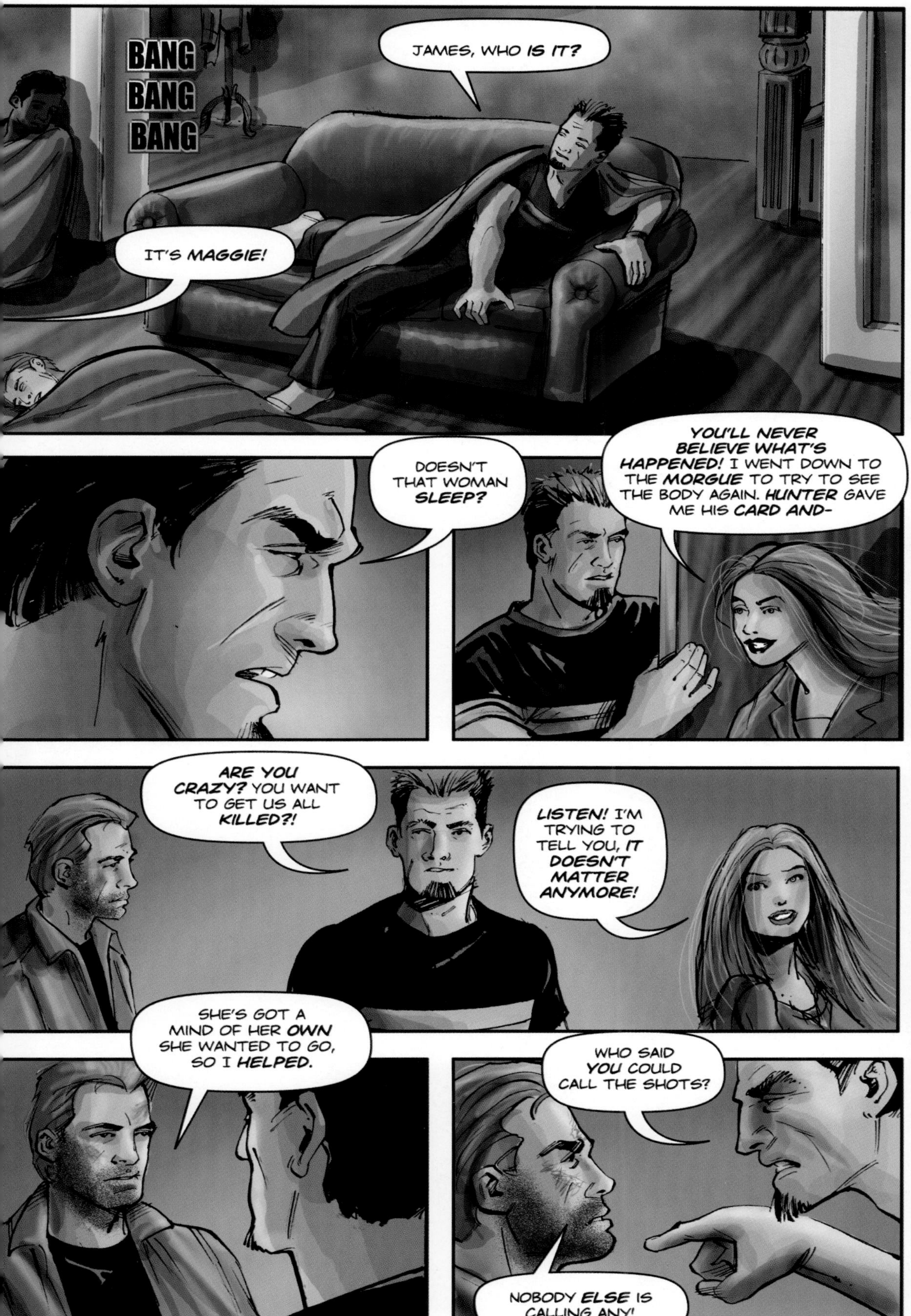
BANG
BANG
BANG
JAMES, WHO IS IT?
IT'S MAGGIE!
DOESN'T THAT WOMAN SLEEP?
YOU'LL NEVER BELIEVE WHAT'S HAPPENED! I WENT DOWN TO THE MORGUE TO TRY TO SEE THE BODY AGAIN. HUNTER GAVE ME HIS CARD AND-
ARE YOU CRAZY? YOU WANT TO GET US ALL KILLED?!
LISTEN! I'M TRYING TO TELL YOU, IT DOESN'T MATTER ANYMORE!
SHE'S GOT A MIND OF HER OWN SHE WANTED TO GO, SO I HELPED.
WHO SAID YOU COULD CALL THE SHOTS?
NOBODY ELSE IS CALLING ANY!

WHAT'S ALL THE *FUSS* ABOUT?

MAMA! IT'S *AMAZING!* HE'S ALIVE! *HERO IS ALIVE!*

MY SON? *ALIVE?*

HE CAN'T BE *ALIVE,* MAGGIE. YOU MUST HAVE *IMAGINED* IT.

NO, I *DIDN'T.* THE *BODY* ISN'T *THERE!* AND I *SAW* HIM--

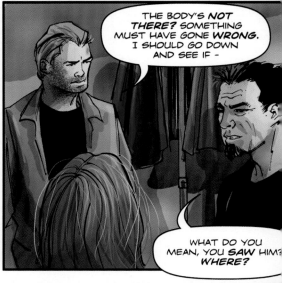

THE BODY'S *NOT THERE?* SOMETHING MUST HAVE GONE *WRONG.* I SHOULD GO DOWN AND SEE IF –

WHAT DO YOU MEAN, YOU *SAW* HIM? *WHERE?*

MAGGIE, STAY HERE AND GET SOME *REST.* PETROV AND I WILL GO AND SEE IF WE CAN FIND OUT WHAT'S *GOING ON.*

YOU'RE NOT LISTENING TO ME! HE ISN'T *THERE!*

DO YOU THINK IT'S SAFE FOR ME TO GO AS WELL? I MEAN, AFTER *ALL THAT...*

FINE, STAY HERE. I'LL *CALL* IF–

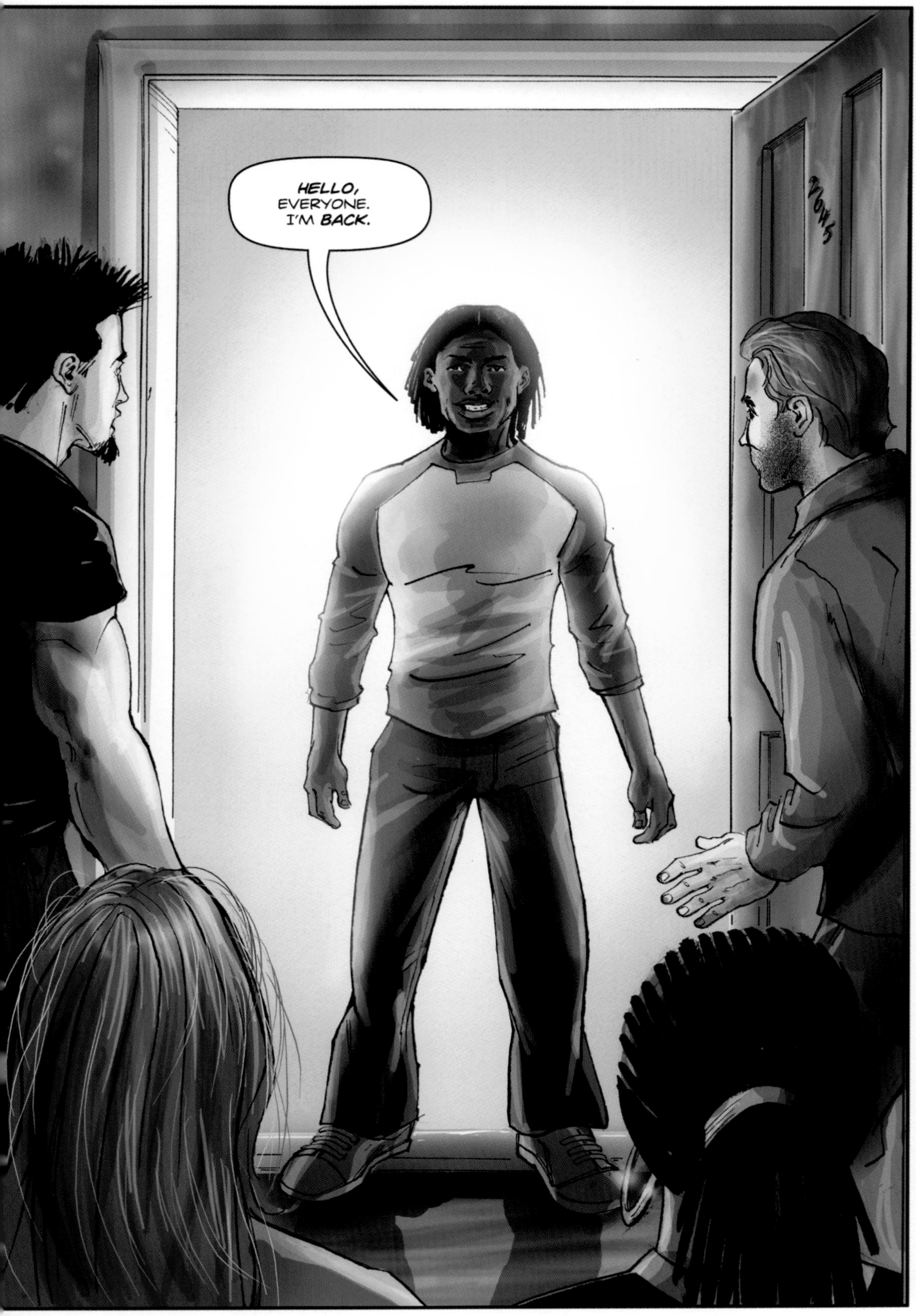
HELLO, EVERYONE. I'M BACK.

!HERO Co

ISSUE
1
NEW YORK
!HE RO
THE EMPIRE STATE
by Stephen
R. Lawhead
& Ross
Lawhead
THINK
Adapted from the original story by Eddie DeGarmo & Bob Farrell

ISSUE
2
NEW YORK
!HE RO
THE EMPIRE STATE
by Stephen
R. Lawhead
& Ross
Lawhead
THINK
Adapted from the original story by Eddie DeGarmo & Bob Farrell

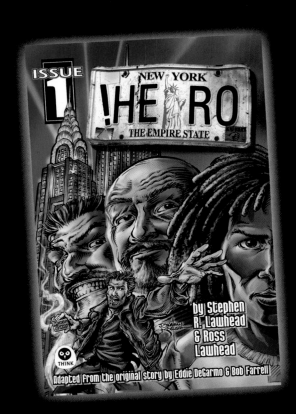

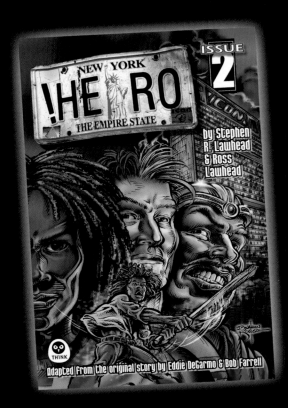

ver Gallery

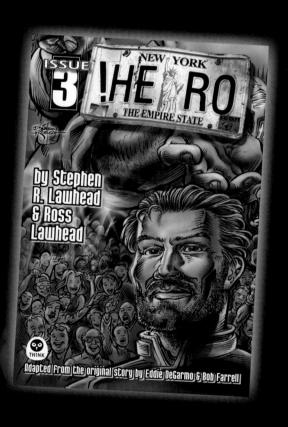

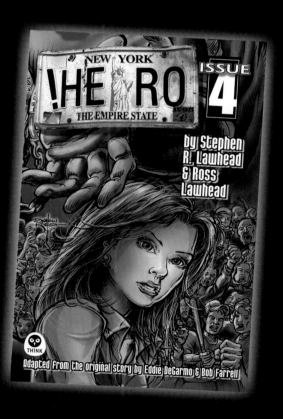

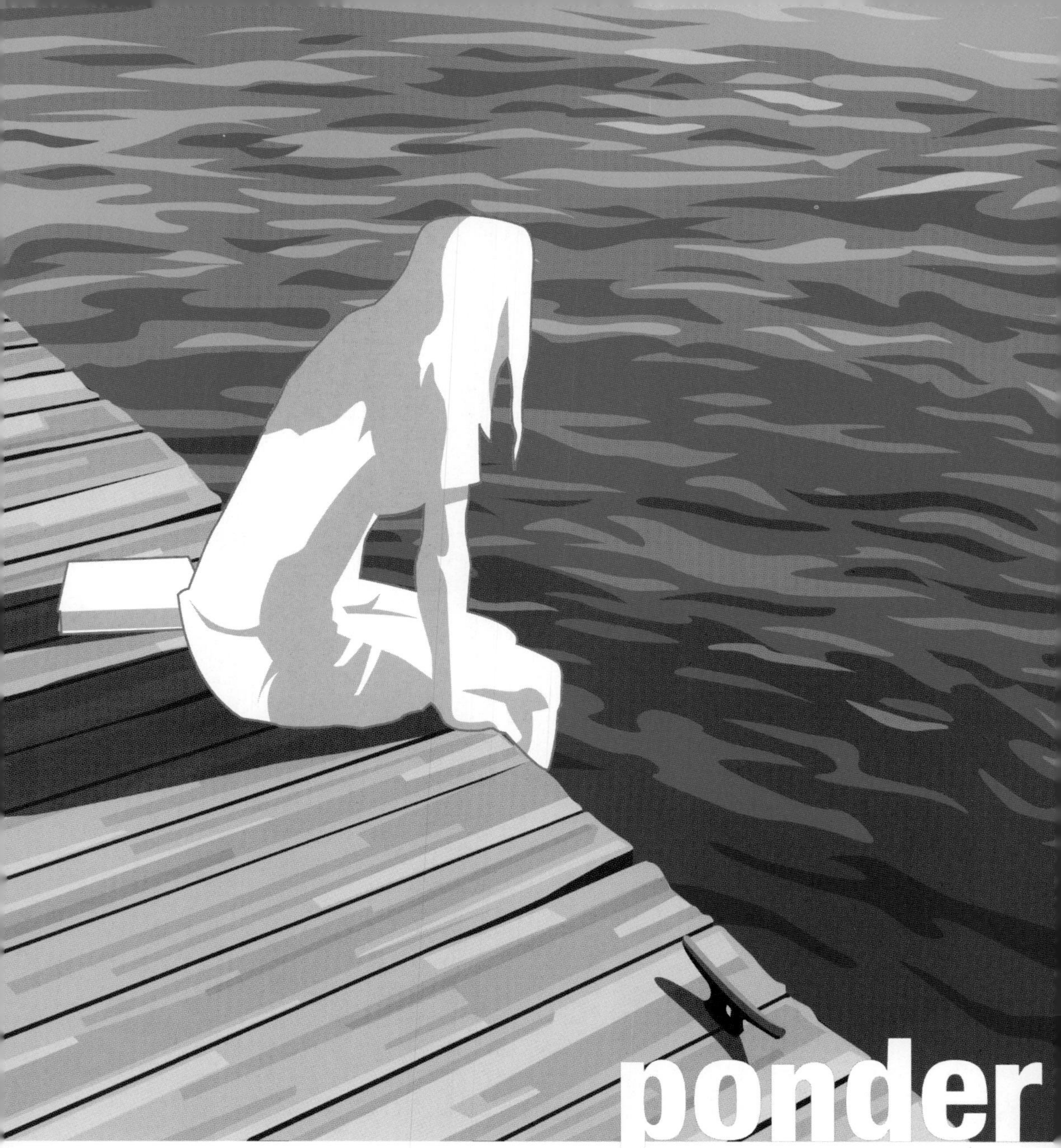
ponder

The NavPress TH1NK line gets into the tough, relevant questions that you encounter every day. It is our hope that by engaging your beliefs, wrestling with your questions, and never settling for fluff over substance, your faith will be put into action to reach your generation.

As much as we try, we'll never fool God with the games we play or the masks we wear. The best part is, we don't need to. The Father already knows and accepts us exactly as we are.

Posers, Fakers, & Wannabes
Unmasking the Real You
Brennan Manning with Jim Hancock
1-57683-465-4

For hundreds of years, contemplative Bible reading has been used by Christians as an essential way to know the Father. Through this method of study, called *lectio divina*, you can know God in a more personal way.

read, think, pray, live
a guide to reading the Bible in a new way
Tony Jones
1-57683-453-0

Do you ever feel a little stumped about prayer? Take a close look at some powerful prayers of the Bible and the early church—you'll see how effective prayer can be.

Pray
Tony Jones
1-57683-452-2

God's Word was meant to be read and understood. It was first written in the language of the people—of fishermen, shopkeepers, and carpenters. *The Message Remix* gets back to that feel. Plus the new verse-numbered paragraphs make it easier to study.

The Message Remix
Eugene H. Peterson
Hardback: 1-57683-434-4
Navy Alligator Bonded Leather:
1-57683-450-6

Taken from the NavPress classic *The Pursuit of Holiness*, this book shows you how "running as to get the prize" isn't just possible, it's what life is all about.

The Chase
Pursuing Holiness in Your Everyday Life
Jerry Bridges with Jay and Jen Howver
1-57683-468-9

Take a look at God's promises—promises of a real life and a future. See how knowing them can change your life.

Promises. Promises. Promises.
Eugene H. Peterson
1-57683-466-2

How did Jesus handle temptation? He quoted God's Word in its face. A specialized version of NavPress' successful *Topical Memory System*, this book will help you deal with whatever life throws at you.

Memorize This
TMS 3.0
1-57683-457-3

With brutal honesty and biblical wisdom, you will finally be free from feelings of guilt and shame related to masturbation.

The Struggle
Steve Gerali
1-57683-455-7

WHAT IF HE WERE BORN IN BETHLEHEM... PENNSYLVANIA

NEW YORK .HE RO
THE ROCK OPERA

It's a Rock Opera, a Novel Trilogy, a Comic Books Series, a double-disc CD— And it's going to change the way you think about the gospel.

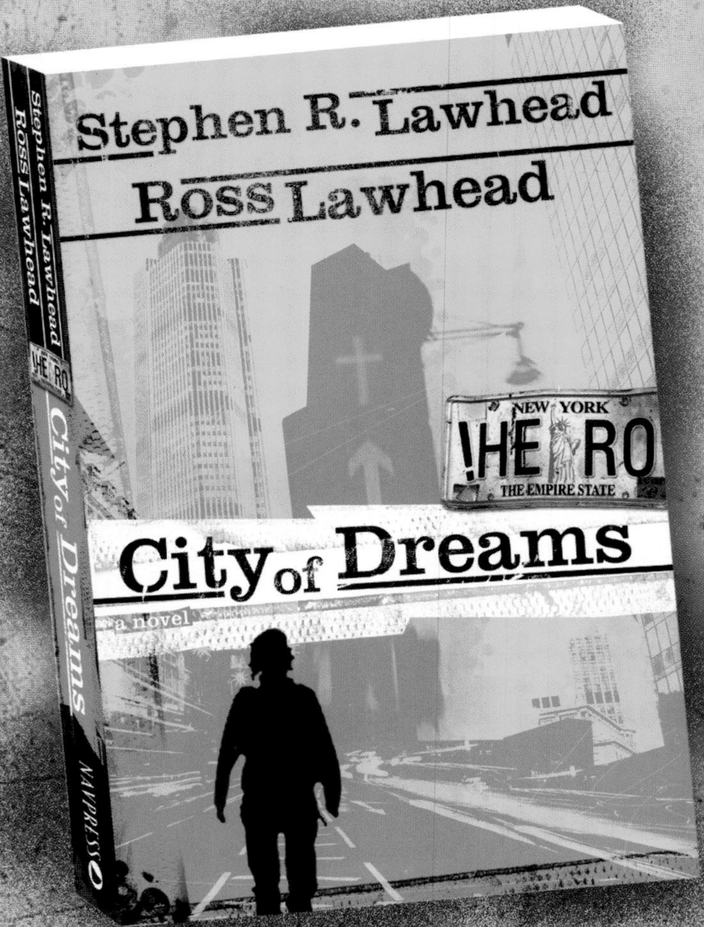

Stephen R. Lawhead
Ross Lawhead

NEW YORK !HE RO
THE EMPIRE STATE

City of Dreams
a novel

NAVPRESS

"A TOUR DE FORCE...HERO CREATIVELY BRINGS THE GOSPEL INTO THE 21ST CENTURY."
—CHRISTIANITY TODAY MAGAZINE

"POWERFUL"
—CHRISTIAN MUSIC PLANET MAGAZINE

"A CULTURALLY RELEVANT PRESENTATION OF THE GREATEST STORY EVER TOLD."
—CAMPUS LIFE MAGAZINE

In this explosive adventure, best-selling author Stephen R. Lawhead and Ross Lawhead show us what it would be like if He were born in Bethlehem...Pennsylvania.